In the
Shadow
Garden

In the Shadow Garden

LIZ PARKER

FOREVER

NEW YORK   BOSTON

Cover art and design by Daniela Medina. Cover images © Trevillion Images; Shutterstock. Cover copyright © 2022 by Hachette Book Group, Inc.

Forever
Hachette Book Group
1290 Avenue of the Americas, New York, NY 10104
read-forever.com
twitter.com/readforeverpub

First Edition: September 2022

Forever is an imprint of Grand Central Publishing. The Forever name and logo are trademarks of Hachette Book Group, Inc.

The publisher is not responsible for websites (or their content) that are not owned by the publisher.

The Hachette Speakers Bureau provides a wide range of authors for speaking events. To find out more, go to www.hachettespeakersbureau.com or call (866) 376-6591.

Library of Congress Cataloging-in-Publication Data

Names: Parker, Liz, 1988- author.
Title: In the shadow garden / Liz Parker.
Description: First edition. | New York : Forever, 2022.
Identifiers: LCCN 2022010839 | ISBN 9781538708798 (trade paperback) | ISBN 9781538708804 (ebook)
Subjects: LCGFT: Witch fiction. | Magic realist fiction. | Novels.
Classification: LCC PS3616.A74534 I5 2022 | DDC 813/.6—dc23/eng/20220310
LC record available at https://lccn.loc.gov/2022010839

ISBNs: 9781538708798 (trade paperback), 9781538708804 (ebook)

Printed in Canada

FRI

10 9 8 7 6 5 4 3 2 1

*For everyone who wishes they could remember
and to those who would give anything to forget.
And, especially, for Nick.*

Yarrow's Founding Families

The Haywoods

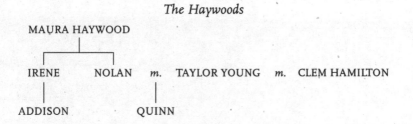

MAURA HAYWOOD

IRENE   NOLAN   *m.*   TAYLOR YOUNG   *m.*   CLEM HAMILTON

ADDISON   QUINN

The Bonners

SYLVIA BONNER   *m.*   CHRISTIAN DURANT

NATE   KADEN

The Bakers

ROLAND BAKER   *m.*   ELENA WILLIAMS

CASEY   *m.*   SUSHEILA DAS

RIVER   HARPER

Chapter 1

Addison

Yarrow, Kentucky, was big enough that you didn't know everyone, but small enough that it felt like everyone knew you. For Addison Haywood, it wasn't just a feeling. The entire town of Yarrow did know her. Just like they'd known her mother and her grandmother and each generation of Haywood women as far back as anyone could remember.

For years, the people of Yarrow would bring their heartache to the cottage at the edge of town, where a Haywood would take one look at them and see the pain that had sprouted from their hearts—the yellow carnation petals of disappointment, a petunia hinting at resentment, the trailing leaves of a willow revealing a sadness, soft and deep. All one had to do was ask, and a Haywood would uproot the suffering from their heart and ease their sorrow.

The Haywoods would then take that pain out the back door, bury their hands beneath the soil, and offer it to the earth. The more pain their shadow garden took, the more it thrived. Though summer had come, the garden produced cabbage and greens in abundance, as if the oppressive heat didn't touch them. Even in winter, as frost gripped the rest of the land, within the shadow garden, peppers bloomed, blackberries fattened on the vine, and sunflowers opened wide beneath the snow.

But not every pain required magic to be remedied. Sometimes a simple cup of tea would do, and so, twenty-five years ago, Irene Haywood opened Lavender & Lemon Balm. In the tea shop, the Haywoods paired nonmagical plants' inherent properties with each customer's needs. Chamomile for anxiety. Valerian for insomnia. Lemon balm for sadness. Then they'd look to the tea leaves left at the bottom of the cup for insight into their customers' lives and share what the universe had to offer.

Of course, when a cup of tea wasn't enough, the Haywood magic was there to help—and it would be, as long as each generation had a Haywood born with that magic.

At least, that's how it was supposed to work.

At age twenty-four, Addison should've been well established with the family gift, but after one disastrous incident, she couldn't be trusted to go digging around in anyone's heart without her mother or her grams at her side.

She'd worked in her mother's tea shop less and less since then, every moment spent inside its doors a reminder that she couldn't offer her neighbors the healing they sought without risking taking more than she should. These days, Addison had to have a very good reason to visit her mother at work.

With a deep breath, Addison squared her shoulders and stepped through Lavender & Lemon Balm's door.

The shop's heady herbal scent enveloped her, all florals and leaves, and though for years nothing smelled more like home, now it only reminded her of the uncertainty of the future and her magic right along with it. But today she let herself breathe it in, because for the first time in a long time, Addison had hope.

Two midcentury armchairs were nestled in the corner of the room between shelves packed with jars upon jars of leaves and roots and flowers. Small wooden tables sat in strategic spots, littered with dirty mugs.

A hand-scripted sign hung above the register.

Lavender & Lemon Balm
Teas and Tinctures: Priced as Marked

Tea-Leaf Readings:
— 15 Minutes: $25
— 30 Minutes: $40
— 60 Minutes: $70

Healing Sessions (Local Customers Only):
— Anger/Frustration: $50
— General Sadness: $75
— Shame/Disappointment: $100
— Fear/Anxiety: $125
— Grief/Loss: $150
— Trauma: $200

We retain the right to adjust pricing based on difficulty. Equal-value trades accepted as payment on a case-by-case basis. Healing will not remove all pain but will help ease suffering. Subscriptions for mental health-related appointments can be arranged at a discounted rate.

Closed for tea-leaf readings and healing sessions
on Thursdays.

Addison spotted her mother sitting at a table in the back. Irene Haywood had her long orange hair tied in a thick braid that she'd pulled over her shoulder, and she wore a loose crew-neck T-shirt tucked into her jeans. At the sound of the bell tinkling above the door, she glanced up. Then, she waved for Addison to join her.

Sarah Roberts sat across from Irene. The woman was older than Addison but younger than her mother. Begonias bloomed in her aura, a sign that she was experiencing unwanted thoughts. While the Haywoods were unable to remove her trauma completely—their magic couldn't take away the memory of what happened to her or eliminate the very real scar it had left on her heart—they'd been able to ease the weight of it so much that while she used to visit them weekly, now they only saw her every few months at most.

She held a teacup in her hands.

"Why don't you sit in on this healing session?" Irene asked.

Addison knew what her mother was doing. It was a safe space for Addison to try her hand at healing again. She almost refused, but if she let her mom walk her through her magic the same way she'd done when Addison was a kid, Irene might be more amenable to the real reason Addison had come into the shop that morning.

To her customer, Irene said, "You don't mind if Addison joins us, do you?"

Sarah smiled sadly and shook her head. "Not at all. Some-day it'll be you I come to for this anyway."

"Hopefully by then the chamomile will be more than enough," Addison said, as Sarah set her teacup on the table. "Anything specific bring you in today?"

Sarah laughed softly. "The usual triggers have me in a bit of a dread spiral. Maybe one day I'll have my confidence back without worrying about a stray thought taking it right out from under me."

"Let's see what we can do about that," Irene said.

She held one hand out faceup. Addison mirrored her, and Sarah placed her palms in theirs. Addison closed her eyes and felt her mother's energy beside her.

"You see the anxiety?" Irene asked.

Addison nodded, then remembered her mother's eyes would've been closed, too, and said, "Yes."

Addison followed the erratic pulse of fear from the tips of the woman's fingers, along her veins, and to her heart. Already Addison could see the result of her mother's work, the lingering scars from where Irene had pulled the effects of the trauma free. Right at the center, a fresh crop of pain had sprouted from Sarah's heart, its leaves just starting to unfurl, its roots attaching themselves to her joy, her confidence, her self-worth.

"Now gently lift the roots from the soil," Irene said.

Addison started to tug, but as she did, the full root ball shook loose. She inhaled, sharp. Then, she froze, terrified if she made another move, she'd remove too much. Again.

"Mom," Addison whispered.

Beside her, Irene whispered softly, "Don't worry. I'll take it from here."

Addison watched as her mom gently pulled the roots free, and all the parts Addison had brought up with them stayed behind where they belonged. Then, Irene transplanted Sarah's anxiety into her own heart, where it would sit until she got home and handed it over to the shadow garden.

When Addison opened her eyes, the tight set of Sarah's

mouth had melted, and she smiled softly. Her aura of begonias had shifted so it now radiated from Irene.

"Thank you," Sarah breathed as she squeezed both of their hands one last time before she pushed back from the table and stood.

"Always," Irene said.

Addison waited until the door closed behind her and the shop was empty before she turned to her mother.

"It's okay," Irene said. "We'll figure out your magic."

"That's actually what I wanted to talk to you about," Addison said. "Sylvia Bonner has a request."

Her mother's eyes widened. She opened her mouth, closed it, then shook her head, before she walked away and started preparing herself a cup of tea without another word.

Chapter 2

Irene

There were two things every Haywood woman knew: never trust a Bonner, and always trust the leaves.

"I don't care what Sylvia Bonner is asking. The answer is no," Irene said. The teakettle's whine emphasized her words.

"Mom, her husband died. Shouldn't we at least think about it? She just wants an order of rosemary from the garden for the funeral. Apparently she plans to do a toast or something."

"We will not be selling that woman a single thing from our garden."

A Bonner's betrayal had changed her life forever, and the well of rage still boiled deep inside her. Irene was not about to let her daughter make the same mistakes. She hoped the tea would help tamp enough of that anger down so she could focus on getting through to Addison.

But Addison just rolled her eyes, opened a jar of lemon balm, and tossed a few leaves into Irene's mug. "I should've waited until you put Sarah's pain in the shadow garden."

Though Irene's heart raced, she knew the anxiety wasn't her own. She'd been doing this work long enough to not let others' suffering affect her—too much. "That wouldn't have made a difference. Sylvia Bonner wants to make sure there isn't a dry eye at that funeral, and I will not let her use our magic to help people feel artificial grief for a man who won't really be missed."

Each fruit, vegetable, and herb from the shadow garden slightly amplified a person's emotions, making joy sing a bit brighter and melancholy hum a touch deeper. It wouldn't be enough to leave the funeral's guests feeling fully bereaved, but it would certainly help set the mood.

"Maybe it's finally time for you to get over what her son did to you," Addison said as she circled around to the front of the counter. "It's been more than twenty years."

"This *isn't* about him," Irene said. "It doesn't matter how long it's been. Sylvia came to you because she knew I'd say no."

Addison rested her elbows on the countertop, her brown hair falling into her face. She might not have the strawberry-blond curls and hazel-green eyes that marked every other Haywood woman, but she had Irene's freckles, her sun-kissed shoulders, and her stubbornness.

"Maybe it's time we started saying yes to the universe," Addison said.

"This is *not* the universe," Irene said through clenched teeth.

"That's where you're wrong," Addison said. She pulled out her phone, swiped through her photos, then placed the screen in front of Irene.

"What's this?" Irene asked.

"My reading from this morning."

"And why is it relevant?" Irene asked as she looked at the symbols the leaves formed at the bottom of Addison's teacup.

A ladybug. A fern frond. A hand pointing to an ear of corn crossed with a sprig of rosemary.

"Sylvia specifically asked for rosemary," Addison reminded her.

As much as Irene wanted to, she couldn't explain the reading away. Not when the tea leaves were so clear. But that didn't mean she wasn't going to try. "So, the universe warned you she was going to ask for rosemary from the shadow garden," Irene said. "That doesn't mean we sell it to her."

"The hand is pointing for me to do exactly that and you know it."

Ladybugs had been attracted to Irene's daughter since she was an infant. Now, whenever they appeared in the leaves, they meant Addison. Irene knew this. The fern, a symbol of magic, spoke to the troubles Addison was having with the family gift. And the corn, a sign of bourbon, usually meant the Bonners, who ran the distillery that brought so many tourists to Yarrow.

"I don't like it," Irene huffed.

"You don't have to," Addison said. "But I can't ignore it and turn her away."

Irene pressed her eyes closed. Irises bloomed in Addison's aura, and Irene couldn't bring herself to crush the fragile hope building in her daughter. "You know your grams isn't going to be happy about this."

"Maybe the Bonners aren't as terrible as you and Grams say."

"The Bonners are *exactly* that terrible," Irene said. "They offer this town empty magic, as if forgetting your darkest memory is the same as healing."

"They offer magic *our* garden gave them through the dark corn," Addison said. "Magic you willingly used that summer twenty-five years ago."

"But that I *didn't* use to forget the pain Nate Bonner caused me."

"I've heard that story a hundred times," Addison said.

"Clearly it hasn't sunk in." Irene took a seat in one of the armchairs and motioned for Addison to join her. She held her teacup in both hands and stared at her daughter over the rim. "If I'm going to agree to this, then let me remind you, once again, exactly what kind of people you're doing business with."

"Here we go . . ." Addison said.

1997 was supposed to be the start of my happy ending. I'd carved out my own bit of Yarrow, a little shop right on the town square, and the grand opening had been a success. Tomorrow would mark the unofficial start of summer, my favorite season of the year, and I wasn't about to let a snail and a snake in the dregs of my tea take that from me, even if I couldn't shake the twisting in the pit of my stomach. The snail—a sign of infidelity—I'd been seeing for almost a year, but I'd yet to find any proof that the reading was true. I'd been engaged to Nate for a full month, I was truly, deeply in love, and he was as faithful as the sunrise.

I was sure of it.

But if the symbols in my cup were to be believed, I was in for betrayal.

That night, Nate was supposed to have stopped by to help me close up before taking me to dinner. It was our first night alone in almost a month. I'd bought a little special something for the occasion and couldn't wait to see the look on his face when I stripped down to it.

We'd had no time for each other in the weeks leading up to the ribbon cutting. It had just been me and Clem and—

Irene paused and shook her head as she tried to put the pieces together, but she just couldn't remember any of the summer after that night.

"Please spare me the details about your lingerie purchases," Addison said, breaking Irene's concentration.

"This is my story. I'll tell it how I want to tell it."

I looked out over the town square as I locked the door. Backyard roosters crowed the sun into the sky, and hounds woke the moon with their songs. Fireflies broke up the gloom from the Bonner bourbon distillery—their light just enough to chase away the darkness that clung to windows and walls and branches like soot, a thin dusting of shadow.

Clem came up beside me and flipped the Open sign to Closed. She'd ditched her black leather jacket as soon as the humidity had settled in, and she had on her favorite Cranberries T-shirt. We'd gotten it together at a concert in the fall.

I forced my worry over the tea leaves away. It probably wasn't even my own fear anyway. Just that morning, I'd healed a young mother's anxiety over her son being slow to start walking, and until I could get home and give the emotions to the shadow garden, they'd sit right in the center of my chest, putting down roots in my heart as if the anxiety I'd taken from her was my own. It had to be that.

"Our first day on the books," Clem said.

I turned and leaned the back of my head against the glass. "We did it."

Though Clem wasn't family, she might as well have been. We'd been best friends since we were kids, and opening a tea shop together had been our dream, as fewer and fewer people were showing up at my mother's door, choosing instead to give their darkest memories up at the annual bourbon festival, rather than heal slowly over time, their suffering eased by Haywood magic.

Clem looped her arm through mine.

"Honestly, I didn't think we'd pull this off until our thirties," Clem said.

"All of our dreams are coming true," I said.

"Some might say you've peaked." Clem grinned and looked at the Bonner-family diamond on my left hand. "Speaking of which, wasn't Nate supposed to be here an hour ago?"

I looked at the shop's answering machine. There were no new messages.

"This isn't like him," I said.

Clem arched an eyebrow. "If you wanted a man who showed up on time—"

Irene paused and looked down into her mug. Again, she felt like she was grasping at straws—at something she couldn't quite place.

"So, the Bonners don't know how to keep track of time," Addison shrugged. "That doesn't make them bad people."

"You know that's not how the story ends."

"I just think you're looking to point out how terrible they are," Addison said.

"Because they're terrible," Irene said, then she continued.

Clem sighed. "If Nate's not here by the time we're done closing up, you and I are going for milkshakes."

"Milkshakes were not what I had in mind," I said.

"Spiked milkshakes." The two of us had given up bourbon in the final weeks leading up to the shop's opening. We had too much to focus on to be drinking.

As Clem headed behind the register to count the drawer, I picked up dirty teacups. I started for the sink in the back, when a black Porsche in the alley caught my eye. It sat a few shops down, hidden behind a dumpster. Had I not been at just the right angle, I might not have seen it at all.

"Nate's here!" I set the dishes down in a hurry and wiped my hands on the sides of my denim overalls before brushing my curls out of my eyes.

When I stepped into the alley, the summer heat hit me like a physical thing. I hurried toward Nate's car. But with each step I took, I slowed, the feeling in my stomach twisting deeper.

The car looked almost hidden the way he'd parked it.

The windows were fogged.

The frame shook.

I froze. Blinked.

I took a deep breath, fists clenched. Cicadas hummed as they landed on the pavement around me.

I'd asked Nate if there was another woman after I'd seen that first omen. I'd asked him again, and again. But he'd wrapped his arms around me and told me how much he loved me and promised me a life together. And every time, I'd believed him.

Until now.

I should've listened to the tea leaves. I should've listened to my mother.

"And you should listen to me now," Irene said.

"Really, Mom?" Addison said.

"She was right," Irene said. "I could have saved myself a lot of heartache."

A cicada perched on the back windshield, rubbing its wings and humming in time with the angry beat of my heart. I tried to open the car door. Inside, a woman lay sprawled in the back seat, barely visible through the dark tint of the windows. The look on her face was enough to tell me exactly where Nate was.

I only half recognized her, the way you might recall someone you'd seen at the grocery store or pumping gas at one of the town's two filling stations. She was no one I knew. I didn't know if that made it better or worse.

I pulled the front door open wide, and the woman shrieked.

Cicadas descended on the car in a swarm.

As the woman closed her knees, Nate got caught in her tartan skirt. Once he'd managed to untangle himself, he turned to look at me with wide eyes and flushed cheeks. His hair stuck out at odd angles.

"Irene?"

He made his way out of the car. When he took a step toward me, I held up a hand.

"I thought you loved me." I choked on the words.

"I do." He rubbed the back of his hand over his mouth, and I grimaced. "This was a mistake."

The woman in the car leaned forward. "A mistake?"

I almost felt bad for her.

Almost.

Nate looked back at her. "I'm marrying Irene Haywood," he said.

"You're . . ." the woman started, then shook her head as she pushed the passenger seat forward and jumped out of the car, skirt askew. "So, this past year meant nothing to you?"

The words rattled around in my head as the cicadas' song reached a crescendo.

"I've done everything for you." My voice was a whisper. "I've ruined my relationship with my mother. For you."

I should've known better.

It was a rare person in Yarrow who had anything but good to say about the family who owned the town's world-famous bourbon distillery. But not the Haywoods. You had to be careful around a Bonner. One word and they'll have you eating out of their hand. All the things my mother had told me were true.

I'd ignored her. I let a friendship bloom into something more and—

"I just don't know how you couldn't have seen he was going to be one of those guys," Addison interrupted.

Irene pressed her lips together. When she tried to think of her friendship with Nate before they got together, even that felt tainted. Like it had all been a dream. Hazy, but not completely blank like the rest of the summer that had changed the course of her life forever—she ended up pregnant, her brother was dead, and no one in town remembered a thing.

I stepped closer to Nate until he stumbled back against the car, and we were face-to-face. I could smell the pungent scent of marigolds that was all him—mixed with sweat and bourbon and god knew what else.

"Why don't we forget about all this?" he said.

I pulled back my hand, and the world moved in slow motion. My fist collided with his nose. Cartilage cracked and it felt good. Blood spilled from his nostrils, down his face, and onto his white button-up.

I shook out my hand. Then I twisted the ring off my finger and threw it at him. It hit the ground. Light glinted off the diamond, and he dropped to his knees to retrieve it.

A voice came from behind me, just loud enough to be heard over the cicadas. "What the hell?"

I stepped back without a word and turned to find Clem standing there in her black combat boots, eyes narrowed as they skipped from me to Nate to the woman by the car. Nate stood, one hand clutched around the ring and the other cradling his face. The woman grabbed her purse and took off down the alley.

"You're lucky Irene's the one who found you," Clem said as she looked him over. She narrowed her eyes and cracked her knuckles. "If it had been me..."

Nate slid into the front seat. Blood dribbled down his chin. He pulled the door shut as he fumbled with his keys. The engine roared to life and he took off.

Clem wrapped her arm around me as he sped away. "Let's get out of here."

The rest, of course, was history—even if Irene couldn't remember it—and she sure as hell wasn't going to let Addison repeat it.

Chapter 3

Kaden

There are exactly five things that make a bourbon more than just a whiskey, and Kaden Bonner had learned them before he could read or write or count. When other children said their prayers before bed, Kaden had repeated the laws of bourbon back to his mother as she tucked him in to sleep.

As much as he'd tried to erase them from his mind over the past twenty-five years since he fled his hometown, it wasn't the type of thing you forgot, even if, like a religion, it was something you desperately wanted to leave behind.

1. Bourbon has to be made in America (not specifically Kentucky, even though everyone knows Kentucky bourbon is the best bourbon).

2. Corn must make up 51 percent or more of the grain used.

3. It must be aged in new charred-oak barrels.

4. The liquor can't be distilled at more than 160 proof. It can't enter the barrel at higher than 125 proof, and it can't enter the bottle at less than 80 proof.

5. Nothing can be added to it but water.

Even now, as he sat at the dive bar down the street from his apartment, the laws played on a loop in his mind. He'd planned to spend the night with a good book and a beer, but he'd opted for something stronger after listening to his mother's voice mail. How she found his number after all this time, he had no idea, but hearing her words crackle through the speaker had ruined any chance of enjoying his book.

Your father passed away last night from liver cancer. I didn't tell you he was dying because I knew you wouldn't want to see him, but I hope you'll change your mind and come home for the funeral. You belong with your family, Kaden. Come take your place at the head of the distillery.

Then a long, pregnant pause. A sigh and—click.

He'd started it over. Played it again. And again.

Kaden had promised himself he'd never go back to Yarrow. He'd sworn he'd never take up the family business.

His father, Christian Durant, had married into the Bonner family. The son of one of the largest coal-mining moguls in Kentucky, he had the breeding and the fortune the Bonners required for a husband to the sole heir of the Bonner estate. It was Christian's money that kept the distillery afloat in the early '80s while the country turned its taste to clearer liquors. Yet Kaden's mom had never taken Christian's last name and hadn't allowed him to pass that name on to his sons. Not that Kaden would've wanted it. His father hefted words like fists, and when words were no longer enough, he threw actual punches.

And his mom stood by and let it happen.

As the eldest, Kaden had been first in line to take over the distillery. Instead, when he was twenty-two, he had it out with his father one last time, then fled. All these years later, he couldn't remember the specifics of the fight, only that his mother and his brother took his father's side, and Kaden left Yarrow and the Bonner legacy behind for good.

He hadn't tasted their bourbon since that summer. But after learning his father was dead, he decided—just once—to order a glass of Bonner's. It was a silent, private celebration that the man was finally gone. Christian Durant got what was coming to him. He'd loved bourbon so much he married a Bonner, and in the end, it was the alcohol that killed him.

It felt like a small sort of justice.

Kaden held his glass up to the light and swirled it as a woman slid onto the stool beside him. She wore a short-sleeve dress and black boots and leaned toward him in a cloud of perfume that smelled like pineapple and lemon.

"What're you drinking?" she asked.

"I'm drinking alone," he said.

She scooted closer. Her knee brushed his. With a nod to Kaden's glass, she said to the bartender, "I'll have one of those."

"Bonner bourbon, straight?" the bartender asked, sizing her up. The way he looked her over irritated Kaden.

"Add a splash of water," she said.

At least she knew how she liked her whiskey.

"Heavy alcohol to be drinking alone," she said once the bartender turned his back on them.

Kaden shrugged. After the bartender set her drink in front of her, Kaden raised his glass.

"My dad died," he said, matter-of-fact.

She frowned but lifted her glass all the same. "Sorry for your loss."

Kaden nodded and threw back his drink as if it were a shot. The bourbon hit his tongue like sweet honey, burning just a little at the back of his throat on the way down. It left his mouth with a hint of smoke and wood, but his head was already reeling.

It was like he was right back in Yarrow, before the abuse. Before the lies. Nostalgia mixed with a bit of hope.

He pressed his palms to the countertop. Maybe this hadn't been such a good idea.

"I love this stuff," the woman said, and Kaden glanced over to find her sipping it slowly, the way he should have. "Wish I could afford the family reserve, but the four-year gets the job done. Takes me back to my wedding day—without any of the bad that came after. At least, not until the next morning when I wake up hung over and alone, and the memory of the car accident hits me all over again." She threw back the rest of her drink.

When she held up the empty glass, the bartender crossed over to them and lifted the bottle. "Another?"

She nodded. He raised the bottle in Kaden's direction, and Kaden nodded, too. The label read *Jesse*. Rather than calling their bourbons by year, or by harvest, the Bonners named them. Kaden always thought it was pretentious.

"Sorry," the woman said as she nursed her second round. "You didn't come here for my sob story. It's just...today would've been our anniversary."

Kaden stared into his empty glass and felt like a complete ass for trying to brush her off.

"I'd say I get it, but I can't imagine losing your husband is anything like losing your father," Kaden said.

She took another sip. "Sorry again about your dad."

It wasn't worth explaining why he was anything but sorry. "Thanks," he murmured.

"I spiraled after my husband died." She looked down at her hands, then back up into Kaden's eyes. "I guess I'm still spiraling. Sometimes I wish I could give up all my memories of him."

"Even the good ones?" he asked.

She shrugged. "Maybe then I'd finally be at peace, you know?"

"Just forget it all," he said, more to himself than her, thinking of his father, his manipulative mother, his younger brother who got all the bad parts of both their parents. His chest warmed as the words left his mouth, like he'd swallowed another glass of bourbon, the burn sharp and heady.

The woman leaned toward him, eyes soft. Her lips parted. A puff of black smoke escaped her mouth and hovered in the air between them. Kaden rubbed his eyes, and when he opened them, it was gone. But the bar seemed darker somehow.

"Maybe it'll help," he said. "Talking about the good times." It was better than thinking about his disaster of a family.

The woman blinked. "The good times?"

"With your husband," he said.

She shook her head slowly. "Not much to talk about." She rubbed her temples. "When I think about him, my mind sort of comes up blank. You know?"

The warmth he'd felt in his chest disappeared. Kaden's eyes widened. "You told me Bonner's gives you all the feelings from your wedding day."

She blinked. "I did say that, didn't I?" She shook her head slowly. "It feels like there's something there—something I forgot." Then she laughed. "I don't really remember much of it at all. I was married, he died. It's sad when you say it out loud, but you're right. It's all in the past now." She took another sip. "Want to grab dinner?"

"You don't remember...any of it?" Kaden asked. Fear clawed at his throat.

"It's like you said," she mused. "I should just...forget it all."

Chapter 4

Addison

Addison knew the shadow garden like an old friend. How it savored the sorrow the women in her family poured into its soil like a fine wine. The way it let anger slowly soak through its roots like a cat basking in the sun. Its habit of downing anxiety all at once, like a shot with no chaser.

Being here felt like home, and home made Addison's heart happy. The ladybugs crawling across her knuckles were a testament to that.

The Haywoods' healing powers made them uniquely suited to care for the garden. With their magic, they eased their neighbors' suffering. Then, the shadow garden took that pain and transformed it into something more.

While Addison might not have any misery to offer the plants in that moment, she could help them in other ways. She pulled on her gloves and started weeding the rows of fruits and vegetables and herbs, the summer sun warm against her back. She pulled a snail from a vine of ink-dark chocolate strawberries. She gently squeezed black raspberries that hid just a hint of mint. She watered deep purple tomatoes infused with basil, oregano, and thyme.

When she'd finished her rounds, she wormed her hands beneath the dirt. Roots prodded at her fingertips. A blackberry vine started toward her. It spiraled up her arm, night-dark blossoms soft against her cheek, their touch feather light.

The garden was her place of retreat. Two years ago, after she'd tried a healing on her own and messed everything up, she'd come here. Her magic broken, her heart broken. The shadow garden was the one place where Addison found solace, and the plants responded in kind. It was as if they could feel her pain and sought to comfort her. But while the garden eagerly accepted the heartache the Haywoods eased in others, the plants were powerless to heal the Haywood women themselves.

A vine rose in front of Addison, blackberries hanging from its tip. She tilted her head, held out a hand, and one of the berries dropped into her palm.

Normally, Addison didn't eat from the shadow garden. The last thing she needed was to intensify her pain. But who was she to turn away a gift from the garden?

She dropped the berry into her mouth, and it hit her tongue with the barest hint of vanilla. At first, her own sadness welled up inside her. It settled into her chest, where it grew and grew, making her vision swim. She brushed back tears, but when she blinked her eyes open, all she saw was darkness.

She tried to stand, but her legs wouldn't respond.

Panic had only just settled in when she started to see again. Dirt and worms and pill bugs. Grubs and millipedes and roots, so many roots.

These weren't Addison's thoughts.

They belonged to the shadow garden.

Addison traveled along the root system as if she, too, were

buried in that magical earth. Each plant fed into the other...
and all of them were weak and frightened. She moved from tendril to tendril for what felt like miles. The further she went, the
weaker she felt. The soil had once been rich with sorrow. Now
it was empty. Depleted.

Soon, there would be nothing left.

Addison stopped. The roots twisted down, down, down. They
stretched farther than any plant should. The soil couldn't feed
them, so they'd turned on each other, desperate and starving.

Rows of black cornstalks stretched as far as Addison could
see—the dark corn the Bonners grew for their bourbon—and
wisps of inky silk bled from them, up into clouds of gloom.

Addison blinked, fighting for breath as the vision loosened
its hold on her. She tried to make sense of it, her mind going
back to yesterday's tea-leaf reading.

The garden had never given her any sort of vision before. If
it weren't for the argument with her mother, Addison would
have gone straight to Irene with this. But with the signs of the tea
leaves on her side, she had managed to convince her mom to sell
their rosemary to the Bonners for the funeral. No matter how
much they hated the Bonners, none of the Haywood women
dared ignore the power of their readings. And if Addison was
right about the tea leaves, this was her chance to fix her magic.
She wasn't about to give her mother a reason to back out now.
Whatever this vision was, it could wait until after the funeral.

The vine slowly unwound and returned to its place on the
trellis. She ran her fingers through a row of dusky chives, their
flowers already in bloom, and let out a heavy sigh when her
phone started to vibrate. She fished it from her pocket. Her
cousin's face stared up at her.

Addison furrowed her brow. Quinn usually texted. Addison held the phone up to her ear. "Quinn?"

"You were supposed to be here with that shipment an hour ago," Quinn said. While Addison tended to the plants, Quinn managed the garden's sales. "The chefs are going to arrive any minute. Please tell me you're on your way."

"Shit," Addison said as she scrambled up from the dirt. "The Bronco's already loaded. I'm coming now." She took off at a run across the yard, tossing her sun hat in the back as she slid into the driver's seat. She tugged a scrunchie from her wrist and pulled her dark hair back.

Ten minutes later, Addison met Quinn by the loading dock at Baker's Grocery. Quinn was the closest thing Addison had to a sister. The two cousins had grown up together, side by side, running through the rows of vegetables in the shadow garden and digging into jars of tea at Lavender & Lemon Balm.

While Addison was the first Haywood in generations without the family's traditional red hair, Quinn looked every bit the Haywood, all straight lines and long, sun-bleached curls. Quinn leaned against the bed of her yellow 1980 Ford F-150. The truck had belonged to her dad before he died. She fixed it up in high school and had been driving it ever since. It was her way of keeping a bit of him alive.

Sometimes Addison wondered if it was easier for Quinn, at least knowing who her father was even if he was gone, barely a memory. At least there was a name, a history. Addison's mother had told her that after she broke up with Nate Bonner, she went on a terrible rebound—spent that fall trying to erase Nate from her soul. It had been a relief ten months later when Addison showed up, because she knew beyond a shadow of a doubt, Addison wasn't Nate's, and even Addison's birth had become another cautionary tale.

She jumped out of her Bronco, and the two of them unloaded the crates from that morning's harvest. She tugged a pair of scissors from her canvas apron and snipped the ties around the boxes.

"A little light today," Quinn said.

"I pulled all the rosemary for the funeral," Addison said.

Quinn clicked her tongue and shook her head. Rosemary was one of their best sellers. With notes of lemon, it paired perfectly with bourbon, which was likely why Sylvia had wanted it in the first place.

"I can't believe you talked Grams and Aunt Irene into it."

"You can thank the tea leaves," Addison said. "Speaking of which, the garden gave me a blackberry today."

"The garden... gave you a berry?" Quinn repeated.

"That wasn't even the weirdest part," Addison said. "I ate it, and I think I had a vision."

Quinn arched her eyebrows. "Has that ever happened before?"

Addison shook her head, but before she could explain what she'd seen, four cars pulled into the back lot, right on time. Thanks to the booming bourbon industry, Yarrow had also become a culinary hub, boasting four Michelin-star restaurants, all of which were the shadow garden's primary customers.

It didn't take them long to go through what Addison had brought—with a few grumbles that the day's harvest had no rosemary—but they took what the garden had to give, paid, and drove away.

Addison glanced at the back door, trying not to think of the days when her ex-boyfriend River would walk through it, would inventory what was left over by the restaurants to put in a special display inside—most of which would be sold before noon. Though River had been gone from Yarrow for almost two years, working on his master's, Addison thought of him every time she visited his family's store. She still couldn't forgive herself for what she'd done.

"So about this vision," Quinn said after the chefs left. "Want to go grab a cup of tea and talk about it?"

"I'm not sure I want anyone at the shop overhearing this," Addison said.

Quinn's eyebrows shot up. "Coffee, then?"

"Or we could go inside and talk right now," Addison said.

Quinn tugged a strawberry-blond curl between her lips the way she did when she was nervous.

"What's going on?" Addison asked.

Before Quinn could answer, the back door opened. River Baker stood on the threshold. His skin glowed brown in the mid-morning sun, but he'd changed his hair. He wore his bangs parted down one side, curling just past his ears.

Addison's heart dropped into her stomach, and as soon as his eyes landed on her, his smile turned to a frown.

Chapter 5

Addison

River didn't hold Addison's gaze. Instead, he looked over her shoulder at Quinn. "Have you seen my sister?" He held up a slip of paper. "Dad asked me to give this to her before I head out."

No *Hello*. No *How are you*. Not even a hint of a smile.

Addison wasn't surprised, but it still stung.

"You're back," she breathed.

River's eyes slid to Addison, but when they met hers, they held no warmth.

The last time Addison had spoken to him, he'd made it perfectly clear he never wanted to see her again. Now the memory from that day reared up, and she was back outside Baker's, the sky orange and full of smoke.

We'd planned to go out for drinks after River got off work, but I fell asleep on the couch. I was so unused to the sound of my phone that the ringing almost didn't wake me. When it did, River was crying and yelling about a fire. Sirens blared in the background.

I got there as fast as I could. As I pulled onto Main Street, an ambulance drove past, away from downtown. It slowed to a stop at the traffic light, and I caught a glimpse of the driver through the window. Hyacinths bloomed in her aura. My heart sank at the sign of her grief, but at least she wasn't in a hurry. She wouldn't be leaving the scene like that if anyone had been hurt. She would've barreled through, racing for the hospital.

River was okay. He had to be.

Main Street had fallen into chaos. I parked along the sidewalk and ran the rest of the way to Baker's. People lined the road, trying to get a look at the store. I pushed through them, but their words followed behind me.

"How did it happen?"

"How long has it been burning?"

"Was anyone in there?"

Flames danced inside the windows of the grocery as the firemen worked to put out the blaze. Ash swirled in the air, coloring the town white. I searched for River in the chaos until I spotted him sitting on the sidewalk, arms around his knees. Sadness and guilt hung from him like the leaves of a weeping willow. I ran for him, but when I got there, he didn't even look up.

I sat down next to him and threaded my fingers through his. "Are you hurt?"

"I'm fine," he said. "I wasn't inside." The words had no force to them.

"The ambulance...?"

He pulled his grip from mine and dropped his head into his hands. "My grandfather."

"No," I whispered.

He only nodded.

"Let me drive you to the hospital," I said. "You should be with him."

He shook his head. "There's nothing for me there." A sob escaped his lips. "He's already gone, and it's all my fault."

My heart cracked at his words.

"You didn't do this," I said.

"I went for a walk after I closed up. When I came back..." He held out a hand in front of him.

"If you'd been there, you—"

"I could've saved him." River cut me off. "He'd fallen asleep in the back office. I didn't want to wake him just yet. And now he's gone."

I wrapped an arm around him, and after a few seconds River leaned against my chest. He shook with his tears, and I wanted more than anything to help ease his suffering. I couldn't remove his grief completely—but the blame? The guilt? I didn't want him to carry that for the rest of his life. What was the point of being a Haywood if I couldn't help the people I loved?

"Let me help you."

I knew I shouldn't have offered. Not without Mom or Grams. I still hadn't mastered the family magic, but this was different. I was a Haywood, and River needed me.

He turned to look at me with wide eyes. "Help how? It's not like you can bring him back."

"I can at least ease your guilt. Get you through to tomorrow."

He glanced at me, his eyelashes wet with tears, and nodded.

I leaned forward, brushed my lips against his cheek. "It's going to be okay."

River shrugged and held out his hands.

He rested his palms in mine. I closed my eyes and followed the trail of guilt all the way to his heart. It had already buried itself deep—wrapped around joy and pride and everything his family's business had ever meant to him. Worse, it had sunk its roots into the love he had for his grandfather, the love his grandfather had for him. If left unchecked, River might never be able to separate the weight of what had happened tonight from years of cherished memories.

This wouldn't be an easy fix, and it wasn't one I should have attempted alone. But if I was ever going to come into my magic, this was the moment.

It had to be.

Carefully, I began the work of pulling his pain free, biting my lip in concentration. I tugged and lifted and shook River's guilt from the soil of his heart. I knew I couldn't take it all, but I desperately wanted to. Still, the pain held fast.

"Come on," I whispered. "Let go."

It loosened its hold, and all at once I uprooted it. River gasped.

But my work wasn't done.

I transplanted it into my own heart. It wound itself around me like wisteria choking a young tree, tinging the world a little darker. I clenched my teeth against the weight of it. I wouldn't have to endure it for long. I'd hand it over to the shadow garden as soon as I could.

I struggled to breathe.

I blinked—once, twice.

The world came back into focus.

I'd done it. All on my own.

"See?" I tried not to choke on the question, as if River's crushing guilt was nothing to me.

River stared at me, eyes wide. A hand over his heart.

I was proud of the Baker family—the legacy they'd built, the shop that one day River would take over. Even more, I knew just how much his grandfather loved him. The look of pride in his eyes every time River walked through the grocery's doors, the assuredness that River would carry on what his grandfather had built, yes, but also *twenty-two years of love that even his grandfather's death couldn't erase.*

I felt those feelings as if they were my own, my heart full to bursting.

"What did you do?" River asked. I'd expected to hear relief in his voice, maybe even gratitude. But rather than the tension draining from his shoulders, he sat rigid beside me. Bindweed sprouted in his aura, the small, trumpet-like flowers blooming all at once until olean-der replaced them. Uncertainty turned to distrust.

My chest filled with ice as I realized the sense of pride and love I was feeling wasn't my own.

It shouldn't have been possible. A Haywood could take a person's pain, nothing more, and that only when freely offered.

I grabbed his hand tighter and closed my eyes, searching his heart once more. My family didn't remove a person's suffering completely. Though we eased it, making the process of healing on your own more tolerable, always, some trace of those feelings remained. Surely these things I'd taken would grow back.

But there was nothing left in the hole I'd dug in River's heart.

I tried to pull the feelings out of myself, to bury them back where I'd found them. But I couldn't get my hands around them. Once another person's pain entered a Haywood's heart, the only place for it to go was the shadow garden.

What I'd taken from River was irreversible.

He'd never feel his grandfather's love again.

This was the closest Addison had been to River since that night. She could see the golden flecks in his hazel eyes, almost trace the strong line of his nose, and smell the sharp scent of thyme that he always carried.

"I wish my sister had warned me you'd be here," he said.

His eyes held hers, and the ache Addison had done her best to stitch up started to split open at the seam. She'd been tempted to hand over her pain from the whole ordeal during the bourbon memory harvest—to offer up what she'd done to River and never remember it again—but heartache was all she had left of him, and she refused to give it away.

"We're here at the same time every day," Addison said.

"Yeah, well, it's been a while since I've been in the shop. Seems I've forgotten a few things," River said. "And we both know who I have to thank for that."

Addison's head dropped. "My magic...I didn't understand what was happening. I didn't mean to take what I did. I broke myself just as much as I broke you. I made a mistake. I don't know how many times I can tell you how sorry I am."

"You made a mistake?" He laughed, the sound low and grating. "You broke something in me."

A cicada landed on the pavement, rubbing its wings in a soft warning.

Addison, too, felt like she lost something every single time he came back to Yarrow and she only found out because Quinn told her. She lost something every time he crossed the street to avoid her, and every time he refused to make eye contact if she did manage to see him when he was in town.

"I needed you, too, River. You left me, like what we had meant nothing...like I meant nothing to you."

He shook his head. "You stole something from me that I'll never get back. I don't even remember what it feels like to want to be here. In Yarrow, in this building. I know at one point I'd hoped to help run the grocery with Harper, to carry on our grandfather's legacy, but now, whenever I try to think about it,

I come up empty. No matter how many times my grandmother tells me how much he loved me, it doesn't sink in. It doesn't feel real. I don't even remember it. You took that from me. From my family."

"I never meant to hurt you, River." Her voice cracked, and tears pricked the corners of her eyes.

He shook his head, then left without another word.

Addison braced herself against the truck. Quinn put an arm around her.

"I wish I weren't still in love with him," Addison said after the door closed behind him.

"If it helps," Quinn said, "I'm pretty sure he's still in love with you, too."

"It does *not* help," Addison said.

It helped a little.

"Why didn't you tell me he was back?" she asked. "Didn't Harper mention it?" Quinn and River's sister had been dating for a few years.

Quinn scratched at the back of her neck.

"She told you not to tell me," Addison said.

"River asked her not to," Quinn said. "He's back in Yarrow for the summer. He's going to be apprenticing under Nate Bonner now that he's completed his master's in distilling."

Addison laughed. It felt better than crying. First her tea leaves, then the vision in the garden, now River. Everything in Addison's life was coming up bourbon.

Chapter 6

Quinn

When Quinn Haywood said a person rubbed her the wrong way, it wasn't a figure of speech. It was a literal, physical sensation.

She may not have been born with the traditional Haywood magic, but she still had a sense about people. When Harper looked at her, it felt like the first spring morning after a particularly cold winter. Being around her mom gave her the sensation of the perfect cup of tea right before bed. Clem, Quinn's stepmom, felt like driving fast with the windows down and the radio on high. And Addison, like she'd shoved her hands beneath the cool, damp dirt after a day baking beneath the summer sun.

Right then? Quinn's hands felt like they were on fire.

She knew she should try to pull Addison back from the edge—to help her move on from River instead of focusing on how her healing had gone all wrong. But delving into the wild part of her magic was exactly what Quinn wanted her cousin to do.

What happened with River had been impossible by all Haywood accounts, which meant that Addison was the only one who might be able to help Quinn with her own problem: nightmares from the summer her father died. Over the past two years, Addison had been too fragile for Quinn to risk broaching the subject, but after her cousin's recent tea-leaf reading, now might finally be the time to bring it up.

Addison tilted her head back against Quinn's truck, her dark hair falling over her shoulders. She rubbed the back of her hand over her eyes and sighed. "What am I supposed to do, ignore River all summer?"

"Maybe you can figure out what went wrong," Quinn said, "try to understand how you were able to take so much from him in the first place."

Addison shot her a look. "What do you think I've been doing for the past two years?"

"Hiding in the shadow garden," Quinn said softly.

"I have not been hiding," Addison said, but they both knew that wasn't true.

"I don't blame you," Quinn said.

"At least someone doesn't," Addison murmured.

"But things are changing," Quinn said. "Your tea leaves pointed toward your magic—magic that allows you to take more than you should be able to."

"Thank you for that reminder," Addison said.

"What if there was a way you could test it?" Quinn asked. "To practice without putting anyone at risk."

Addison narrowed her eyes. "And how exactly would I do that?"

With a deep breath, Quinn said, "You could try it on my nightmares."

Quinn didn't remember much about her father—she'd only been a little over a year old when he died—but every summer, dark dreams plagued her sleep. Even now, all she had to do was close her eyes and she could see the images.

Daddy lay in a puddle of his own blood beside me.

It soaked my clothes.

Dripped from my hands.

My tiny fist brushed his shoulder.

His hand slipped from his chest.

I wailed. I didn't understand; I knew nothing about death or blood or loss.

But it had come for me all the same.

Then I was in my Aunt Irene's arms. Cicadas surrounded us, their wings blocking out the sun. People stood all around, plastic cups pressed to their mouths. Lips stained with chocolate. Horror in their eyes.

On the stage before us: the Bonners.

A scream pierced the buzzing as my mom ran toward us.

The cicadas went still. All the faces around me went slack. As the bourbon went down, the memories rose from the townsfolk like a sigh and formed a dark heavy rain cloud of gloom.

Quinn knew she shouldn't be able to remember that memory harvest. No one else in Yarrow did; even the children and teenagers who'd been too young to drink had consumed sweet chocolate bourbon balls that wiped it all away.

She'd spent most of her childhood believing her father had been murdered. She was convinced the Bonners were involved. It had been their festival, after all. But as her mom healed and found new love with Clem—as their little family grew—Quinn found herself wishing she could do away with the dreams altogether.

She tossed her hair over her shoulder and rubbed the sole of one boot against the side of the other as she waited for her cousin's response.

Addison shook her head slowly. "You're immune to Haywood magic."

"I'm immune to Irene and Grams," Quinn said. "But your magic is different."

"Even if it could work on you, I take emotions, not dreams," Addison said.

"What if it's not a dream?" Quinn asked. "What if it's a memory?"

Addison pressed her lips together. "I want to help, I really do, but giving up your worst memories is bourbon magic, not Haywood magic."

"And that bourbon uses corn that first grew in the shadow garden," Quinn said. "Corn you saw in your tea-leaf reading."

"I'm not sure I'm following," Addison said.

Quinn pulled up the photo Addison had texted her the day before. Quinn might not have the family magic, but even she drank a cup of tea each morning. Reading the leaves at least gave her a bit of satisfaction that she knew the symbols as well as any Haywood.

"You said this was about Sylvia," Quinn said.

"Because it was," Addison said.

Quinn pointed at the sprig of rosemary. "Rosemary is *also* a symbol for memory."

"Quinn..."

"Come on," Quinn said. "Can you at least try?"

"You're taking advantage of my distressed emotional state," Addison said.

"I'm being the sister you never had," Quinn said.

With a sigh, Addison relented. "Fine," she said.

Quinn grinned, and a dragonfly flitted toward them. It landed on Quinn's shoulder.

"At least one of us is happy about this," Addison said.

She held out her hands palm up, Quinn rested her own on top of them, and Addison closed her eyes. They stood like that for a few seconds, the summer air thick against Quinn's denim. Sweat pooled at the waistband of her shorts.

"Well?" Quinn asked.

Addison cracked open one of her eyes. "Nothing," Addison said. "You're like an abyss."

"I'm not giving up on this," Quinn said.

"It's not going to work," Addison said. "And now I have a headache. Please leave me alone so I can cry for the rest of the day."

"Not gonna happen. Let's head over to the tea shop. I need to drop off these payments, and we can get you a cup of chamomile," Quinn said.

∽⦿⌣

As they rounded the corner that led to the Lavender & Lemon Balm tea shop, Quinn felt a prickle like a nettle sting, like tiny shards of glass burrowing beneath her skin. Only one family had ever given her that sensation, and sure enough, when the door to the shop opened, Sylvia Bonner stepped out onto the sidewalk, head held high. Her short gray hair gleamed in the sunlight as she turned and said to Irene, "I really do appreciate you making an exception, and I hope we'll see you at the funeral." The door closed behind her.

She started in their direction. Her thin-lipped grimace

transformed into a sad smile as her eyes landed on Addison. "I was hoping I'd run into you."

Quinn rubbed at the space between her eyes. Every word out of Sylvia's mouth pressed against her skull. It looked like she was on her way to a headache that matched Addison's.

"I appreciate you convincing your family to let us buy from your garden," Sylvia said.

"I'm so sorry for your loss," Addison said.

When Quinn didn't say anything, Addison elbowed her gently.

"We all are," Quinn mumbled.

Sylvia glanced back toward the shop. "Somehow I doubt that." With a heavy sigh, she rested a hand on Addison's shoulder. "Thank you. I've never forgotten the debt we owe to your family. If it weren't for your grandmother, this whole town would've gone under."

"We've heard," Quinn said.

"Quinn," Addison warned.

"I was just stopping by to let your mother know I would welcome her presence at the funeral," Sylvia said. "I'll always regret that things didn't work out between her and Nate. I know her being there would mean a lot to him. I hope you'll all attend," she finished before she started down the sidewalk to a Mercedes parked just a few shops down.

Quinn and Addison shared a look once her back was to them.

Addison pointed to a handful of cicadas singing on the window ledge.

"Ah, shit," Quinn said.

Addison nodded. "Mom's never going to forgive me for agreeing to help her."

Chapter 7

Irene

The mason jars Lavender & Lemon Balm used to store teas and herbs were not made for slamming against countertops. After the first one cracked, Clem started following Irene around the shop, taking each jar out of her hands before she could break another.

"I cannot *believe* that woman." Irene wasn't yelling, because Irene didn't yell. She let the cicadas do the talking. "She has the nerve to go behind my back to my daughter for something she *knew* I'd never sell her. Then she comes in here bemoaning the marriage that never was? Like I give a shit if it would mean a lot to Nate to see me at that funeral."

"You know your reaction is exactly what she wants," Clem said as she rescued the dill from Irene's grip and gingerly set it on the table. "To get you riled up so that you'll decide you *will* go to the funeral just to be the bigger person."

"Not helping." Irene scooped a tablespoon of dill into her three-cup granite mortar. She tilted her head to the side, considered the amount, and added three more heaping spoonfuls. Dill helped protect against dark forces, and when it came to the Bonners, she needed all the protection she could get.

Unlike the produce they sold to the restaurants and at Baker's Grocery, the herbs and teas in the shop were sourced more broadly or came out of the family garden that ran the perimeter of the house, before the land gave way to darkness. There was no shadow magic in them, just old-fashioned homeopathy and green witchery.

"And that *is* helping?" Clem gestured to the mess Irene had made of the table.

Irene was only half listening. She tapped a finger against her lip, then strode across the room and grabbed the jar of dried blueberries.

"I'll take that." Clem swiped it from her. She glanced down at the label, then back up at Irene. "Dill and blueberry? This sounds terrible."

"It isn't about the taste." Irene continued making her rounds. "Blueberry provides protection against psychic attacks."

"Which you need why?" Clem asked.

"Sylvia clearly came in here to get under my skin."

"Is this some sort of revenge thing? Like a potion or a spell?" Clem said.

"You know I'm not that kind of witch."

Clem wasn't a Haywood, but she'd been around Irene's family long enough to know as much. Still, Irene quirked her lips before she rifled through another row of herbs. Cloves to clear a lingering charm. Angelica to fight bewitchment. Sylvia clearly had her own sort of influence—Addison selling her the rosemary and her mother ever agreeing to give the woman corn seeds from the shadow garden all those years ago were both a testament to that.

Irene spooned the concoction into a teacup and added boiling water.

Clem stepped up beside her and wafted the steam toward her. "Doesn't smell as bad as I expected," Clem said. "You want to sell this?" That was Clem, always thinking about their business. It was part of what made Lavender & Lemon Balm so successful outside of Irene's magic. While Irene could put together teas on instinct, Clem could see the opportunity behind them.

"I don't see why not," Irene said. "With the sort of energy that woman carries around? Everyone in town should drink this daily. Just to be safe."

She crossed the shop and grabbed the bottle of Bonner's ten-year that Sylvia had dropped off as a thank you. The label read *Danielle*. Irene held it high and examined the amber-colored liquid beneath the warm, yellow light.

"No, you don't!" Clem jumped into action, running across the room to rescue the bourbon. They may have had no intention of ever touching the stuff, but it was worth almost two hundred dollars. "I'll take that," Clem said. "Since I know you won't be drinking it."

Irene rolled her eyes and sat down at the table. Once the tea finished steeping, she took a sip, letting the herbs that floated to the top of the cup press against her lips, but not swallowing them. She needed every last leaf for her reading.

The front door opened, and Addison and Quinn stepped through. Quinn went around to the other side of the register and stashed the paperwork from that morning's shadow garden haul, then wrapped an arm around Clem's waist and planted a kiss on her cheek.

"Hey, Mama," Quinn said.

Clem ruffled her hair. It was only a couple years after the death of Irene's brother that Clem had started dating Quinn's mother, Taylor. They'd been together ever since, and though they hadn't been able to get married until 2015, it hadn't made them any less of a family.

"Take this to your mom at the bed and breakfast, will you?" Clem handed over the bottle of bourbon to her stepdaughter. Quinn's mother ran the second-largest estate in Yarrow, an old governor's mansion turned inn that her family inherited. It was *the* place to stay in Yarrow, and with a death in the Bonner family, the rooms had booked up fast. It was not going to be an easy week for Taylor or Quinn, especially with the Annual Yarrow Bourbon Festival coming.

"Bonner's?" Quinn arched an eyebrow.

"Not you, too," Clem said. She snatched the bottle back and stashed it under the register.

"Everything okay?" Addison asked as she surveyed the table.

Irene sipped her tea. "I'm sure you saw Sylvia."

Addison nodded and reached for the jars. "Dill? This is because of her, isn't it?"

"It is," Irene said. "And it's delicious."

"I was going to have a cup of chamomile, but this might be more what I need." With a heavy sigh, Addison said, "River's back in town."

Irene set her cup down. "You're better off without him." She wrapped an arm around Addison. "You've got everything you need right here."

Irene poured a cup of tea for her daughter. While it steeped, she took one last sip of her own until there was only about a tablespoon of liquid left. She swirled the cup three times to the right before upending it on the saucer.

"You're doing a reading?" Addison asked.

"With everything going on, I want some specific answers about what's coming."

"Because of my tea leaves?" Addison prodded.

Clem answered, "Because Sylvia Bonner ruffled her feathers."

Irene rolled her eyes. "I want to know what to expect."

Tasseography was a natural extension of what they did in the garden. Outside, they talked to the plants. In the teacup, the plants talked back.

Addison leaned forward as Irene flipped the cup. Some of the leaves stuck to the sides of the porcelain, others gathered in the bottom. She tilted it this way and that.

"Well?" Clem asked.

Irene shook her head. The symbols didn't make sense, and they certainly didn't shed light on anything.

"It's not clear." She pointed to leaves at the bottom. "There's a man who looks like he's carrying flowers."

"Ooh. A visitor?" Quinn asked.

Addison clapped her hands. "Bringing *love*. One of us is going to have a good summer."

"Oh, this *is* going to be good," Clem said.

But Irene shook her head and pointed to another pattern of leaves. "That could be an owl."

"Ah, yes, an owl," Clem said, nodding sagely.

Quinn laughed. "Deception, that sort of thing. Maybe a secret lover?"

"This," Irene continued as she traced the tip of her finger along an arc at the top of the cup, "looks like a comet, which suggests treachery."

"So, Sylvia Bonner," Clem said.

Addison rolled her eyes. "She's a grieving widow *and* a paying customer."

"It could be tied to the man," Quinn said.

"We're rooting for love here." Clem smacked Quinn's shoulder playfully.

Irene bit her lip. Small patterns of leaves dotted the sides and bottom of the porcelain. "There are flowers all over this reading, which should be good, except for all the dark clouds." She tilted the cup a few more times. "Maybe it's not an owl at all."

"Could be a swan." Addison grinned.

"Right, a swan," Clem said.

"It's a sign of loyalty," Irene explained.

Clem laughed. "So, the universe is bringing us the perfect man and there's nothing you can do about it. Are you done yet?"

Irene hadn't seen her best friend's aura so full of excitement since her and Taylor's wedding, and damn it if it wasn't contagious. She tried to hide her smile as she said, "I'm not looking for a man. Or a woman. Or anyone. I just want to help Addison sort out her magic—whatever this funeral has to do with it—and then be done with the Bonners for good."

Addison crossed her arms. "Is that why your aura is bleeding red and yellow roses?"

Irene rolled her eyes. "Fine," she admitted. "It's a little exciting."

"And there's nothing there about Sylvia Bonner. Nothing at all," Addison said, smugly.

"If the universe sees fit to bring you love…" Quinn trailed off.

"Then you take it," Clem finished. "And it's about damn time."

Chapter 8

The Shadow Garden

As Yarrow slept and the moon rose high in the sky, a breeze rustled through stalks of onyx-hued basil and deep gray sage, tall as sunflowers. Starlight fell in slants across petals of black violets. A night-dark strawberry rolled across the ground. A plum-colored tomato fell from its stem. Borage and pansies and nasturtium in varying shades of black and gray turned the darkness into its own kind of rainbow.

Beneath the soil lurked something even darker. Generations of pain saturated the earth, fed each stem and fruit and flower. In the soft, thick leaves of sage: loss. In the blackened basil: broken hearts. Tucked inside the husks of charcoal corn: anger and betrayal. Trapped within the bell of burgundy calla lilies: stolen innocence.

The garden didn't just absorb pain, it thrived on it. And the town of Yarrow had always had more than enough to spare.

In the earth, feelings had a life all their own. Roots shuddered. They knew sorrow was no easy burden to bear. There was a powerful magic in pain—transformative, if you managed to survive it. In the garden, balance was everything.

For centuries, flowers blossomed and fell and gave way to

fruit. Thanks to the Haywoods, the plants had flourished, an equal exchange of heartache for harvest. The witches only ever took what the garden offered when the garden offered it, never forcing the plants to produce more than they were capable of.

But now, the vines twisted and turned. Stems stretched skyward, leaves splayed their fingers through the air. Fireflies landed on buds, spreading gloom, and the plants drank it up greedily as if the darkness that hung over the town was itself thick with melancholy and the creatures knew the garden needed it. Though the sun had long since set, heavy black blossoms turned toward the chain-link fence at the far edge of the Haywood property. It was only a tiny bit of land that separated the shadow garden from the Bonner corn. Ebony vines crawled up the metal, stretching toward the other side, where the gloom was heaviest.

As the branches reached toward the Bonner distillery aboveground, the roots dug deeper and deeper into the earth below. Blackened stalks of corn, once a gift from the Haywoods to the Bonners, might've respected their place in carefully planned rows, but the hunger in the roots knew no boundaries.

Chapter 9

Kaden

Kaden had not planned to attend his father's funeral, but after that night in the bar, he couldn't stop thinking about home. He'd gone to bed, tried to convince himself he'd had too much to drink. But he couldn't shake it.

He'd stolen that woman's memories.

It couldn't be possible.

The Bonners didn't have any magic. The only magic in Yarrow rested in the hands of the Haywoods and their shadow garden. It was that first dark batch of corn they'd used when Kaden was a kid that turned Bonner bourbon into something special. Everyone knew that.

Now, Kaden tore down Interstate 75, crossing the Ohio border into Kentucky. His dread grew with each mile marker he passed. A memory tugged at the back of his mind. He tried to pull it forward, but those years before he left Yarrow only came back in pieces. It had always hurt too much to think about his father's abuse, his mother's decision to look the other way. But now, as he was heading back into the vipers' nest that was Yarrow, looking back was the only option.

*   *   *

"This distillery was supposed to be mine." My father towered over me, his voice measured, his face red, his fists clenched. I should've been scared. I should've backed down or scrambled away or tried to run out the back door, but I was never one for doing what he wanted.

Maybe that's where our problems began.

Just that morning, my mom let me work in the grain house. I was still underage, so it wasn't entirely legal, but that didn't matter to her. It mattered to him.

"Then take it," I said from where I lay on the living room floor. "I don't want it anyway." Books and coasters were strewn across the carpet. The coffee table was splintered. Blood seeped through the side of my T-shirt. I was going to need stitches. Again.

I wondered what story my mother would tell the doctor this time.

My father laughed softly. "You know Sylvia will never give it to me." He shook his head. "Clean this up."

My father turned and walked out of the room.

Kaden rubbed at his temple. That part of the memory, at least, was crystal clear. It had been part of the many nightmares he'd been having for years.

I waited for the front door to slam shut before pulling myself up. My mother stepped into the room and leaned against the frame in a crisp white dress. She made no effort to help me up, though she did cast a worried glance at the carpet where blood dripped from the hem of my shirt.

"You could put a stop to this," she said.

As if I was strong enough to stand up to a full-grown man.

"You could put a stop to it, too," I said. "Report him. Divorce him."

"That's not an option," Mom said. *"If I leave him, we'll lose half of what we have—more, thanks to the money he's put in."*

Pressure built up behind my eyes, but I wouldn't cry. Not again. "Then let him run the distillery. I don't want it."

"We both know that's not true," Sylvia said.

She was right. Bourbon was in my blood. I loved the smell of the sour mash, the feel of the kernels in my palm. I'd always looked forward to taking over one day. My family wasn't all that different from the Haywoods. People gave up their darkest moments to our bourbon and found peace. It was its own sort of healing. It was something I wanted to be a part of. But not at any cost.

"What if it is?" I asked. "I'll graduate, I'll leave. You'll have Nate."

"I want you, Kaden. This is your birthright," she said. *"You'd really leave your family behind?"*

He stuck around for another five years. His mom had a way of convincing people to do what she wanted, and his father never laid a hand on him again.

But it hadn't been enough. His mother's machinations and his father's disapproval were a different kind of abuse. And after the memory harvest of '97, he was done.

Yet here he was, on his way home.

Within a few minutes, he'd passed the sign that said, "Welcome to Yarrow, Bourbontown USA!" The day was all sunshine and humidity, but as soon as he crossed the city limits, a faint fog descended. The gloom clung to everything. The trees, the road, even the clouds.

The speed-limit signs shifted from fifty-five to forty-five to thirty-five, and among the wild trees and kudzu, he could see a smattering of colonial and Victorian homes until they gave way to the town square. Brick buildings lined the street. Banners hung from lampposts, announcing the upcoming Yarrow festival. Just past the courthouse and one left turn was all it would take to reach his family's estate. He could already see the five-story still house rising up over the trees.

He drummed his hands against the wheel, taking in what he'd left behind more than two decades ago. Unfamiliar restaurants lined the road, and though the grocery he remembered from childhood still carried the same name, the brickwork looked recently laid, despite a thin layer of gloom. Once, he'd recognized every face in Yarrow, even if he didn't know the names that went along with them. These people were new, and many carried gift bags stamped with the Bonner bourbon logo.

He pulled over into a parking spot. Then he tugged his sunglasses from the visor. Without them, anyone looking closely enough would recognize him for the Bonner he was. His dark brown hair, his equally dark eyes, his mother's strong jaw.

He grabbed his jacket from the front seat despite the heat and stepped out into the warm sun. He shrugged on the leather as a chalkboard sign caught his eye.

Lavender & Lemon Balm
Come have tea with us!

It sparked a familiar feeling—warmth, like coming home, if home were anywhere but here. It was better than facing his mother right away. He started for the door, when a young woman stepped through it carrying a simple arrangement of black flowers. She wore a pair of denim overall shorts cut off at the thigh and worn work boots. If it weren't for her dark hair, he'd have thought her a Haywood.

She held the door open as he approached.

"Thanks," Kaden said.

"No problem," she said, before she took off down the sidewalk.

A bell tinkled overhead as Kaden stepped inside. Herbs hung from the ceiling and jars of teas lined the walls. He pulled his sunglasses free and tucked them into his jacket pocket. Slowly, he turned in a circle, taking it all in. With each step, his mouth fell open a bit more.

A voice came from down the hallway along with a flash of red hair. "Be right there!" There was a grunt and the sound of something heavy hitting the ground. "Just need to bring one more thing in from the truck. Feel free to look around."

Rather than wait, Kaden followed the voice to a set of stairs that led to an alley. Here, time had worn away the asphalt, revealing brick underneath. Old Yarrow.

Red hair stuck up over the cab of a small white pickup. He jogged down the stairs, but when he reached the other side of the truck, the woman had disappeared.

"Where did she go..." he whispered, when he saw the back of a pair of Crocs underneath the bed of the truck. He dropped into a crouch. "Need any help down there?"

The woman hit her head on the muffler with a thump. "Damn it." She groaned.

"Are you all right?"

She opened her eyes with a mumbled "I'm alive."

"Sorry," Kaden said. "I didn't mean to distract you. I thought I could help carry this in."

It wasn't until she'd rolled out from underneath the truck,

her freckles on full display, that Kaden recognized her and realized he may have been right about the woman at the door.

"Irene?"

He was assailed by flashes of her—long curls, flannel shirts, overalls. She'd been engaged to his brother. Judging by the lack of a ring on her finger, that hadn't ended well. She looked up at him and narrowed her eyes. She'd paired loose denim with a simple burnt-orange tank top, and just a hint of gray threaded through her thick, strawberry-blond braid.

"You look...Do I know you?" she said.

"Kaden." He reached out his hand.

She shook her head slowly. "Bonner?"

After a few seconds she started to laugh. The sound was throaty and deep. Bitter. It hit him hard in the chest like a sip of white dog—the pure, sharp alcohol that came out of a still before it was aged in the barrel. It was not a pleasant thing.

Kaden took a step back.

"A visitor." Irene shoved her hands into her pockets. "A damn visitor."

He pressed his lips together as he tried to understand her words and tilted his head to one side. "Excuse me?"

"Of course it's a Bonner."

She said his name like a curse, and his cheeks burned. She stumbled as she stood. Kaden offered an arm to steady her, but she righted herself on the truck instead.

"Can I help you bring these boxes in or...?"

"It can't have meant you." She worried at her lip as she looked him over, but he didn't think the words were for him. Then, eyes locked on his, she said, "Sylvia sent you."

Kaden wasn't following. "My mom?"

"I'm not coming to the funeral. Sending the son I don't hate to ask on her behalf isn't going to change that."

A cicada landed on the truck.

Kaden held up his hands. "I, um...came for a cup of tea. I didn't know this was your place, and I haven't seen my mom in twenty-five years."

Irene blinked a few times. Her green eyes caught the sunlight and threw it back at him.

"You're here...for tea?"

Kaden rubbed at the back of his neck. "Technically I'm here because my father's dead, but I wasn't ready to see my family just yet."

All at once, Irene's eyes went wide. "Kaden Bonner." She whispered his name like she only just realized what it meant to have him standing in front of her. "You're back."

"I am." He hesitated, not sure how far to push her. "And it sounds like you're pissed at my mom. Why am I not surprised?"

"She doesn't know you're here?"

"She doesn't," Kaden said.

"And you don't want to be here," Irene said.

"Not particularly."

Irene considered him. "Maybe it *is* you."

"Maybe what is me?"

She shook her head and the cicada took off. "Help me bring this case inside, and I'll get you a cup of tea."

Kaden lifted the crate and carried it up the stairs through the back door. Irene nodded to a stack of similar boxes in the corner. "Set it there for now."

Then she headed into the shop, pulling jars from the shelves. Kaden followed her.

"Where did I put the lavender?" She bit her lip. "Never mind." She reached for one of the circular racks overhead and pulled a few purple flowers free. "Sit," she said with a nod at a pair of armchairs in the corner.

So he sat, watching as she filled a mug with leaves and flowers and water. Her eyes lifted from the rim, met his across the room, and she shook her head. "Unbelievable."

"Out there," he said, unsure how to ask the question, "did you ... remember me?"

Irene's eyebrows rose. "Actually, no. I mean, once you told me who you were, I remembered Nate had an older brother. But you left so long ago."

Kaden nodded slowly. "Summer of '97."

"No wonder I don't remember you actually leaving." She crossed the room and sat down in the chair beside him. She pressed the mug into his hands. "Drink."

"How much?"

"All of it except for a tablespoon."

"No, I mean how much for the tea."

"On the house," she said. "As long as you'll let me read your leaves."

Kaden glanced up at the sign over the register and the price this place charged for a tea-leaf reading. "What's in it?"

"Lemon balm. Dandelion. Stinging nettle."

"And lavender," Kaden said.

Irene's lips tilted up. "And lavender."

Kaden lifted the teacup toward her in a toast. The contents tasted like forest and sunshine and warmed him all the way down.

"It's good to see you, by the way. How've you been?" He

attempted to make conversation, trying to understand what had happened since he'd been gone. It had been a long time. Long enough, apparently, for him to be forgotten. The thought stung, but it's what he'd wanted. To leave Yarrow behind forever.

Irene arched an eyebrow. "Don't swallow the leaves."

He took another sip and considered her. "I'm guessing you and my brother broke things off?"

Irene's smile slipped. A cicada started singing outside the window. "Drink," Irene said. "Before I change my mind."

"One last thing?"

Irene crossed her arms and leaned back in her chair.

"I like the shop. It suits you."

"I...Thank you." She tossed her braid over her shoulder, then stood and started putting the jars back in their places.

Kaden sipped in silence. When he'd almost finished, Irene reached for the cup. Her fingers brushed his, and something in his chest hitched. Her eyes held his for a second before she pulled the mug away. She swirled it three times and upended it on a saucer. Then she flipped it back over, quick.

Kaden leaned toward her, close enough to smell the lavender sticking to the porcelain. But she didn't pull away as he looked over her shoulder and into the cup. A few noncommittal sounds slipped from her mouth, and she pressed her lips together. Without warning, she stood, cup in hand. She crossed to the front door and flipped the sign to Closed.

"You have plans this afternoon?" she asked.

"Just avoiding an inevitable family reunion."

"Good. I need more-practiced eyes on this." She started down the hallway and toward the back door. "Come with me."

Kaden scrambled out of his chair and followed her, though

he wasn't really sure why. When he reached the bottom of the stairs, a sedan had pulled in beside Irene's pickup, and Clem Hamilton stepped out of the driver's side door.

She glanced from Kaden to Irene and back to Kaden.

She tilted her head to the side. "Friend of yours?"

"You remember Kaden Bonner?" Irene asked.

Clem's eyes went wide.

He lifted a hand in greeting.

"Surprised to see you back in Yarrow," Clem said.

"You and me both," Kaden said.

"What brings you home?" Then her face paled. "Oh, shit. You're here for the funeral."

"I'm here for a lot of things," he said.

"Sorry for your loss," Clem mumbled.

"Don't be," Kaden said. "I'm not. My dad was a dick."

Clem's eyebrows rose, but she nodded. "Guess it runs in the family." Then to Irene, "Is this your visitor?"

Irene let out a long sigh and held out his teacup. "That's what I'm hoping to find out." She glanced at Kaden. "Get in."

He looked from her to the truck, then to Clem.

"I wouldn't keep her waiting," Clem said.

Chapter 10

Irene

Irene glanced at Kaden as she drove. Took in his leather jacket, his brown hair shot through with a slight dusting of silver, his salt-and-pepper beard. She'd put him around her age, forty-six, maybe a year or two older—strange that she couldn't remember just how much older he was than his brother. He was devilishly handsome, like all the Bonners. His dark eyes narrowed as they drove past the wrought-iron fence of his family's estate.

Her focus drifted back to the flowers in her teacup.

"I never thought I'd come back here." Kaden's words came out hushed. He ran a hand through his hair and held it there. The furrowed lines along his forehead deepened. The air in the car grew heavy.

Irene wondered what would make a man leave his family behind. But right then, she was more concerned with why the universe had seen fit to thrust another Bonner into her life.

Once the distillery was out of sight, Kaden shook his head, as if coming out of a spell. He turned toward her. "What did my brother do to you?"

One of the first things Irene had learned about her gift as a child was how to put a wall up around her heart to keep from getting overwhelmed by other people's emotions. Now, she let it drop and took a quick look at Kaden, long enough to see dead leaves fluttering from his shoulders—sadness, disappointment. Behind his eyes were stalks of purple, bell-shaped flowers. Monkshood always indicated hatred.

If this man hated his brother, they might have more in common than Irene realized.

"We're getting right into it, then," she said.

"You tell me. I came in for a cup of tea and you kidnapped me." His eyes on her skin warmed her in a way she hadn't felt in a long time. "You could be taking me to the woods to kill me for all I know."

She smiled.

"What's all this about?" he pressed.

She wasn't ready to tell him. Not until she knew if she could trust the reading. "Could be nothing."

He crossed his arms and leaned back in his seat. "All this for nothing? At least tell me what my brother did."

It was just like Nate to never have told Kaden what had happened between them.

When she didn't answer, Kaden said, "He hurt you." He turned around in his seat and looked back the way they came.

"I found him in his car with another woman and broke off our engagement."

Kaden took a sharp breath. He opened his mouth, then closed it.

"It was years ago," Irene said.

"I doubt that makes it hurt any less."

She sighed. It didn't.

"I hoped he'd turn out better than the rest of my family," Kaden said.

Irene's eyes cut to him. "You don't like your family?"

"That's putting it mildly," he said as Irene pulled up the gravel drive of her mother's old Victorian home. She let the truck idle and turned toward Kaden.

"Is that why you left?" Irene had very few memories of him, almost like he'd never been there at all.

"I didn't want to be a Bonner anymore."

"Simple as that?"

He laughed softly. "Once you tell me why I'm really here, I'll consider telling *you* why being a Bonner is anything but simple."

Irene narrowed her eyes. "Let's get this over with."

She hopped out of the car and started along the winding path that led up to the house. Though it was worn and long past the need for a fresh coat of paint, flowers and greenery more than made up for the chipped wood. English ivy climbed thin, round columns that kept most of the overhang from sagging except after a particularly heavy rain. Honeysuckle shrubs grew on either side of the front staircase. Their offshoots wrapped around the rails, fire-orange blooms promising happiness and love. Oakleaf hydrangeas spread beneath the windows, the flowers already turned sepia beneath the summer sun. Bees buzzed from branch to branch.

She started for the stairs, and when she reached the door, she found Kaden still standing by the truck, hands in his pockets, head tilted back as he took in the house. Irene considered him for a second. His shadowed eyes. His open smile. It was the look of a man coming home, and it pulled at something in her that wasn't pain or sadness.

"I didn't miss much about Yarrow, but this..." Kaden trailed off.

The Victorian structure had been expanded over the generations—most recently by her mom, and before that by her grandparents. But rather than making the original architecture unrecognizable, the bay windows, transoms, and chimneys added to the house's character. The roof hung low over a front porch that wrapped around the back of the home. Even the garden out front, though not shadow dark, felt a little bit magical.

"It really is something," she agreed. "Now come on."

Before Irene had opened her shop, if her neighbors needed help with their pain, they came right to her family's doorstep. For a long time, it had been just her mother, Maura, easing the weight of their sorrow. The Haywood gift didn't hit everyone. Most often, it skipped the boys and their children, like it had with her brother and Quinn, then came back when a daughter was born of a daughter—although there had been a handful of men and those who didn't identify as either gender over the generations who'd had it.

"I'd have never left Yarrow if this is what I had to come back to."

Irene glanced back at him and saw that he wasn't staring at the house anymore. It had been a long time since someone looked at Irene with wonder rather than expectation. The awe in his voice stirred something in her, and a slow smile spread across her face. She held out a hand and a butterfly landed on her palm.

"Never seen a butterfly do that before," he said.

Irene laughed. "They show up when I'm happy."

Kaden reached a hand toward her. "Can I?"

She nodded and shifted the insect to Kaden's fingers. He lifted it close to his face. Watching him thawed something inside her. This moment—Kaden's wonder—seemed achingly familiar, but when she tried to grasp the feeling, it felt smothered, covered in cobwebs.

"Shall we?" Kaden asked.

"I almost forgot!" She ran back to the truck and grabbed the teacup. Then she started for the stairs.

Kaden followed. "You're really interested in my tea leaves."

"I'm interested in answers," Irene said as she pulled open the door.

"Hello there." Irene nearly jumped at the sound of her mother's voice. Maura Haywood stood in the entry hall, dusting a shelf that hadn't been touched by a rag in at least two months. She wore her hair—more white than red—in a thick braid that mirrored Irene's. Except for her crow's feet and deep laugh lines, she and Irene could've been sisters.

"You were expecting us?" Irene asked.

Maura tucked the rag into one of her belt loops. "Magic," she said with a shrug.

Irene raised an eyebrow.

"Clem texted," Maura said. She gave Kaden a cursory glance. "She knows how I feel about having a Bonner under my roof."

"He showed up at the tea shop," Irene said.

Maura crossed her arms, lips pressed thin. "So, what is he doing *here* now?"

Kaden leaned forward until he was in Maura's line of sight. "*He* was asked to come here. Well, he wasn't really asked. He was told to get in that truck, and since your daughter gave him a free cup of tea and he *really* doesn't want to see his own mother just yet, he agreed to it."

Maura's eyes widened. "I like him more than the last Bonner you brought home, but I still think you can do better."

Heat crept up Irene's neck.

"I thought you'd learned your lesson," Maura continued. "To think, I'd almost forgotten Nate had an older brother. You attract Bonner boys like honey attracts flies."

"Enough, Mother." Irene thrust the mug at her. "That's not why he's here."

Maura unfolded her reading glasses and settled them on the tip of her nose. She clasped the cup and glanced down at its contents, where the still-damp leaves clung to the porcelain. "Oh," she said, eyes widening. "Tricky. His, I presume?"

"Mine," Kaden agreed.

Maura rolled her eyes. "Come in, then." She turned on her heel and started down the hallway, spinning the cup around and around in her hands all the while. "Very, very tricky."

Irene followed her into the kitchen. Plants were drying on circular racks that dangled from the ten-foot ceilings, and the white walls had images of vines painted on them, creeping up along the cabinets and toward the old chandelier.

As Maura took a seat, Irene set the kettle on to boil. Might as well have her mother read her leaves, too.

"Well?" Kaden said, taking up the spot across from Maura. "What's my fortune say?"

"More like intuition, omens, that sort of thing," Irene said from the other side of the room, where she spooned herbs and tea into a mug of her own. A soft whistle filled the air, and she poured boiling water over the mixture.

"Why do my tea leaves matter to either of you?" Kaden asked.

Irene ignored him and sat down next to her mother. "What do you see?"

"His future has happiness and pain in it. A great love, but a great sorrow."

"So, you think it's an owl," Irene said.

"Could be a swan," Maura mused, and Irene laughed.

Her mother arched an eyebrow and said, "Why did you want me to read it?"

"I read my leaves the other day after Sylvia stopped by the shop."

"Bitch," Maura murmured. She cast a cursory glance at Kaden but didn't apologize.

"The comet, the clouds, the flowers, the bird, all identical to this," Irene continued. "The only difference was that mine showed a visitor. A man."

Maura's eyes widened. "I see." She looked back in the cup. "There's more. This hawk suggests a spiteful enemy."

She tilted the cup toward Irene. When Irene had looked earlier, that particular smattering of herbs had looked like nothing to her, but at her mother's words, the shape took form.

"And this at the bottom," Maura said with a quick glance at Kaden, "looks like a fern."

Irene took the cup from her mother and pressed the tip of her finger to the clump of leaves. Addison had seen the same thing in her leaves before this whole mess with the Bonner funeral started.

"This has been fun and all, but if you're not going to explain it to me—" Kaden started to push his chair back, and Irene clamped her hand down on top of his. His eyes flashed, the forsythia blooming behind them a sign of anticipation.

"Don't go," she said. The universe had sent him here. Irene may have had no intention of falling for another Bonner, but that didn't mean she was going to let this man walk out that door after they had almost exactly the same reading.

"Tell me what this is about," Kaden pressed.

Maura glanced at them, the lines between her eyebrows growing deeper. She took off her glasses, folded the sides in. For the first time since she'd addressed him at the front door, she looked right at Kaden when she spoke to him. "A fern is a sign of magic."

"Haywood magic?" he asked.

"I'm not sure what else it could be," Irene said.

"Why do you ask?" Maura said.

He shook his head. "I've been gone for a long time. Wasn't sure if things had changed."

He sat back down, slowly, his gaze dropping to Irene's hand on his. She grinned, and a butterfly flitted in through the back door. Once she finished off her tea, she swirled her mug, tipped it, and with a deep breath flipped it back over. The leaves had formed a perfect frond at the bottom, an exact match for the one in Kaden's cup. She pushed them toward him, and his eyes widened.

"You see it," she said.

"Kind of hard to miss." He looked into his own cup. "Not sure how you didn't see it in mine."

Maura huffed out a laugh.

Nonplussed, he asked Irene, "What's this mean?"

"That there's a reason you're back in Yarrow," she said.

"Oh, yeah?" Kaden asked. "Hmm. Like maybe a funeral?"

Irene shook her head. "It's more than that. And whatever it is, I'm a part of it."

He tilted his head to the side and considered her. "You don't sound disappointed."

Irene wasn't sure how she felt.

Kaden reached for his teacup and twirled it around in his hands. "Great love *and* great sorrow? Couldn't it just be one or the other?"

"You've clearly never been in love," Maura said.

Kaden rolled his eyes at her, and Irene laughed.

The only way to deal with the leaves pointing her to this man was to face them head-on. "Do you have dinner plans tonight?" she asked him.

"I was probably going to get takeout and eat it in my hotel room alone while working up the courage to go see my mom. Binge-watch something on Netflix. Cry a bit." He shrugged. "You know, the usual."

"You are *not* inviting him to family dinner night," Maura said.

"That's exactly what I'm doing," Irene said. "You like pizza?"

Kaden grinned. "Who doesn't like pizza?"

Chapter 11

Addison

While the Haywoods may have been the only ones in Yarrow with real magic, the Bonner distillery gave off an enchanted air. As Addison pulled her Bronco through the ivy-wrapped gates and followed the signs toward visitor parking, she couldn't help but notice the gloom. It was thick in the air and strongest near the distillery—settling over everything like a mist. She cranked her window down and let the fog float into the cab of her SUV. The car grew heavy with nostalgia.

Both her mother and her grandmother had spent Addison's teen years warning her about drinking Bonner bourbon, and, like a good girl, she'd listened. She'd trusted them.

But after things turned sour with River, all that had changed. She'd bought her first bottle of Bonner's. While she drank, she remembered every one of the good moments with River. Bonner bourbon did that, fostered sentimentality. It was part of what had made it so popular and something the town attributed to the dark-corn mash, but the next morning, without fail, she woke up with a killer hangover. Not that it had stopped her from drinking again.

Her family would've blamed it on the bourbon. Addison had blamed it on herself. These days, she always had a bottle of Bonner's on hand in her kitchen.

She shifted the car into park and leaned back against the head-rest. Her heart twisted in her chest, and she welcomed the ache. One breath. Two. She said a quick prayer to the universe that she'd run into River again. And a second prayer that if she did run into him, she'd say the right thing for once.

Then she grabbed the flowers her grams had asked her to hand deliver. Maura and Irene may have hated Sylvia with a passion, but in Yarrow, you killed your enemies with kindness.

She started for the distillery's main offices. The bourbon festival preparations were underway. The Bonners would be going straight from the funeral to the celebration, kicking things off with the annual memory harvest, but maybe that's how Christian would've wanted to be remembered.

Her eyes snagged on a silver Mazda in the employee-marked spaces with a bumper sticker that read, "Save the bees!" She smiled. River hadn't removed every part of her from his life.

When she walked through the doors to the office, she was greeted by a lobby covered in floral arrangements. Yet, as elaborate and expensive as most of them were, none of them carried the power of the shadow garden. The Haywoods' bouquet put the others to shame with its black hollyhock and sunflowers, inky lilies and dark, star-shaped borage blossoms.

"Welcome to Bonner—" The young woman behind the front desk stopped short as she looked up. "Oh! Miss Haywood."

Addison smiled. "My family asked me to drop these off for Sylvia."

"Certainly, let me just ring Mrs. Bonner."

"That's not necessary," Addison said. She didn't want to get caught up in the drama.

"I insist." She lifted the receiver from the phone on her desk. "Mrs. Bonner? Yes, Addison Haywood's here with flowers."

Before Addison could sit on one of the plush couches out front, Sylvia stepped through the door just past the reception area. "Addison," she said. "This is a surprise."

"My grams wanted to send her sympathy." Addison lifted the vase Maura had painstakingly arranged.

"Maura did this?" Sylvia accepted the flowers. She gently touched her fingers to the petals. Though she smiled, Addison could see it for the mask it was. Maura would've said Sylvia was a woman full of falsehoods, but to Addison, she only looked like a woman grieving her husband. "For me?"

"We're sorry for your loss," Addison said. The words felt hollow, but none of the condolences her grams had suggested had been even close to appropriate.

Sylvia set the arrangement on the receptionist's desk. "Please call someone down from the house to pick this up. I'd like to put them in my room."

"I'll be sure to tell her that you like them," Addison said as she stepped away.

"Leaving so soon?" Sylvia asked. "While you're here, at least let me show you around. Have you ever been on a tour of the distillery?"

Addison shook her head. "I've always been interested, especially knowing the corn started with seeds from our crops. But I'm sure now isn't the best time."

"This will be fun, then," Sylvia said.

"Oh, no, I couldn't possibly..." Addison protested.

But Sylvia took Addison by the hand and led her out the door and onto the distillery grounds. A golf cart sat in a parking space marked with Sylvia's name. She patted the seat beside her, and Addison slid into place.

"Maura's lucky to have you taking care of that garden for her," Sylvia said. "I wish Nate had decided to have children. I'd hoped to leave all of this to a granddaughter someday. He does well with the bourbon, but he doesn't have a woman's touch. You wouldn't happen to be interested in making bourbon, would you?"

Addison laughed softly, not sure what to say. "My hands belong in the dirt."

Sylvia stopped the golf cart in front of one of the buildings right along the river. This close, Addison could see the thin, sooty lines the gloom had left in the brick.

"You want to look at the corn?" Sylvia asked.

"I was hoping to see the fields, actually."

"We'll start here. This is where the magic really happens," she said with a wink.

Inside, Sylvia led her to a large vat. Nate Bonner stood several feet above them on the catwalk beside it. His brown hair was thinning on top, and though the cut of his shirt looked expensive, it didn't quite hide the gut that came from too many years of too much bourbon. Addison squinted and tilted her head to the side. It was hard for her to imagine her mother with this man.

"Mom," he said with a nod to Sylvia. "Giving a private tour?" He narrowed his eyes at Addison. "Damn, never thought I'd see the day you'd be walking a Haywood through here. Addison, right?"

"Right," Addison said.

"Your mom still hate me?"

Addison winced.

He laughed, big and loud. "Your family sure knows how to hold a grudge."

"Nate," Sylvia said. "Addison dropped off flowers from Maura. From their shadow garden. Be nice."

"I'm always nice." His grin—petunias blooming purple with resentment—unsettled Addison. "Want some swag? Tell the gift shop you can have whatever you'd like—on me."

Before she could decline, the door at the opposite end of the catwalk opened wide. River stepped through it in a black T-shirt marked with the Bonner's logo. Addison's heart dropped, and when her eyes met his, it sank further.

"I was hoping your apprentice would be here," Sylvia said. "River, this is Addison."

"We've met." His eyes flashed.

"I didn't realize..." Sylvia trailed off, then shook her head. "But of course you have. Elena's grandson, Maura's granddaughter. Weren't you two dating at one point?"

River gave a smile that didn't quite reach his eyes. "At one point." Then with a short nod in Addison's direction he said, "Good to see you."

Addison knew she should block out his emotions, but she couldn't help herself.

River was all anger and bitterness. It wasn't pure hatred, but it might as well have been. If his bosses hadn't been standing there, she could tell he would've been out that door in a heartbeat.

Nate glanced between the two of them. "We've got quite a lot to do here. Hope the rest of the tour is as exciting as this has been."

"No worries at all," Addison said. "I actually need to get going. Thanks for showing me around, Mrs. Bonner."

"Please," she said. "Call me Sylvia."

"And Addison?" Nate called from the catwalk.

She glanced up at him, trying not to let tears fall.

"Tell your mom I said hello."

Addison didn't allow herself to think as she ran back to her car and sped away as fast as possible. It wasn't until she'd pulled back onto her family's land that she let herself breathe freely.

"We've *met*," she mumbled to herself. "What an absolute dick."

Instead of heading out to the shadow garden, she knelt right out front beside her grams's tomatoes, taking her frustration out on the weeds that had the audacity to try and make a home there. She gripped one with her full hand, then cursed when she realized it was a yellow thistle rather than a dandelion. She stuck her pricked fingers in her mouth. When they finally stopped throbbing, she grabbed her gloves from her pocket, tugged them on, and mercilessly pulled it from the ground.

"Serves you right, masquerading as a harmless weed."

"You're back later than I expected," Maura said as the screen door slammed shut behind her and she stepped onto the front porch with a mint-filled pitcher. "Lemonade?"

"Please," Addison said.

"Sylvia put you in this state?"

"I'm not," Addison said as she huffed and pulled up another weed, "in a state."

Maura arched her eyebrow as a cicada landed on the banister.

With a heavy sigh, Addison sat back on her heels. "River was there."

Maura poured Addison a glass of lemonade. Addison wiped

the sweat from her forehead, leaving a trail of dirt along her skin. She brushed her hands on her overalls and started up the front steps.

"It's not your fault what happened to him," Maura said as she lifted the straw hat from her head and settled down in one of the front porch rockers.

Addison had heard this before—from both her grams and her mom.

"There's no one else to blame," Addison said. "It was my magic that broke him."

"It was Haywood magic," Maura said.

"Not like yours," Addison said. "If I had yours . . ."

"You're not me. And you're not your mother."

"I'm only fit to work in the garden. I know that now."

"You work the garden because it likes you better than it likes either of us," Maura said.

Addison sipped her lemonade. "At least someone likes me."

Maura set her glass down beside her and leaned forward in her chair. "We're proud of you. You know that, don't you?"

Addison tipped her head back. "When mom was my age, she had a two-year-old and a successful tea shop. When you were my age—"

"I had two children and the whole town coming to my door to take away their pain."

Maura flashed her a grin, and Addison let out a small laugh as she tried to ignore the tears welling in her eyes. "I should be further along. I should have something of my own by now."

"You're twenty-four."

"And?" Addison said.

"Who do you think is going to manage all this when I'm too

old to bend over and pull the weeds myself?" Maura asked. "I didn't entrust the garden to you because you can't heal people as well as your mother and I can. I entrusted it to you because you belong here, beneath the sun, not trapped behind the walls of a brick building."

"If my tea leaves are right, selling that rosemary..." She paused as her grandmother stiffened in the chair beside her, and decided against mentioning Sylvia. "I might finally figure out what's wrong with my magic."

"You're not the only one whose tea leaves are bringing unwanted guests to our door," Maura said.

"Guests?" Addison asked.

"Your mother's invited someone for family dinner," Maura said.

Addison's eyebrows shot up. "Someone we know? Or...a visitor?"

Maura crossed her arms. "I see she told *you* about her tea leaves."

"Yet you know about them, too," Addison said.

"Because she brought him *here*." She clucked her tongue. "A Bonner."

"How?" Addison asked. She'd been with the Bonners all afternoon.

"Sylvia's long-lost son, Kaden, has returned to Yarrow. There was magic in his leaves."

Addison leaned back in her rocker and took a long sip of her lemonade. Maybe Quinn was right. Maybe there'd been more to her own reading than she'd thought.

Chapter 12

Kaden

It had been harder than Kaden had expected to find a hotel room. With the Annual Yarrow Bourbon Festival coming up, all the affordable spots were booked. He'd ended up in the only open room at the Yarrow Bed & Breakfast, complete with a twin bed so short his feet hung off the edge and a standing shower that only came as high as his shoulder—so much for historic charm.

It cost what a king would've run him at a chain hotel.

But, like everyone else he'd run into, the woman working the desk hadn't recognized him. So, instead of letting word get out he was back in town, he'd run to an ATM and paid in cash. He hadn't decided how he wanted his reunion with his mother to go, but he wanted it to be on his terms. If she didn't realize he was here, he might be able to make that happen.

He found himself pulling up the gravel drive to the Haywood home once again, half expecting to discover Irene's invitation had been a joke.

He drummed his hands against the steering wheel and checked his hair in the rearview mirror. He wasn't quite sure what he was doing here. He'd come to Yarrow looking for answers, but he wasn't ready to go looking for them with his own family.

As he opened his door, another car pulled into the driveway. The woman who exited the vehicle was the same person who'd checked him into his room. She wore a yellow-and-white checkered blazer and dark jeans. Her hair was pulled up in a bun that didn't quite manage to capture every strand. She'd introduced herself as Taylor at the bed and breakfast. If she was here, then she was Taylor *Haywood*—Nolan Haywood's wife. Kaden might not have been close with the Haywoods, but he remembered that much.

"*You're* Irene's visitor?" she said.

He gave her a half smile. "Does everyone in town know about the tea leaves?"

"Yours or hers?" Taylor asked.

"That's a yes," Kaden said.

"That's a yes," she agreed before she started up the steps, her yellow heels clacking all the way. "Come on, then."

Kaden jogged after her.

She slipped off her shoes and left them by the door. Kaden did the same.

"Found your visitor in the driveway!" she called out as she led him to the kitchen.

The room smelled of tomato sauce and pepperoni. A basket of garlic bread sat on the counter. Taylor swiped a piece before she slipped out of her jacket and kissed Clem full on the mouth.

Kaden narrowed his eyes. Had he misremembered?

Across from them sat two young women—a redhead wearing black boots and equally black lipstick who was clearly a Haywood, and a young woman with light brown skin and dark hair that fell to her chin—both in their twenties. Another young woman with dark hair pulled back at the nape of her neck stood chopping fresh vegetables at the counter, and beside her Irene was pulling a pizza out of the oven.

She tugged off her oven mitts, turned to him, and said, "I didn't think you'd show."

"I want to see how the leaves play out," he said, which put a smile on Irene's lips.

"*This* is the guy?" asked the woman at the cutting board as she set down the knife.

"You've met?" Irene asked her.

"I saw him heading into the shop earlier today. If I'd realized it was him, I might've stuck around." She extended a hand. "Addison Haywood."

Kaden glanced from Addison to Irene. "Your daughter?"

"I'm full of surprises today, apparently," Irene said. "That's my niece, Quinn—Taylor's daughter. Her girlfriend, Harper. Clem and Taylor you already know."

"Kaden Bonner," he said. "Nice to meet all of you."

"Wait," Taylor said, "that's definitely not the name you gave at the bed and breakfast. You're a Bonner?"

"I still don't understand why you invited him for dinner," Addison said. She blushed and looked to Kaden. "Sorry. You seem nice enough."

He shrugged and somehow felt like he should be the one apologizing.

"All I wanted to do was sell rosemary to Sylvia Bonner, and you about lost your shit," Addison said to her mother. "Now you've invited a Bonner into our home?"

"Twice!" Maura called as she stuck her head into the kitchen.

Kaden raised his hand in a wave. She arched an eyebrow.

"Kaden is here because I saw him in my leaves," Irene said. "And you know what we say."

"Always trust the leaves," Quinn said.

Addison crossed her arms. "And never trust a Bonner."

"You told me your name was Mike Smith," Taylor said.

"I lied," Kaden said.

"Not a great start," Maura called from the other room.

"He's Nate's older brother," Irene said to the younger women in the room. "He left town back in the '90s."

"I take it you don't want your mom knowing you're here?" Taylor asked.

"Not just yet," Kaden said. "And since no one I've run into today seems to remember me, I'm doing pretty good so far."

"I recognize you," Quinn said.

Maura stepped into the kitchen, poured herself a drink, and took the spot at the head of the table. "Probably because he looks like his brother."

"Maybe. If Nate hadn't spent the last twenty-five years drinking as much bourbon as he makes," Clem said.

Quinn shook her head. "No, I mean..." She pressed her lips together, closed her eyes, tugged a lock of hair between her teeth. "Never mind."

Kaden took a seat across from her. "You're Quinn?"

She nodded.

"Our daughter," Taylor and Clem said at the same time.

That definitely didn't line up with Kaden's memories.

"You remember me?" Kaden asked.

"I think so?" Quinn said, letting the hair go. "It's a little hazy."

"Please tell me," he said. "I got back in town this morning, and every person I've talked to has told me they forgot I even existed. It's a little disorienting."

Quinn held a hand over her face. "I get these nightmares."

Taylor reached across the table for her daughter's hand. "Those bothering you again?"

"It's just...there was a man in them I didn't recognize. Flashes, anyway. And I think it could be you?" She shook her head. "I need a drink." Harper offered Quinn hers, and Quinn took a long sip.

They all stared at Kaden for a minute.

"Were you here that summer?" Quinn asked. "'97?"

"I was, but I only remember leaving," he said.

Irene pressed her lips together. "You didn't even remember me calling off the engagement with your brother."

Kaden shook his head slowly. "All I know is something happened that was bad enough for me to give it all up. My family, the distillery, and I..." He looked around at all of them. "Let's just say I'd thought about leaving for a long time. When I realized I'd willingly handed over an entire summer to the memory harvest, I knew I didn't want to be a part of whatever led me to do that anymore."

"What was so bad? Did you, like, kill someone?" Quinn asked.

Kaden stared at her blankly.

Addison dropped her face into her hands. "Really?"

"What do you mean?" Kaden said.

"She's convinced your family murdered her dad," Harper said matter-of-factly.

Kaden blanched. "*Murder?*" His eyes slid to Clem and Taylor. That explained why Nolan wasn't there.

"He was gone by the time Nolan's body was found," Taylor said.

"He was there *before* Dad disappeared," Quinn countered.

"Well, this got dark awful fast," Clem said. "More bourbon, anyone?"

"Wait, you're drinking *bourbon*?" Kaden asked.

"Not Bonner's," Maura said. "We don't touch that stuff in this house."

Clem held up the bottle, and Kaden nodded. "Neat," he said as he rubbed at his temples and turned his focus back to Maura. "You're the one who sold my family that corn."

"A lot of good that did Yarrow," Maura huffed. "Don't think I don't regret that decision every day."

"Excuse me," Quinn said. "I'm waiting to hear if Kaden murdered my father."

Irene sighed, heavy, as Clem topped off her drink. "The Bonners are an absolute bag of dicks—"

"No argument there," Kaden said, which earned him an appraising look from every woman in the room.

"—but they didn't kill your dad," Irene finished.

"We don't *know* that," Quinn said.

"We do know that the entire town gave up their memories that summer and decided not to write a single thing down," Taylor said with a hand on Quinn's shoulder. "If I'd known what would happen to your father, there's no way I'd have gone along with it. None of us would have."

"And yet you don't remember Kaden," Quinn said.

Kaden tapped his fingers against the tabletop as he tried to keep up.

"As much as I'd love to blame my son's death on the

Bonners, your mom's right," Maura said with a sympathetic look in Quinn's direction.

"Why *did* you come back to Yarrow if you hate your family so much?" Addison asked.

"I . . ." He hesitated. Quinn's accusation settled into him. Had this been a week ago, he might have brushed off the idea. Of course, had this been a week ago, he'd never be here, at this table. It was only that night in the bar that convinced him to come home.

If he could take a woman's memories, what else might he be capable of? He needed to find out more.

He watched as Irene exchanged a look with her mother. Maura went back to staring at him over the rim of her glass.

"I've been having some weird things happening with memory," Kaden said. "I thought maybe I'd find some answers in Yarrow."

Quinn elbowed Addison. "Told you that rosemary meant memory."

"What's this about rosemary?" Maura asked.

Addison grabbed a slice of pizza and set it down in front of Kaden. Then she said, "Quinn wants me to try and get rid of her nightmares—"

"Our magic can't do that," Maura interrupted her, though her tone had softened.

"—and she thinks my reading about the Bonners was about more than just the funeral and my magic," Addison said.

"Maybe it was," Irene said. "Mine said we'd be getting a visitor, and here he is."

All eyes turned to Kaden.

"While we're talking about the Bonners," Addison said,

"Sylvia once again expressed how much it would mean to her if our family was at the funeral."

"We are *not* honoring her dead," Maura said.

"No offense, Kaden," Irene said.

"Offense fully intended," Maura corrected her.

"I, for one, am not offended," Kaden said.

Maura crossed her arms. "Stop being so easygoing about all this. I'm trying to hate you for the Bonner you are."

Kaden considered her. "You know, if you really wanted to get under my mother's skin, you wouldn't skip the funeral. You'd show up with me instead."

Maura narrowed her eyes. "That's actually an excellent idea."

The kitchen fell silent.

"Excuse me?" Irene asked.

"Can you imagine the look on Sylvia's face if she sees her prodigal son sitting with *our* family?" Maura said. "I never thought I'd say this, but I like the way you think, Kaden Bonner."

He let out a long breath. At least he wouldn't have to face the funeral alone. The Haywoods might not be family or even friends, but they were certainly better than what he knew was waiting for him at home.

"It also means we'll get to take credit for the shadow garden rosemary in person," Addison said.

"Maybe we'll even get some new customers," Quinn said.

Maura pointed at each of her granddaughters in turn. "I like the way you *all* think."

"What do you say?" Kaden asked Irene. "It would be nice to have a friendly face there."

"And *I'm* a friendly face?" she said.

"You did invite him to dinner," Clem said.

"And don't forget the leaves," Addison chimed in.

"Is this your way of saying I told you so?" Irene asked.

Her daughter grinned. "You tell me."

Irene rolled her eyes. "I'm not making this decision until after dessert."

❧

Kaden and Irene sat on the back porch, alone. After dinner, everyone had quickly disappeared with excuses that they had to get home or head to the shop or read a book. Even Maura had made herself scarce once the family had agreed they'd attend the funeral.

Yet somehow Kaden was still here. He wasn't ready to be alone yet.

"That was the best strawberry rhubarb pie I've ever had," he said.

"Be sure to tell Harper the next time you see her," Irene said. "It came from Baker's."

"I didn't miss a lot about this town, but I did miss Baker's."

"For good reason," Irene said.

They were quiet for a few moments, the crickets' song soft and low. Fireflies floated on the thick summer air, casting the shadow garden in hues of green. The only place where Kaden had ever seen more in one place was at the bourbon festival. They came out in droves for the harvest.

"Your family is—"

Irene cut him short. "I'm not apologizing for them."

"—the kind of family I wish I'd had growing up."

"Oh," Irene said.

"I like them."

"As you should." She leaned forward in her chair and turned her head toward him. "Your family really did a number on you."

"It was a long time ago," Kaden said.

She looked him over, her eyes catching on his. "There's hope in you, but it's more than that. You're scared."

"You can see all that just by looking at me?" Kaden asked.

"You really have been gone a long time," Irene said.

"Can you read minds?"

"Just feelings," Irene said. "But yours don't make sense to me. Grief's always hard to parse."

"I'm not grieving my dad," Kaden said. But that wasn't fully true. He'd never stopped mourning the father Christian Durant could have been. The family he might have had if they'd chosen love over control.

"I take it things weren't great between the two of you," Irene said.

What could it hurt, baring his heart to this woman who could read it so clearly? The day had already been strange enough.

"He was abusive," Kaden said.

"Nate never told me that." Irene shook her head.

"He wouldn't have," Kaden said. "Dad never raised a hand to him. It was me he went after."

"Did your mom know?" Irene asked.

He let out a strangled laugh. "You know, she told me I could stop what my father was doing to me?" He rubbed at his eyes. "I thought I'd buried all this, but coming back here..."

"If you want me to ease the pain..."

Kaden shook his head. "I think some pain we're meant to keep. To remind us who we never want to be."

Irene sipped her drink. "You surprise me, Kaden Bonner."

He kneaded his knuckles against the side of his neck and stole a quick glance at her. "Why are you doing this for me?"

"Drinking a mint julep and watching the sunset?" Irene asked.

"Inviting me to your family dinner, agreeing to attend my father's funeral," Kaden said. "You don't even know me."

She started to answer, but he cut her short. "And don't tell me it's because of the leaves."

"It *is* because of the leaves," she said.

"From what I heard in there, you hate my family far more than I remember," Kaden said.

"You can thank your brother for that."

"This is about more than Nate."

"My mom doesn't like what the bourbon industry's become. She doesn't like the memory harvest, the gloom, any of it." She sighed. "When you spend enough time pulling sorrow from people's hearts, you start to wonder where it comes from."

"You think my family's responsible?"

Irene shrugged. "My mom thinks they are. And that definitely made it easier for me to write off your entire family after what your brother did to me."

"But you're still willing to help me," Kaden said. "That's what I don't understand."

She let out a heavy sigh and leaned her head back against the chair. "I have this...feeling when I'm around you. I can't really explain it. Like I want to trust you. It doesn't make any sense, but there it is. Combined with the leaves, it's something I can't just ignore."

Kaden didn't know much about readings, but he'd heard what Maura said before. He stood and offered Irene a hand up. She eyed it, warily, but ultimately, she accepted. She rubbed her thumb along his until it caught on his nail, then held tight as he pulled her to her feet.

Irene's eyes held his for a few seconds.

Their readings had been exactly the same.

But he didn't know whether he was the love or the sorrow.

Chapter 13

Addison

Addison knew full well she ran the risk of bumping into River when she went to drop off the crate of shadow garden rosemary, but instead of asking Quinn to handle the delivery, she'd decided to subject herself to that distinct possibility. The universe had put rosemary in her tea leaves for a reason. Maybe this was part of it.

She nestled her sunglasses on top of her head, threw back her shoulders, and stepped into the sunlight. Once she unstrapped the crate, she shouldered it toward the old barn the Bonners had converted into an event space.

She was hefting the crate a little higher as she reached for the door when she heard, "Let me help you with that."

There it was, the universe coming through for her.

"Oh," River said, as he saw her, "it's you."

"You don't have to be a dick every time you see me," she said.

"Things would be a lot easier if I didn't have to see you at all."

Addison shook her head and dropped the crate at his feet. "Your sister is dating my cousin. Our grandmothers are best friends. Avoiding each other isn't going to work. There's got to be another way."

"For you, that means taking no responsibility for what you did," River said.

"How?" Addison asked. "I tried to fix it, and I can't. I've apologized a thousand times. What more do you want?"

"Don't you get it?" River met her eyes. "Every time I see you, I'm reminded of what I lost. I'm reminded that if I'd just stayed there, if I'd decided to wake my grandfather up before it happened, he'd still be alive. I can't get him back. I can't get any of it back."

"I..." She struggled for words. *I feel the same way too*, she wanted to say. *I wish more than anything that I could undo it all.*

Addison and River had known each other their whole lives, but they hadn't started dating until after high school. When things ended, Addison lost more than a four-year relationship. She lost one of her closest friends.

"If you're going to try to defend yourself—"

"I'm not," she said, feeling even worse.

She looked away.

"If you have something to say, say it."

"You're right," Addison said. "I hurt you. I'm sorry. But at a certain point we both have to move on."

It almost felt like one of their old fights—when they were still together. Addison's eyes flicked up to his, and she saw it— an aching sort of affection blooming right behind his irises. This was why she refused to let go, even though everyone told her she should. She knew that he still felt something for her, and she hadn't been ready to give up on that.

"I'll try to stay out of your way," she whispered, feeling utterly defeated.

"Thanks." He propped open the door. Addison's eyes followed

the lines of his fingers, his skin more than summer dark. Fingers that used to touch her, tenderly. She forced her eyes away from his hands, focusing instead on his heather-gray T-shirt that read *I got sMashed in Yarrow, Kentucky.*

She snorted. *Yeah, you and everyone else in this damn town.* "Nice shirt," she murmured.

River looked down at himself. When he glanced back up, his unexpected smile and soft laughter almost undid her. "I have to wear the merch when I work."

"Not terribly funeral appropriate," Addison said.

"Nate suggested it," River said with a shrug as he reached down and picked up the abandoned crate. "I'll take this in for you. I'm sure you'd rather spend as little time here as possible."

"I don't hate the Bonners as much as everyone seems to think," she said. "I actually really like the bourbon. I started drinking it after..."

The words hung in the air between them. River's eyes flashed with that revelation. He cleared his throat. "I should get going," he said, voice thick. "I've got a few more things to do before the funeral."

Addison stared after him as he walked away. Maybe this was why her tea leaves had brought her there, why the fern had appeared in her cup. It hadn't been to help her sort out her magic at all, but to remind her the damage she'd done had been irreparable. That it was finally time to let River go. She started back toward her car, tears smarting in her eyes. She got there just as Kaden pulled in next to her, his eyes darting from Addison to the now-closed barn door.

"Didn't expect to see you here," she said as she quickly fumbled to put her sunglasses on.

"You all right?" he asked. "That guy say something to you?"

She didn't really know this man, but if the universe had sent him to her mother, then maybe he'd been sent to her, too. Either way, it was nice to feel seen.

"We used to be together. I . . ." She blinked to stop the tears. It didn't work, so she started picking at her fingernails. "I messed things up, did things I can never take back."

Kaden pressed his lips together and nodded. "Before I left town, I'd have told you to give all that up to the harvest."

"And now?"

Kaden glanced up the hill and shook his head. "Now I'm not so sure."

Addison gave up on hiding behind her sunglasses. She wiped the tears away with the back of her hand. "Don't think I haven't thought about it."

"What's stopping you?" Kaden asked.

"The memory of losing him is one of the few things I have left of what we used to be," Addison said. "Funny how the worst things about a relationship are the easiest to remember."

"You could always read what you gave up if you ever wanted to," Kaden said.

After the Bonners had tapped the first barrel with the dark-corn mash and people's worst memories disappeared, the town and the Bonners put rules in place. Memory could be tricky, and the last thing they wanted was people walking around with holes in their minds and no way to fill them. While the harvest, it seemed, could only take a person's darkest moments, if you wanted to participate, you had to write that memory down in detail and give the paper to someone close to you for safekeeping.

Addison shrugged. "Reading about what happened isn't the same as having it here." She touched the tip of her finger to her temple.

"It helps some people, forgetting," Kaden said.

"I guess." Addison stared off in the direction River had gone. "It didn't help River."

Fear bled into Kaden's aura. "Did . . . did something happen with the memory harvest?"

"No, it was nothing your family did." Addison closed her eyes and took a deep breath. She didn't need to read this man's emotions. She had enough to deal with.

Addison shook her head. "I don't know why I'm talking to you about this."

"Because I'm a good listener?" Kaden offered.

She laughed softly. "You're a Bonner."

"Let's call me a Bonner in recovery," Kaden said. "Besides, you and I aren't that different."

"How's that?" Addison asked.

"We're both healers," he said.

She knew her grams would have more than a few words to say about that. "You think what your family does heals people?"

"I don't know about my family, but it's what I wanted. When we discovered what the bourbon did after that first dark-corn batch, it scared me. But taking those memories brought people peace," Kaden said.

Addison smiled sadly. Even if Kaden was right, what she'd done to River wasn't the same. "What if you took a memory someone didn't want to give up?"

Kaden tapped his fingers against his car's window frame. "Something like that happen with you and River?"

"Yeah," she said shakily. "I took more than I meant to." Addison glanced back the way River had gone. "There was a fire at Baker's a couple of years ago. His grandfather died, and I wanted to ease his guilt." She leaned her head back against her truck and closed her eyes. "But I took every good feeling tied to that guilt—about his grandfather, about the family business. It's why he's not working at Baker's anymore."

"Shit," Kaden said.

"The worst part is, I still love him." She laughed through her tears. "Sorry. I hardly know you...It's just nice to talk to someone who doesn't have years of preconceived ideas about me and this town and...my abilities—or lack thereof."

"Don't apologize for your pain," Kaden said.

"I wish I could fix it," Addison said. "But I don't know how."

"The shadow garden made all of this possible," he said with a nod toward the distillery. "Maybe there's some way it can help you heal."

Addison shook her head. The garden couldn't take her pain. There was only one way for her to heal from this heartache. The old-fashioned way. On her own—with time.

Chapter 14

Kaden

The gate code separating the Bonner mansion from the rest of the distillery grounds hadn't changed since Kaden left twenty-five years ago—almost as if his mother knew he'd one day be back. He'd considered waiting until the funeral to see her, but after yesterday, he had more questions than answers.

What he'd said to Addison had been true: once, he'd wanted to believe he could be a kind of healer—that he could provide a form of comfort, that what the bourbon did was truly revolutionary. But after stealing that woman's memories in the bar, he wondered if what his family had done was worse. Much worse.

He took one last look over the distillery grounds behind him. The Ohio River hugged the eastern edge of the property, where limestone naturally filtered the water, before the property gave way to the distillery itself. Five warehouses surrounded the periphery of the complex where the barrels expanded in the hot Kentucky summers and contracted in the cold Kentucky winters. The bourbon bled into the wood, the wood into the bourbon, until flavor and nostalgia had aged to perfection.

He'd missed it.

As he started up the drive, the smell of yeast gave way to

freshly cut grass and flowers in bloom. The peach walls of his family home stood bright and striking, like they'd been dipped in candy. Soft pink blossoms lined the winding drive. A Haywood would've recognized them as begonias, but to Kaden they were simply a show of wealth. The only ones he knew by name were the hydrangeas, his mother's favorite, that crowded the beds in front of the white wrap-around porch in globes of bright blue blooms. Above it all stood the rotunda where her bedroom gave her a sweeping view of the entire Bonner estate.

People moved across the lawn, carrying cases of bourbon as they prepared for the evening's event. He'd hoped his mother might have changed. Instead, she was making a show of the whole thing. It turned his stomach.

He was walking right into a spider's web, and the widow wouldn't give him up easily once she had him in her claws. At least his father was gone. The violence he'd encounter inside would be only one of words, not action.

Kaden pulled his car to a stop by the portico. He turned off the ignition and forced a few deep breaths. Then he shrugged on his jacket despite the heat. He knew that nothing could prepare him for walking up those steps, crossing that porch, and holding his fist up to the door, but he had to try.

Before his knuckles brushed wood, the knob turned. A white woman in a black polo shirt emblazoned with the Bonner's logo looked up at him.

"Oh, I'm sorry. We're not expecting guests until this evening. Or are you..." She checked her clipboard. "Samuel? You're supposed to be wearing the uniform." She looked past him with a frown. "And staff must park in the lot down by the venue. Someone should've explained all this to you."

"I'm not here to work the party," he said.

Her eyes widened, and she glanced behind her. "It's not a party."

"By the looks of things, I'm not sure what else it could be."

"It's a funeral," the woman said.

He cleared his throat. "I'm here to see Sylvia."

"Mrs. Bonner isn't taking visitors before the service." She tried to edge him away from the door, but Kaden held his ground. "How did you... Was the gate open?"

"Is someone there?" His mother's voice echoed through the foyer. Dread settled into Kaden's chest.

He pushed past the young woman and through the open door.

"Excuse me, sir..."

She was at the top of the grand staircase. She wore a pair of horn-rimmed glasses accented with gold. Her black skirt and blazer rolled business and mourning all into one. So convenient. Her dark brown hair had gone silver since Kaden last saw her. At the sight of him, she started down the steps, one hand on the railing. Her heels clicked against the wood, slow and measured.

Tap.

Tap.

Tap.

He held his breath as their eyes locked.

"You actually came," she said.

He ached with the desire to believe the lilt in her voice was about him, but every emotion with his mother had only ever been about her.

Her son had listened to her message.

Her son had come home.

Her son loved *her*.

He looked down at his feet, rubbed the toe of one shoe against the carpet. Then he glanced back up and ran a hand through his hair, stopping at the top of his head.

"I got your message."

"I wasn't sure if I'd found the right number, but when I heard your voice on the answering machine..." She hesitated. "It's good to have you home, Kaden."

The woman behind him whispered his name. "Kaden Bonner?" Dazed, she said, "Mrs. Bonner, I'm so sorry. I didn't realize."

Sylvia fluttered a hand at her, as if she couldn't be bothered with a full wave. "Of course not," she said. "Don't let us keep you."

"If you need anything, I'll be just outside," the woman said, making herself smaller as she backed out onto the porch. The door closed behind her with a click.

"Well?" Sylvia asked. "Aren't you going to give your mom a hug?"

Kaden took a step toward her, willing the tension out of his arms before wrapping them around her. She still smelled the same, sweet and smoky like corn and oak. He closed his eyes. He couldn't stop the tears welling up.

When he pulled back, she rested her hands on his shoulders and arched an eyebrow. This close he could see all the lines at the corners of her eyes and feathering out from her lips. It hurt to realize how much she'd aged since he last saw her.

But he wasn't here to make up for time lost.

"I hope those tears aren't for your father," she said.

Kaden thumbed them away. "You know me better than that."

The furrows in her brow mirrored Kaden's. He hated seeing so much of himself in her.

"It's probably too much to hope they're for me." She dropped her hold on him.

He resisted the urge to laugh, which only made the tears fall faster. Talking to her felt like stretching a broken arm that hadn't healed quite right. Of course she *wanted* him to cry for her.

"They're for a lot of things, Mom," he said. "It's been a long time."

"You missed me," she said, almost childlike. "That's why you're here? Not for him?"

"I'm not here for him." As much as he'd tried to put all this behind him, he was still angry. He was still broken. "But I didn't come home because I missed you, either."

Hurt flashed across her face. "What, then? You thought you'd come collect some sort of inheritance? I've got news for you. Your father didn't love either of you boys." She paused, let the words sink in. "Not the way I did."

It was just like her to twist everything like that. To couple her love with pain.

"Right. By letting him hurt me?" The words escaped Kaden's lips before he could stop them. He knew she'd been one of his father's victims, too, but that didn't lessen the weight of his pain. She'd chosen her husband over him. Again, and again, and again.

"By making you stronger," Sylvia said.

He shoved his hands into his pockets and took a step back.

"Strong enough to leave, maybe." He laughed bitterly. "But now that I've come back to Yarrow, no one remembers me unless I tell them my name. You wouldn't happen to have anything to do with that, would you?"

"The memory harvest took that summer from everyone," Sylvia said. "The town chose not to write it down because they didn't—because we didn't—want to remember, ever."

"So I keep hearing." He leaned back on his heels.

"Let's sit down and catch up," she said. "Maybe a little early for a glass of bourbon, though we are burying your father today..."

He shook his head.

"Coffee, then."

He didn't tell her that all he wanted was tea.

She led him through the grand entryway, past the ballroom, and to the kitchen, where the staff was preparing food for his father's funeral. Death was supposed to be marked by home-cooked meals from your neighbors and your heart falling to pieces every time you remembered you'd never see a person again—not catering.

"Mrs. Bonner, is there something you need?" The question came from another woman in a black polo whom Kaden didn't recognize.

"Bring us a pot of coffee in the sitting room, please," Sylvia commanded, her grip on Kaden not quite tight enough to be uncomfortable but close.

"Two cups?" the woman asked.

Sylvia nodded, almost preening, "One for each of us." She gave a small, calculated laugh, so much like the woman of Kaden's childhood. "I'm half tempted to ask for champagne. My son Kaden has returned home."

The woman's eyes widened as she took him in. A few others looked up from around the kitchen. Soon, the news of his return would spread like wildfire. "Should I get a bottle, or..."

"Coffee is fine," Sylvia said.

Kaden let his mom lead him to the sitting room. Here the furniture looked too nice for a casual cup of coffee. The room had always been off limits to him as a kid. A family portrait hung over the fireplace. Kaden wasn't in it.

The woman came in with the carafe and mugs right behind them.

Once they were alone, his mother leaned forward and took his hand between hers. "I've missed you so much."

He stared down at where they touched, closed his eyes, and tried to let himself believe this was a form of love, giving himself one last chance to feel it before he tore it all down. He took a deep breath and pulled his hand free.

His mother frowned.

"I didn't come home for the funeral," he said. "I came home because I took a girl's memories."

Sylvia stared at him with her head tilted to the side. She pursed her lips; then she set her mug on the table. "What do you mean you *took* them?"

"You know what I mean." He searched her eyes. "The same thing you did to everyone in this town that summer—you made them all forget me."

Sylvia shook her head slowly. "All the memories that this town lost were given up willingly. You know that."

"No," he said. "This wasn't like that. I was at a bar. This woman was talking about her dead husband, and I said she could just forget it all. And so she did."

Sylvia leaned forward and rested a hand on his knee. "Are you certain? Maybe you'd had too much to drink?"

"I know what happened."

"It sounds like you *don't* know what happened," Sylvia said softly. "Grief is a funny thing."

"I was *not* grieving him," Kaden said. "I was celebrating the fact that an evil man is gone."

Sylvia winced.

"What, like you're not just as happy to finally be rid of him?"

She looked away and smoothed her hair. "He was your father."

"Was he?" Kaden said. "He beat me. You watched it happen and you did nothing."

The words hung between them.

"Or did you forget that, too?" he said.

She pulled back from him, her eyes narrowed to points. "Don't think I haven't wanted to forget. But I kept every single cut and bruise your father gave you right here." She pressed a hand to her heart, perfectly choreographed, like an actress.

"Little good that did me," Kaden said.

"I thought I was doing what was best for you, for our family. You deserved better," she said, voice sharp. "I never should've let that man lay a hand on you. I should've left him."

She leaned her head back against the couch with a sigh and rubbed at her temples.

"Then why didn't you?"

"My father would've cut me off," she said. "Without Christian's money, Bonner bourbon would have gone under, and worse, my father would've been right about me. Just a girl. Unfit to run the family business. We would have had nothing."

Of course. It always looped back to the money.

"We would've had each other," Kaden said.

"I was so young when Christian started hurting you. It was

the same way my father controlled my mother . . . I didn't see any way out. Christian wanted the marriage. My father wanted the Durant money. And I traded one monster for another."

Kaden pressed a hand to his chest and found himself aching to believe her. But he knew that this was just another manipulation.

"That doesn't explain what I did to that woman in the bar," Kaden said. "Why no one remembers me until I tell them my name, and even then, they barely seem to remember that I ever existed."

"Don't you think that if I could take a person's memories, I'd have used that power to stop your father from hurting you?"

Her words took the wind out of him. "I . . ."

"If no one remembers you, then that was a choice they made," she said. "But I remember you, Kaden. And I was there, at the harvest. I would never forget you. No matter what you did."

"What do you mean?"

"Something horrible happened that summer," she said. "Bad enough the whole town let it go. A month after you left, Nolan Haywood's body was found in the river. Maybe if the town chose to forget you, there was a reason for that."

The words swirled around in Kaden's head. He knew his mother was a viper, knew she was stirring the pot. But his memories from that summer had been fermenting in his head like the corn mash for so long that her words seeded enough doubt to temporarily stun him into silence. What if she was right? Not only had the town forgotten him, but apparently Kaden had given up the memory that Irene and Nate had ever broken things off, something everyone else remembered just fine.

Quinn's accusations from the night before flashed through his mind.

Kaden dropped his head into his hands. It didn't make sense. If he'd somehow been responsible for Nolan's death, people wouldn't *choose* to forget that. They'd want justice.

Unless.

The back of Kaden's neck prickled. Maybe that woman's memories weren't the first ones he'd taken.

He shook his head. It wasn't possible. This was just Sylvia trying to get into his head. How could he feel so at home with the Haywoods if he'd been responsible for Nolan's death? None of this made sense, and yet...

"You don't think...I couldn't have..."

Sylvia stood and crossed over to his couch. She sat beside him and wrapped her arms around him. "No. Of course not." She rubbed her hand along his upper back. "But if you did, it wouldn't make me love you any less."

The door to the sitting room opened, and they jumped apart.

"Just got off the phone with the pastor. Things are coming together. The rosemary you ordered from the Haywoods arrived."

Kaden lifted his head and found his younger brother standing in the doorway. He almost flinched. Nate looked so much like the father of his childhood. The same height, the same build, the same red cheeks.

"Shit," Kaden murmured, and his mother shot him a scandalized look. "He looks a lot like Dad."

Seeing him in that light, it wasn't hard to believe that Nate cheated on Irene. Yet something in Kaden wanted to jump up and grab his younger brother into a hug. Nate looked at Kaden, then glanced at their mother.

"I didn't realize you had company," Nate said.

The words knocked the wind out of Kaden.

"You . . . you don't recognize me?" Kaden got up and crossed the room, bringing them face-to-face. He had forgotten that Nate had a couple of inches on him.

Nate narrowed his eyes. "Should I?"

Even his own brother had forgotten about him. No, not forgotten—let his memories go.

"I'm your brother," Kaden said.

Nate blinked, took a quick breath. "Kaden?" He looked at their mom, who hadn't bothered to get up from the couch.

"He's come home," she said.

"You look a little like Dad, too, I guess?" He closed his eyes, pressed his palms to them, and shook his head. "Why didn't I remember you?"

"You gave him up to the memory harvest," Sylvia said.

"But *you* still remembered him?" Nate asked. "Why didn't you tell me? Why have you never mentioned him?"

"After he left, it was too painful for you." Sylvia sighed. "You made a choice."

Nate rubbed at the space between his eyes. "A choice? I don't . . . But I would've written it down . . . You could've . . ." He trailed off, shook his head. "It's weird," he said. "Hearing your name brought some of it back. Like there was still a part of you in here somewhere."

He took a few steps forward and grabbed Kaden in a hug. Kaden let himself feel the fierceness of his brother's hold, but he knew it wouldn't last. Nate was just as much a snake as his mother.

"When did you leave?" Nate asked.

"The summer of '97," Kaden said.

Nate stumbled backward. "I don't understand."

"It's not just you. It seems like all of Yarrow decided to forget me." Kaden shook his head. "I need to get out of here for a little bit. This is a lot to process."

"But you'll be here for the service?" Sylvia asked.

Kaden hesitated. He'd planned to attend the funeral with the Haywoods, but he didn't know if he could face them again, if he could look any of them in the eye with his fears over Quinn's accusations.

"You came all this way," Nate implored.

"Fine. I'll be there," he said. "But I have to go now."

Sylvia crossed the distance between them and pulled Kaden into another hug before he could get away.

"Welcome home," she said.

Kaden felt like he wanted to vomit.

Chapter 15

Irene

Irene started the morning the way she started every morning—with a cup of tea. When she flipped her mug, she found the same thing she'd seen yesterday in the kitchen with Kaden: a fern.

She couldn't get the man out of her head. As much as she wanted to blame it on the leaves, the uptick in her pulse when her mind turned to him and the way she couldn't burn his smile from her memory spoke to much more than her simply listening to the universe. She wanted to be somewhere he could find her easily, and while she usually didn't work on Thursdays, the tea shop seemed the most likely place he'd come looking. So she grabbed a few collections of poetry and settled into one of the plush armchairs in the corner at Lavender & Lemon Balm.

"You know it's not *really* a day off if you come into work, right?" Clem called to her from the other side of the room.

She should've brought her noise-canceling headphones.

"I'm not working," she said. "Therefore, I am off work."

"You literally just gave that woman a tea recommendation."

"Fine," Irene said. "I'm not *healing*. Therefore, I am off work. Just treat me like any other customer. Speaking of which,

I could use a refill." She held up her mug, and though Clem rolled her eyes, she accepted the cup.

Addison came in from the back room with a box full of herbs, fresh from the drying racks at home. She set it on the counter and looked her mother over. "Aren't you off on Thursdays?"

"She's hoping Kaden will stop in before the funeral," Clem said.

"I saw him when I was leaving the distillery this morning," Addison said.

Irene set the book in her lap. "And? How did he seem?"

Her daughter grinned. "You really *are* into him."

Irene's cheeks flushed as she picked the book back up and flipped through its pages. "I'm just curious about him. That's all."

"Obviously," Addison said. "You have sycamore leaves in your hair."

"Curiosity isn't attraction," Irene said.

Addison pursed her lips. Irene avoided eye contact by pretending to read.

"Maybe not," Clem said, "but the way you kept looking at him at dinner last night definitely was."

"You're supposed to be on my side here."

"Hello? Supporting your crush automatically means I'm on your side."

"You should ask him out for a drink," Addison said.

"He's a Bonner."

"He's a recovering Bonner," Addison said. "That's what he told me, anyway."

It was tempting, but Irene shook her head. "Can you imagine the emotional trauma he's carrying? And the funeral is today. I'm not here to heal him."

Clem raised her eyebrows and looked around their shop. "That's literally what you're here for."

"You know what I mean," Irene said.

"You saw a visitor in your leaves. That visitor is here," Clem said. "Maybe a little excitement wouldn't be so terrible. And if it's not forever, who cares? You deserve to have a good time."

Addison pointed at Clem. "Exactly."

Irene dropped her head back with an exaggerated sigh.

"Look. From what I saw last night, I like him," Clem said. "He's honest."

"So we think," Irene said. "And I want to believe it. But... he's a Bonner."

"I ran into River when I dropped off the rosemary," Addison said. "Kaden stopped when he saw me. I was, um...not at my best. He actually seemed to care. He gave me a bit of a pep talk."

"Besides, if he tries to pull anything like what Nate did, we'll stuff him in a barrel of bourbon and set it on fire," Clem said.

"That sounds a little harsh," Irene said.

Clem shrugged.

The bell over the door jingled, and Kaden walked into the shop. His hair hung limp, like he'd spent the last twenty minutes running his hands through it. Irene hadn't known him long, but the look on his face said it all.

He crumpled onto the bench at the table and dropped his head into his hands. "I'm sorry," he said. "I don't know where else to go."

The three women shared a look. Kaden was the brother of the man who'd cheated on Irene—the reason she'd given up on love. But he wasn't here to be healed, and she didn't know what to do with that.

She left the comfort of her armchair and moved to sit next to him on the bench.

"I went to see my mom," he said.

"That bad?" she asked.

"Worse."

When he didn't elaborate, she said, "You want to talk about it?"

"I don't know why I'm here," Kaden said.

"The universe sent you," Irene said. "Remember?"

He let out a choked laugh. "I'm not so sure about that anymore. I should go."

"The offer's still on the table," she said. "I won't charge you."

Kaden shook his head. "I don't want anyone to take anything away. I need to feel this."

"It wouldn't be forever," Irene said. "Especially not with grief. It would just help you on your way to healing."

But he shook his head.

"The funeral's not until five, right?" Clem said.

He nodded glumly.

"Then let's get out of here and have our own party."

"Go," Addison said, shooing them with her hands. "Both of you. I'll cover the shop."

"You will?" Irene asked. "Are you sure?"

"It's Thursday," Addison said. "No one is going to be coming in for healing today."

"But..." Irene started.

"Mom," Addison said. "I'll be fine."

Clem fished her phone from her pocket and started dialing. A few seconds later she said, "Hey, babe."

"What are you doing?" Irene asked.

Clem held a hand over the speaker. "You'll thank me later."

Kaden slumped even farther onto the table.

"Can you get away from the bed and breakfast for a few hours?" Clem asked into her phone. "Kaden just got back from seeing his mom." She paused, glanced at him and Irene. "That's *exactly* what I was thinking," she said into the phone. "Perfect."

After she hung up, she crouched down behind the register and started rummaging around. A few seconds later, she popped up with a bottle of bourbon in hand. She turned the label to face them. "Don't worry, not Bonner's. What we need is a little bit of gloom-free sunshine." Clem grabbed Irene's keys from beside the register. "Come on."

Irene stood reluctantly from the table. Kaden followed.

"You're sure you don't mind?" Irene asked her daughter.

"Yes." Addison pushed her mom down the hallway and out the back door. "Now, go." She closed it behind them.

"We'll take your truck," Clem said, her grin all mischief. "But I'm driving. You don't mind sitting in the middle, do you?" she said to Irene.

Irene's truck only had a front seat, which meant she'd be squeezing in right between Clem and Kaden. If Clem wanted to help them get their mind off things, that was definitely one way to do it.

"You have towels, right?" Clem asked as Irene slid across the seat.

"Towels? Why?" Irene asked.

"You'll see," Clem said.

Kaden got in the truck. He pressed up against the window and leaned his legs toward the door, but he was still close enough to Irene that their shoulders touched.

"Sorry there's not a lot of room," Irene said.

"It's a short drive," Clem said. "Your truck's better equipped for it than my car." She dropped the visor, pulled Irene's sunglasses free, and handed them to her. "You have another pair?"

Irene glanced toward where Kaden's knees sat a few inches from the glove compartment. "I do."

"Can I borrow them?" Clem asked.

"Do you mind?" Irene asked Kaden.

He shook his head and opened the glove compartment. Irene reached across him to grab the glasses at the same time he leaned forward, and their hands touched. His eyes met hers. His were haunted and tired. He cleared his throat, and she grabbed the sunglasses, then tossed them to Clem, who was doing a terrible job hiding her smile. She turned the key in the ignition, shifted gears, and they were on their way.

The day was all sunshine and humidity, but the gloom clung to the edge of everything in a fog-like haze.

"Why'd you go see your mom anyway?" Clem asked after a few minutes. "I thought the whole point of us going to the funeral with you was to throw it in her face."

"It was," Kaden said.

"And?" Clem asked.

"I was hoping she'd have answers."

"Did she?" Irene asked.

"Not any I liked." Kaden turned to look out the window.

As they left the city limits, the dusting of darkness lifted. Clem turned off the highway along a worn road. Dirt kicked up beneath the tires. Once the path hit the tree line, Clem shifted the truck into park.

Irene leaned forward and planted her hands on the dash. "The rope swing?"

"No better way to cheer Kaden up than a day at the river," Clem said.

Taylor pulled up beside them. She jumped out of the car and held a second bottle of bourbon high along with a couple of inner tubes. She took one look at Kaden and offered him the bottle. "I heard you could use this."

He took it. "Might as well."

After Irene grabbed a few towels out of the back, they started up the footpath. It led them to an offshoot of the Ohio River that ended at the base of a cliff that was too short to be considered a waterfall, but just high enough that a rope tied to an old sycamore provided a safe drop into the water below.

Rapids roared a few feet up the creek, the loud churning serving as the bass line for the birds and frogs singing in the branches overhead.

Irene nestled into the corner of the sycamore where roots extended from the tree like thick ropes clinging to the water a few feet below. Kaden sat beside her.

He pressed the bottle of bourbon to his lips, closed his eyes, and took a long drink. Irene glanced up to find Clem and Taylor sharing a look. Clem wiggled her eyebrows. Irene grabbed a nearby acorn and threw it at her. She missed by at least three feet.

"Hold this for me," Clem said, handing her the other bottle before first she, then Taylor, climbed onto the low-hanging branch above them. Clem reached a hand down. Irene raised the bottle, and Clem grabbed it by the neck.

Kaden relaxed back against the tree trunk. He stared out over the river and took another sip.

"How's this for easing some of the… What's he feeling, Irene?" Clem asked.

"You know, you could ask me," Kaden said.

"Do you care if I look at your aura?" Irene asked, as if she hadn't been watching his shifting feelings with interest since he showed up at the shop.

He arched an eyebrow. "You haven't?"

Irene bit her lip and reached for the bottle. He laughed as he handed it over.

"I'll tell you," Kaden said. "Anger and betrayal mostly. A little sadness."

"Mourning," Irene said. "Which surprised me."

"His dad *died*," Clem said.

"It's not for him," Kaden said. "It's more like…mourning what my life could've been? Who my mom could've become? I'm also more confused than I was before I came to town. All these missing memories. Nobody remembering who I am. And the town just accepts it—an entire summer, gone—because in Yarrow we give up our worst memories and move on. I accepted it, too, for all these years, and never questioned why."

"You think there was something more to it?" Irene asked.

He rubbed the pad of his thumb against his lip. Instead of answering her, he asked, "What's it like when you heal someone?"

Irene didn't explain her magic to outsiders, but something in Kaden made her want to lay her heart bare.

"I start at the roots," Irene said. "I search for them first. As much as I'd love to stick a spade in and scoop up all that pain at once, I have to pry it free one root at a time."

He considered that. "You don't just take it all, like with the memory harvest?"

"Right," Irene said. "And the worst pain can resurface, but as you tend to it, less and less grows back."

"So, pain is like a weed. And what you do is like weeding a garden?" Kaden said.

"You have experience gardening?" Irene asked.

"There's a community garden back home." Kaden's eyes met hers and held them for a few seconds. He rubbed at his lip with his thumb again. Irene forced herself not to stare. "Pretty sure I started going there because of how much I loved the magic in your family's garden."

This type of talk was not helping Irene's resolve not to fall for him.

"Then yes, it's like weeding," she said, taking a sip of the bourbon. She held it up to the light, the amber liquid sloshing against the glass. They'd already worked halfway through it. It had been years since she'd had this much alcohol in one day.

"Enough talk of pain," Clem said from up above them. "We came here to have fun." She dropped down to her feet beside Irene and started tugging off her shirt until she was down to a sports bra and jeans.

Taylor jumped down, too. She pulled off her shirt and shorts, revealing a one-piece bathing suit underneath, before tossing one of the tubes into the water below. Then she grabbed the rope, backed up a few steps, and ran for the river. She let out a yell as she swung over the bank. Clem followed after her.

Kaden made no move to get up.

"You coming in?"

"I . . ." He looked down at the bottle in his hands, then back up to Irene. "Can we talk first?"

Irene sat back down. "About your mom?"

"Sort of," he said. "I've been trying to figure out why everyone forgot I existed."

"Your mom didn't remember you?"

"She did," Kaden said. "But Nate didn't."

"Wow," Irene said. "Kind of shitty for him to give up his memories of you."

"Unless..." Kaden sighed and tilted his head back against the sycamore trunk. "What if he had a reason? What if you all had a reason for wanting to forget me?"

"Do not tell me you let Quinn get in your head."

"Maybe she's right," Kaden said. "I left the same summer your brother died. What if I had something to do with it?"

Irene took the bottle from him, forcing him to look at her. "Yes, something awful happened that summer. But if it wasn't an accident and my brother was murdered, I would've never, under any circumstances, given up the truth of that."

"What if...you didn't give those memories up willingly?" Kaden asked.

Irene shook her head. "I don't understand."

"I can't keep coming around to see you without telling you the truth."

Irene's chest clenched. Of course this man had been too good to be true. He was a Bonner. She should've known better.

"I don't know how to say this other than to just say it," Kaden said.

"So, say it."

"I'm pretty sure I took a woman's memories the other night at a bar."

Irene opened her mouth, then closed it.

"I know how it sounds," Kaden said. "I tried to tell my mom, and she said it wasn't possible, that I must've misremembered."

Kaden's aura was all hyacinths and weeping willows and

king's spear, and though his regret was obvious, as far as Irene could see, he was earnest. He was as lost as she felt.

"I didn't mean to," he said. "I didn't even know I could. Maybe I did it that summer. Maybe the dark thing the town let go of was me."

Irene looked down at the bottle in her hands and took a long drink. Then she closed her eyes and thought back to that year, to finding Nate in the alley.

"The leaves told me over and over again Nate was cheating," Irene said. "I even asked him about it, but there was never any proof until the very end. It didn't make sense for me to just ignore it, but I did because there was no evidence."

"You think he took your memories?" Kaden asked.

"It never occurred to me before, but if you can do it..."

Kaden cringed.

Irene took a deep breath. Part of her wanted to get up and jump into the river and never look back at this man, but the other part of her wanted the truth.

There had been magic in his reading.

"Try it on me," she said.

"What?" Kaden sputtered and covered his face with both of his hands. He shook his head. "Absolutely not."

"You want to know, don't you?" Thanks to his aura, she already knew the answer.

He nodded slowly.

"So, make me forget something."

Kaden searched her eyes. "You're sure?"

"I'm sure."

"Last night," he said, eyes gleaming with fresh tears. "I

helped you up from the chair and you held on to my hand longer than you needed to."

A lump formed in Irene's throat. She couldn't stop thinking about his touch, but she hadn't realized he'd internalized it, too.

Kaden took a deep breath and said, "Just forget it all."

Irene closed her eyes. She blinked them open. He winced.

"Well?" he asked.

She shook her head. The moment was still clear in her mind. "It didn't work."

Kaden shook his head. Then he laughed quietly. "I was so sure it happened."

Irene found herself at once relieved and disappointed. If Kaden had been able to do what he feared—if he'd been involved in her brother's death—it would've explained the tea leaves and given her an excuse to put this all aside and force him from her thoughts.

And the more time she spent with him, the less she wanted to do that.

"Now that that's settled…" She jumped up and offered him a hand. He accepted, and after he was on his feet, neither of them let go.

"We've got to stop holding hands," Irene said.

He laughed. "Do we?"

At first, she didn't respond, and Kaden faltered. "I can back off if you want," he said.

But Irene still didn't let go of him. "I'm not even sure what you'd back off of," she said. "You're just…really nice? Honest? A breath of fresh air in a town full of gloom?"

"You're a gardener *and* a poet," Kaden said.

She hit him on the shoulder. "I'm serious. What kind of man tells a woman he might have stolen her memories and not remembered it?"

"I'm glad I came into your shop," he said. "I couldn't face all of this alone."

"Good thing for you the universe sent you my way, then."

"Speaking of those tea leaves," Kaden said.

"What about them?" Irene asked.

"Are they always right?"

She shook her head. "Not always."

"I don't want to bring you sorrow, Irene."

She smiled. "So, don't."

"Are you two going to come in, or what?" Clem shouted from the water below.

"What do you think?" Irene asked Kaden. The rope swing had been one of her favorite places since she was a kid, but it had been a few years since she'd come out here—especially without a bathing suit.

"If you're going in, I'm going in," Kaden said.

Irene gave his hand a squeeze, dropped it, and started unfastening her overalls. As they fell around her ankles, she glanced up to find Kaden looking anywhere but her legs. She grinned, feeling brave, but not quite brave enough to tug off her tank top, too.

She grabbed the rope, then plunged into the river. It hit her, cold and sharp. When she resurfaced, she found Clem and Taylor treading water, looking up at the sycamore, where Kaden was now stripping down to his boxers.

"I really thought you were going to kiss him," Clem said.

Irene splashed her. "I might have if you hadn't interrupted us."

"There's still time," Taylor said with a wink.

Kaden came swinging over the edge, sending up a wave of water. He popped up and finger-combed his hair back, before swimming toward them, arm over arm. "You're right," he said when he reached them. "This is exactly what I needed."

"Congratulations," Clem said. "You've successfully passed your first test."

"Following you blindly into a river?" Kaden asked.

"Realizing I'm right," she said. "Because I'm always right."

"Noted," Kaden said.

With a laugh, Clem started back for the shore, and the rest of them followed. They continued swinging and swimming until the sun started to make its way across the sky.

Now, Kaden lay back on one of the towels on the riverbank. Sunlight fell through the leaves, making patterns on his bare skin. Irene grabbed one of the water bottles Taylor had packed, and sat next to him. The world spun a little at the edges. It felt like she was in a dream. Like she was just another single woman enjoying the summer with her friends and getting to know a guy.

Because, for the first time in a long time, that's exactly what she was.

A monarch butterfly landed on the towel, its orange wings awash in the afternoon light. A yellow-and-black tiger swallowtail perched atop her still-damp shoulders. One with blue wings hovered over Kaden.

"Hello there," he said, and held up a hand. It landed on his knuckles, and his light laughter had her lips tugging up.

"I've decided I like you, Kaden." She edged a little closer to him, spooking the monarch into flight.

"Well that's good because I don't really have anyone else to hang out with around here."

"Didn't you have friends before you left?" Irene asked.

"They were mostly people who wanted to be my friend because I was a Bonner. No one I'd want to try to rebuild things with. They wouldn't remember any of it anyway," Kaden said. "I usually kept to myself."

"Well, now you have me."

He smiled up at her lazily, and she leaned a little closer to him.

"Now I have you," he said.

It took everything Irene had not to kiss him. *Why do I always fall for a Bonner?* she thought.

She let out a soft breath. Her eyes strayed to Kaden's lips.

"Don't you have a job you need to get back to?" she asked.

"I teach. Except for a few in-service days, the summer's all mine."

He said it like he meant to say *all yours.*

Irene rested her hand on his and twined their fingers together.

This is not a good idea.

He propped himself up on his elbows until they only had a few inches between them. She could smell the bourbon on his breath, and she didn't have to kiss him to know she'd taste it like sweet honey on his tongue. With just a hint of smoke and wood.

"And how do you plan to spend this summer?" She moved closer until she could feel the whisper of his lips against hers. "After the funeral."

Kaden blinked up at her, and his eyes went wide. He sat up,

bumping his forehead against her chin. The butterflies scattered. He shot to his feet.

"Shit," he said. "The funeral."

Irene groaned. "What time is it?"

Kaden crawled over to where they'd left their things and fished his phone out of his pocket. "Service starts in fifteen minutes."

Irene grabbed her overalls and ran to the edge of the riverbank, tugging them on as she went. "We need to go!" she shouted across the water.

Kaden came up beside her, his shirt on backward and inside out. His hair dripping onto his shoulders, soaking through the cotton.

"I am... This is not good." Kaden dropped his head into his hands. "I've definitely had too much to drink. How... I can't... I can't wear this. Who thought this was a good idea?"

"This is fine," Irene said. "It's fine."

"How are we going to get there?" Kaden swayed on his feet.

"Lucky for all of us," Clem said as she climbed up out of the water, "I stopped drinking a few hours ago."

Chapter 16

Addison

Addison had never been to a funeral that had a guest list. The barn had been open since noon for people to pay their respects, but once it came time for the event itself, the venue only had so much capacity. The greeters at the door—"More like bouncers," Maura said—had made that abundantly clear.

The exclusivity of it all had rankled her grams, but Addison hadn't viewed it that way. Of course the entire town had turned out for Christian Durant's funeral. Was it really so bad if his family wanted to create a sense of intimacy?

The room was filled with Kentucky's elite—politicians, celebrities, industry leaders, and the Bonners themselves—it was no surprise to Addison that these people were in the family's inner circle. That Sylvia considered the Haywoods a part of that spoke more to Addison of her gratitude toward her family than anything.

Her grams should be proud that she helped make all this possible. Because without bourbon, there'd be no Yarrow.

Every person who stopped to greet her was evidence of that.

In front of the Haywoods sat the Bakers—all except Harper, who'd taken a seat in the Haywood row with Quinn. Their matriarch, Elena Baker; her son, Casey, who ran the grocery; his wife, Susheila, who edited the *Yarrow Gazette*; and, of course, River.

Addison had done her best to keep her attention on anything but him, which meant responding to every one of her grandmother's complaints.

Maura sat on Addison's left with her arms crossed, her aura blooming with resentment and her eyes weighing each person who walked down the aisle. "If I'd known your mother was going to run off with him and not show up for this funeral, I'd never have put on this damned dress."

"They'll be here," Addison said.

Maura let out a disgruntled huff.

"It's fine, Grams," Quinn said. "It'll make Sylvia even more upset when she realizes that Kaden didn't just show up with our family. He showed up *late* with our family."

Maura settled farther into her seat. "Small mercies."

"I'm a little surprised you came," Addison said to Quinn.

"Kaden seems nice enough," Quinn said.

"You accused him of murder."

"I didn't accuse him," she said. "I simply suggested his disappearance from Yarrow the same summer my father died is highly suspicious."

"You 100 percent accused him of murder," Harper said.

Quinn waved a hand. "He may be my last chance to find out what my nightmares really mean."

"I thought you wanted me to help you get rid of those nightmares," Addison said.

"I do," Quinn said. "But there's magic in the tea leaves! A visitor! Weird memory shit! We can wait a little longer to sort through my trauma if it means I get some answers."

The lights dimmed and servers clad in Bonner's apparel appeared at the end of every row with trays of drinks.

"She never misses a chance to promote her bourbon," Maura grumbled.

Addison reached for a glass.

"Addison!" Maura said, scandalized. "You are *not* going to drink one of their cocktails."

Addison was, in fact, going to drink one of their cocktails. "Of course not," she said. "I just want to see how they used the rosemary."

"Grab me one!" Harper said.

Maura threw up her hands. "Have none of you heard a single word I've said your entire lives?"

"To be fair, you didn't raise Harper," Quinn said.

Harper's grandmother, Elena, leaned back from the row of chairs in front of them. "That doesn't mean Harper didn't grow up with an earful of Maura's disdain..." She glanced around.

River turned to face them. "Could y'all maybe keep this to yourselves?" he whispered. "We *are* at a funeral."

Addison avoided making eye contact, trying not to think about the last funeral she and River had attended as she examined the contents of her glass. There wasn't much to it. Ice, bourbon, a sprig of black rosemary.

Sylvia approached the stage and held up her drink. "We're about to begin," she said. "First, I wanted to thank all of you for coming, and I wanted to extend a special thanks to the Haywoods for providing a little something extra from their garden for this celebration of Christian's life." A spotlight came on over their row, and Addison was fairly certain Grams hissed in response.

When Sylvia didn't continue, Elena whispered, "I think she wants you to wave."

Maura did not wave.

Sylvia cleared her throat and raised a glass. "I know there is a lot of heartache in this room, but I want to ask that you think instead of all the good Christian brought to Yarrow—his love of the bourbon industry and this town. Pick your best memory of him and focus on it. Then, once we've finished, we'll all toast together."

Addison held her glass to her lips, mirroring the movements of most everyone in the room.

"Not just yet," Sylvia said. "I'd like us all to drink all at once as a final send-off. For now, just think on those memories."

Addison had no real memories of Christian Durant beyond the fact that he spoke at the Yarrow festival every year. Instead, her mind strayed toward River sitting within arm's reach. She knew thinking of him right before indulging in anything touched by the shadow garden was maybe not the best idea, but she did it anyway. It was a funeral. Here it was okay to cry.

Though Sylvia had told them to wait, Addison snuck a sip anyway. The bourbon hit her tongue sharp and sweet. Not only did the rosemary spice the drink, but the hint of lemon from the shadow garden gave it a sour quality. Addison closed her eyes as she swallowed, not wanting her grandmother's judgment to ruin an otherwise perfect cocktail.

She leaned back in her seat as the shadow magic started to work through her. Addison's heartache bloomed fast, and she started to tremble. Her chest weighed her down. Her mind felt thick with sorrow.

She set her glass under her chair to keep from dropping it

as she fought to stabilize her breathing. She'd felt the sadness the moment her eyes had landed on River, and the shadow garden amplified what you were already feeling. But this was more than an emotion.

This was an onslaught.

Chapter 17

Kaden

The drive from the rope swing to the distillery had done little to help them dry out. Kaden stumbled out of the truck, Irene right behind him. Her willingness to let him try to take her memories—and his subsequent inability to do so—had calmed his roiling thoughts, but something about the collective hole in Yarrow's memory still unsettled him.

Irene tugged on the hem of his T-shirt, and he turned back toward her. He could almost pretend things were normal if she weren't looking at him like that. He leaned a little closer to her.

"You might want to flip this around," she said.

He hadn't even noticed he'd failed to put his shirt on right. He laughed and shrugged out of it. Irene didn't take her eyes off him as he fixed it, and he considered ditching the funeral altogether.

It was only once Clem cleared her throat that they started toward the door. As they reached it, Nate stepped out of an alcove, and Kaden walked right into him.

"Shit," Kaden said. "You scared me."

"I was afraid you weren't going to show," Nate said. "I certainly didn't expect you to turn up with them."

Irene arched an eyebrow. "Your brother does have friends in this town."

Nate flicked the ashes of his cigarette. Irene made an exaggerated gesture of blowing the smoke away from them. Nate looked from Kaden to her. "Funny, I thought no one remembered him."

"New friends," Clem said.

Nate dropped what was left of his cigarette on the pavement and crushed the smoldering tip under his shoe. "You look like shit."

Kaden glanced down at himself. "I feel like shit."

Nate laughed softly. He shrugged out of his suit jacket and held it out toward his brother. "Here." Then to Irene he said, "See? I'm not all bad."

Kaden looked down at the jacket, then back up at Nate. As he reached for it, he listed a little to the left.

"Are you drunk?" Nate asked.

"Maybe a little?" Kaden said, sheepish.

"Mom's not going to be happy about that," Nate said.

"I don't know what you remember, but I *really* hated Dad."

Nate shrugged. "He's always been kind of a dick."

Kaden hitched his shirt up where a scar ran the length of his side. "Remember this?"

Nate pursed his lips and shook his head. "Dad did that?"

Before Kaden could answer, the door opened behind them. "Mr. Bonner?" It was one of the assistant pastors from the Baptist church on the town square, a white man in his forties. "We've begun. Your mother's already on stage."

"Be right in," Nate said. "You three may want to stand in the back."

"Fuck off," Clem said.

The pastor's eyebrows shot into his receding hairline, but he held the door open for them all the same.

Irene leaned in. "Kaden's sitting with us."

Nate gave Kaden a wounded look.

Kaden shrugged. "Thanks for the jacket," he said, even though it came down a little too far over his wrists.

"You're going to need it," Nate said.

Kaden arched an eyebrow, but before he could ask, Irene had grabbed his hand and was dragging him into the venue. As they walked in, servers were distributing trays of cocktails.

"No, thanks." He'd had more bourbon this week than he'd had in the past ten years combined. He took a deep breath and pinched the bridge of his nose.

"Had enough to drink already, have we?" Clem asked with a wicked grin as she reached for one of the glasses.

Irene smacked her hand. "We don't drink Bonner's."

"*You* don't drink Bonner's," Clem said. "*I* don't turn down free bourbon." She and Taylor each grabbed a glass.

Kaden's mother stood front and center on the stage, a drink in hand. All around the room, people stared at their cocktails.

As Kaden started to sit with Irene's family, his mother's voice echoed throughout the room. "Today isn't only a day for recognizing my late husband's life, it's also a day of reconciliation for my family." A spotlight landed on him, the brightness blinding. He shielded his eyes. "My son Kaden has returned home to help lay his father to rest."

A collective gasp echoed off the vaulted ceiling as his father's mourners turned around to face him and his brother.

"I was hoping you'd say a few words," Sylvia said.

Kaden stared at her. Nate gave him a little push, and before he knew it, Kaden was walking down the center aisle, his brother at his side. Acid burned at the back of his throat as the day's choices threatened to come up in one giant wave. He swallowed hard. What little color was left in his cheeks faded.

"I can't do this," Kaden whispered to his brother. "I don't have anything good to say about him."

"Then lie," Nate whispered back.

When Kaden reached the front of the room, his eyes went to the giant portrait of his father, which had been set up on an easel at the center of the stage. Kaden recognized it from the distillery's main office. Christian may not have had any real hand in making the bourbon, but it had hung there as long as Kaden could remember. He doubted it would ever find its way back to that place.

Sylvia greeted Kaden with a cold hug, then took his hand and pulled him up the stairs to the stage. Nate started to follow, but Sylvia shook her head and he stepped back, his lips pressed in a flat line of annoyance. Sylvia stepped up to the microphone and forced one of the bourbon and rosemary cocktails into his hands. "Go ahead," she urged. "Make a toast."

He stared down at the drink, then up at his mother.

"My father," he started, paused, tried to find the right words when he realized how hilarious all of this was, "is dead."

A small laugh escaped the otherwise silent crowd, and people turned toward the source. At the back of the room, where the Haywoods had gathered, Clem had her hands over her face and had started coughing. Taylor ducked her head.

Irene bit her lip when Kaden's eyes met hers. Kaden bit his

own in response, sure any second he would start laughing. Already he could feel it rising up from his belly.

He cleared his throat.

"You already know that," he said. "Obviously you know that. You're all here to...recognize him." He gestured to his side where his father stared out at them from that portrait. He gripped the podium tighter, tried to keep the laughter down. "I'm Kaden, by the way. I know none of you—" He cut himself short as his mother cleared her throat behind him. "I mean... it's been a while. You, uh, may not remember me well. But Christian Durant is dead. So, here I am."

Again, Clem's laugh-coughing started up, and now Taylor joined her, and it was the funniest thing Kaden had ever seen. He grinned and held a hand over his mouth to hide it.

He held up his drink to the crowd. "To Christian Durant."

They raised their glasses. They sipped.

"My father," he said, his laughter bubbling up. He clenched his teeth and ground out, "What a man."

He couldn't keep it in any longer. His stomach rumbled with it and he thought, what was the worst that could happen from laughing at his father's funeral? He opened his mouth.

And he puked all over the stage.

Chapter 18

Addison

Addison stared blankly as the power of the rosemary worked its way through her, pulling every dark thought, every fear from that night she'd stolen River's joy to the surface.

She hadn't wanted this.

Her whole body ached with the shame and the guilt and the helplessness of it all. The pain sat heavy in her chest, pressed against her throat, making it hard to breathe.

Addison felt a tingling and an itching beneath her skin.

Somewhere in the back of her mind she knew she should've been concerned. Normally, you'd have to eat a whole basket of shadow fruit to feel this way. It should've worried her. But all she could think about was this ache that wrapped around her heart, setting its roots in deep.

She blinked, and the world came into focus. Beside her, Clem and Taylor were laughing so hard they had tears in their eyes. Up ahead, Kaden stared out at the room in horror, his hands held over his mouth, a puddle of vomit on the stage. Irene had burst out of their row of chairs and was making her way toward him.

River turned in his seat. His eyes met hers. Just minutes ago his aura had carried the mild annoyance and general frustration he always had when she saw him, but now it overran him like crabgrass.

"Really?" he asked. "*You're* crying?"

"We're at a funeral," Addison said. She didn't bother to wipe the tears away and instead found her chest heaving with an unexpected sob.

"What, like you cared about the Bonners?"

"I cared about *you*. I still care about you, but all you can do is look at me with hate."

"Why do you always have to make my pain about you?" River rubbed at the tears in his own eyes.

"Because it's my pain, too," she said.

"You hurting me is *your* pain?"

Addison shook her head. "This isn't what I came here for."

"And yet you're bringing it up," River said. "At a funeral for the family I'm working for. Are you planning to take another thing I love from me?"

Harper started peppering Quinn's cheek with kisses.

"Is that really appropriate right now?" River asked.

Harper glared at him. "I'm in love, and Quinn looks hot in a suit."

"This is more than a little shadow garden magic," Quinn said.

"Of course it's your family's garden that's making you act like this," River said to Addison.

"Sure," Addison sniffled. "Because it's not enough for there to only be something wrong with my magic. It has to be the garden, too."

"I think this is going to be a lot better for both of you if you don't speak to each other right now," Quinn said.

"He started it," Addison replied as she tried and failed to hold back another sob.

"*I* started this?" River asked. "You're the one who fucked with my head."

Quinn gripped Addison's shoulder. "Something's not right."

"Clearly." Addison nodded. "My heart feels like it's breaking all over again."

Maura grabbed Addison's hand and tugged her up. "Come on, before Irene does something we'll all regret."

Chapter 19

Irene

Irene had always had what she considered to be an extraordinary constitution. She'd spent almost forty-six years turning compost and spreading mulch, and it took a lot to get her stomach to curl, but as she stood from her chair and started toward Kaden, the encroaching smell of vomit threatened to do her in.

With each step she took, cries rose around her. People wailed, pulled at their hair. Some rocked back and forth in their seats. Others started shouting. She sidestepped a fight that broke out in the center aisle.

Clem followed behind her, laughing so hard she was crying. "What the hell is happening?"

Irene shook her head. "I have no idea."

She hoisted herself up over the edge of the stage. Kaden swayed as he offered her a hand.

"I thought I was just going to laugh," he mumbled, gripping Irene like he was afraid she'd leave him up there alone.

"It's okay," Irene said. "Let's get you out of here."

He buried his head in her hair and whimpered softly.

"Well this is a surprise," Sylvia said. "The two of you...?"

"Yeah," Irene said. Kaden was a mess, but it didn't change any of the affection she felt for him. "The two of us."

"Now is not the time for this," Nate said. "It's been over twenty years. So I cheated on you. Big deal. Did you really think showing up here with my brother was going to get under my skin?"

His face had gone red with anger. Petunias bloomed in his aura so quickly it was a wonder the venue wasn't full of them.

"This has nothing to do with you, but it looks like I got under your skin anyway," Irene said.

He started to reply when Sylvia placed a hand on his arm. "Not the time or place, Nate."

"I only came up here to help get Kaden off this stage," Irene said.

"In case you forgot, we're burying my father," Nate spat at her.

"In case I forgot?" Irene threw out a hand at the room full of mourners.

As Sylvia shifted her focus from Kaden to the people before them, her eyes widened. She stepped up to the microphone.

"If everyone could please sit down."

But her voice was lost in the din.

Clem's laughter reached a peak.

Irene tried to blink away the haze, thinking all that bourbon earlier was messing with her head. She leaned toward Kaden. "Are you seeing this?"

Down the center aisle, Maura pushed her way through the writhing mass, Addison on her heels. When they reached the stage, Irene saw the tears streaming down Addison's face. Taylor had fallen into the same laughing fit that Clem couldn't shake. Harper was running her hands all over Quinn, pressing kisses to her neck in a frenzy. Only Maura and Quinn seemed put together.

Sylvia shook her head in dismay and brought her glass to her lips when Nate knocked it out of her hands.

"I was looking forward to that." She glared at him.

"Unless you want to end up like them, I wouldn't," Nate said. He held up his own drink and pointed the glass at Maura; liquor sloshed over the edge. "You did this!"

Maura held up her hands. "I'm only here to pay my respects."

"I know shadow magic when I feel it." He rounded on Irene. "This was your plan all along."

Irene gaped at him. "You think the shadow garden caused this?"

"Actually, Mom, I think he's right," Addison said. She held herself tightly. "I took a sip and...the rosemary..."

Irene wanted to wrap an arm around her, but she was unsteady on her feet as it was. She didn't want to send both of them toppling over the edge of the stage.

"The rosemary is fine," Maura said. "We can't control the garden's effects at an event where emotions run high. You signed the waiver. You knew the risk."

Nate shook his head. "No, this is something else. This was clearly deliberate."

"The only thing wrong here was my decision not to put my foot down," Maura said. "We never should've sold you a single sprig."

Addison winced.

Sylvia reached out and rested a hand on Addison's shoulder. "It's all right," she said. "Your grandmother's right. We knew the risks."

All at once, the room went quiet.

Clem's laughter ceased.

Addison's tears dried up.

Nate's red face went back to its normal flush.

Irene may have been a bit tipsy, but she knew that was definitely *not* how shadow garden magic worked. It was meant to be a sustained amplification—to last a couple of hours at least—not a burst that hit you all at once, then disappeared.

The crowd turned their focus toward the stage.

Sylvia stepped up to the mic. "Thank you all for pouring your hearts into that toast."

Irene stared at her. Why was she covering for them?

But Maura was already herding her family out of the room. Irene held Kaden's hand tight.

"Kaden, wait," Sylvia called after them.

He shook his head. "Sorry, Mom," he said. "I…" He glanced down at a fleck of puke on his lapel. "I have to go."

He let Irene lead him down the row of chairs and out of the venue. It wasn't until they were all standing together in the parking lot that Maura's calm exterior shattered.

"What the hell happened in there? Did you know that something was wrong with the rosemary, Addison?"

"You're blaming *me*?" Addison said.

"You were the one so intent on selling it to her," Maura said.

Addison burst into tears.

"Back off, Mom," Irene said, and pulled her daughter into her arms. She whispered to Addison, "Did you happen to notice anything off in the garden?"

Addison pulled away from her, her eyes growing wide. She glanced at Quinn and bit her lip.

"You have to tell them," Quinn said.

"Tell us what?" Maura asked.

"I..." Addison hesitated, fear blooming in her aura.

"It's okay," Irene said. "We're in this together."

Addison crossed her arms, retreating into herself as she said, "The garden gave me a vision."

"The garden doesn't—" Maura started, but Irene's glare stopped her short.

"Something was wrong with the soil," Addison continued. "There wasn't enough sorrow to feed the plants...It felt like they were starving."

"You didn't think it might be important to mention this?" Maura asked.

"I was going to," Addison said. "After the funeral. I didn't want you to change your mind about the rosemary."

"Which is exactly what we should've done!" Maura said.

"Your grams is right," Irene said. "You should've told us."

"What about my tea-leaf reading?" Addison asked.

"Maybe you misread it," Maura said.

"You saw it! All of you did." Addison dropped her eyes to the ground and rubbed at her forearms. "What if it's my fault? I can't take anyone's pain on my own, so I can't feed the garden as much as it needs."

"Your magic..." Irene started. But she couldn't find the words, so she just stood there staring at her daughter and shaking her head.

Addison looked up at her, eyes narrowed. "You think I'm right."

When Irene didn't respond, Addison turned to Quinn and Harper. "I need to get out of here. Can I stay with y'all tonight?

I've had enough of this interrogation." She shot Irene and Maura a withering look.

Maura crossed her arms and cocked her head to the side as Addison turned her back on them and stalked toward Quinn's truck. Quinn and Harper followed.

Irene stared at Addison, almost started after her, when Clem rested a hand on her shoulder. "Give her time," she said.

"But..."

"I don't think you're at your best right now," Clem said gently.

Irene turned on her own mother. "Did you really have to start in on her?"

"You did your own fair bit," Maura said. "Drinking before a funeral? Really, Irene?"

"Let's go," Irene said.

Clem glanced from Maura to Irene and Kaden, and then to Taylor. "Okay, let's go. See you, Maura."

Irene pulled open the passenger door to her truck when Maura called out, "You know you'll have to see me at home!"

She shouted back, "Not if I don't come inside!" Then she crawled into the cab of the truck.

Clem climbed into the driver's side and the engine roared to life. "Well, that was fun."

Irene leaned her head against Clem's shoulder. "I really screwed that up, didn't I?"

"Your mom was worse."

"That's not a no," Irene said, and she dropped her head in her hands.

"At least you didn't throw up while giving a speech at your abusive father's funeral," Kaden said. "Is there anything in here I can use to rinse my mouth out?"

Irene reached under the seat and pulled out an almost-empty bottle of bourbon.

"That's the last thing I need," Kaden said, but he popped off the lid and took a pull anyway. Then he rolled down the window and spit it out. He looked at the bottle again, shrugged, and took another drink. "Now what?"

Irene groaned. "Now I want to go to sleep and pretend none of this ever happened."

Kaden leaned his head back against the seat. "Yes."

"But first, I need to look at the garden. If Addison's right..." Irene didn't finish the sentence, because she didn't want to think it through to the end.

Chapter 20

Irene

Clem and Kaden dropped Irene off at home before heading into town to pick up takeout. As soon as Irene got out of the truck, she went around back. The garden rose up before her, the gloom hanging a little heavier over the plants.

She made her way to the hedge of rosemary where Addison had cut the herbs for the funeral, taking a sprig between her fingers. The shrub had started to turn gray at the tips, and when she rubbed the leaves, they crumbled into dust. It was as if the plant had poured all its magic into the harvest and had nothing left to give.

Irene's eyebrows drew together. It would explain what had happened at the funeral, why the magic had hit everyone in one big burst, then dried up almost as quickly as it came—a sort of cry for help.

She fell to her knees in the dirt and plunged a hand deep into the soil, looking for whatever Addison had found there. "What is it?" she asked the plants. "What did you show her?" She closed her eyes, tried to imagine what it would feel like to receive a vision, but nothing appeared.

The roots tickled her skin, a little slower than usual. They wrapped around her fingers, prodded at her knuckles, but

Irene had no sorrow to offer them. As quickly as they'd come, they retreated deeper into the dirt and out of reach. It was like Addison said. They felt hungry.

With her free hand, Irene rubbed at her face and tried to gather her thoughts. Over the past few years, Maura had pulled back from healing, her own sort of retirement as she left the family magic to Irene. Addison had never been able to take care of their customers alone, which meant there were fewer Haywoods pouring pain into the earth. But that wasn't all. People who once brought their heartache to the Haywoods had turned, instead, to the memory harvest. After all, why enlist a witch to tend to your suffering when you could give it all up in one moment, forgotten forever?

Maybe the garden *was* starving, Irene realized. It was a sobering thought, but not one that Irene was ready to sort through on her own. She glanced back at the house, where she saw Maura watching her from the attic window. Irene certainly wasn't going to be able to get her mother and daughter to work together until everyone had time to cool off.

At the sound of tires on gravel, Irene pushed herself to her feet. She wiped the dirt from her hands and went to meet Clem and Kaden. As promised, Clem had gotten them a feast, but as soon as she arrived, she left with a wink and an excuse that she needed to take inventory at the shop.

Irene grabbed a quilt and set it up on a bare patch of dirt toward the edge of the shadow garden where the plants grew low to the ground, offering a view of the forest beyond, far from where her family's land met the cornfields.

Even after everything that happened at the funeral— including her lingering guilt, her worry over the garden, and a handful of unanswered apology texts to Addison—Irene's mind kept straying back to the afternoon at the rope swing, her lips so close to Kaden's.

Yes, she'd been drunk then, but she couldn't deny there was something between them—something she wanted to turn over in her hands and explore, because Kaden was everything Irene hadn't known she was looking for in a partner. And the first person she'd been interested in in twenty-five years. She'd always thought that Nate broke whatever romantic impulse she'd ever had. But when she saw Kaden, she felt her body light up in places she'd thought had long since gone dormant.

He lay on his stomach, watching a large black beetle scuttle across the dirt. Though they'd both cleaned up before they ate— with Maura stomping around overhead and pointedly avoiding the main floor—he still looked like he'd spent the day at the river. His dark hair had dried in waves that he'd pushed back over his forehead, and his cheeks were tinged pink by the sun.

He glanced up to find Irene watching him.

"What's this one do?" he asked, pointing at the bug.

"That's a ground beetle," Irene said. "It eats slugs and snails and caterpillars. Basically all the things we don't want munching on the plants."

Years ago, she'd shown Nate around the garden, and he'd stepped on one deliberately, as if anything he didn't like the look of didn't belong in his world.

"It's cute." Kaden poked it gently with the tip of his finger. The beetle paused and twitched its antenna before scurrying off.

"You're not what I expected," Irene said.

He turned onto his side. "How's that?"

Irene gestured at him as if that explained it.

With a half smile, Kaden pushed himself up from the ground and offered her a hand. "I want to see more."

Together they slipped into one of the nearby rows of ink-dark plants, Kaden trailing his fingers along the leaves as they went. In this part of the garden, the blooms still held their darkness, no fading color or wilted leaves. Irene filed the thought away for later as Kaden stopped in front of her and pressed his nose into a black hollyhock flower. He took a slow, deep breath.

"I was so afraid that I'd really taken that woman's memories, or yours, or Clem's, or this whole town's. But maybe magic isn't so bad if it can be like this." He brushed the petals, then dropped into a crouch and eased his hand beneath the earth. "Hard to believe that this beauty could somehow be responsible for what happened at the funeral."

Irene sat beside him and leaned her shoulder against his, the cotton of his T-shirt soft on her arm. "It's strange, that's for sure," Irene said.

"Did you find anything earlier?" Kaden asked.

Irene nodded slowly. "Something's definitely off," she said. "But whatever the garden showed Addison, it didn't show me."

"You're worried," he said.

"I am," Irene agreed. "But the garden has been here for generations. Whatever is happening, I'm sure we'll get through it." At least, she hoped they would. But with the problems of Addison's magic, the warnings in the tea leaves, and now this, she feared change might have come for the Haywoods.

"It doesn't feel like magic," Kaden mused as he held out a handful of soil, then breathed that in, too. He glanced up at her, nose smudged with dirt. Without thinking, she brushed it away. His eyes widened, and she froze, fingertips still on his skin.

"You had some dirt on your face..."

She lowered her hand slowly, her eyes darting to his lips as he grinned and said, "It just smells like dirt."

Irene laughed. "That's because it *is* dirt." She dipped her own hand into the ground.

"Magic dirt," Kaden said with a grin.

"All dirt has a little magic in it."

"The Haywood dirt just has a little more?"

"It holds the town's sorrow. Everything we take from the people who come to us, we put here, and the plants give us back fruits and vegetables, blooms and herbs in return."

The plant seemed to be turning toward her, offering its petals. Irene plucked a flower and held it out to Kaden.

He eyed it warily. "I'm not sure I want to amplify my emotions again after what happened at the funeral. I'm sort of a mess right now..." His eyes flicked to hers.

"Even if the rosemary was responsible for what happened, it only amplifies what you're already feeling. So, maybe you should hold on to it. You can eat it when you find something you *do* want to feel."

Kaden arched an eyebrow. "Reading my aura, are you?" He leaned a little closer to her.

"Did I get it wrong?" she whispered.

Kaden glanced down at the flower she held between them. "Not at all."

He took it from her. There was a glint in his dark eyes, a small smile playing at his lips as he marveled at the bloom like it held all the magic in the world.

He was about to pop it into his mouth, but instead he pulled his wallet from his pocket and tucked the flower between two punch cards. Then he held his hands out to her.

A sensation trilled through Irene—a little bit like magic. She held out her hand as a butterfly flew toward her. It landed on her knuckles. A second followed. It had been a long time since she'd felt this quiet sort of happiness.

"If I am going to kiss you, I'd rather feel it without any magic between us," he said.

And that was it.

Irene's heart was done for.

Kaden stood and offered her a hand up. His skin was rough and dry and gritty with dirt, and when she touched it, her own skin came alive. He led her back to the blanket they'd set up, where the setting sun was about to slip below the horizon.

"As much as I want to kiss you now," he said, "once I start, I don't know that I'll be able to stop, and I don't want to miss the show."

The fireflies arrived right on time, zigzagging through the air like they'd been waiting all day for the fading blue light. Kaden settled back onto the old quilt, and Irene followed, close enough that their legs brushed. A lightning bug hovered a few inches in front of her, its abdomen pulsing a steady beat as sunset faded to dusk. She leaned forward and gently cupped her hands around it. Wings fluttered against her fingers. Tiny legs pressed into her skin as it landed at the base of her palm.

"Kaden." His name was a whisper.

He turned toward her as the light faded. Irene brought her hands within a few inches of his face. "What . . . ?"

Slowly, she peeled back her thumbs. The firefly climbed

along the soft pad of her palm, unsteady. Kaden brought his hand to hers gently, but before he could take the insect, it fluttered its wings and flew off into the night.

"Magic," Irene said, as she tracked its movement across the yard.

Kaden nodded, but his eyes were on her.

Her lips tilted up, and she reached for his hand. When her fingers grazed his, he threaded them together. They stared out at the world around them, the music of the night soft and low, Irene's worries over the garden settling into the back of her mind, where she could deal with them tomorrow.

A butterfly landed on her overalls. Another came to rest on her knee. Kaden held out his hand as a third settled on his outstretched fingers.

He glanced at her. "Am I the one making you this happy?"

"You just might be."

The crickets' songs grew louder as darkness fell. Stars sprouted in the sky, their pinpricks of light reflected in his eyes.

She leaned toward him. The butterfly took flight as he tucked a stray curl that had escaped her braid behind her ear and held his hand there, the tips of his callused fingers soft against her skin.

Then, he kissed her. Gentle at first, a brush of lips moving against lips. Irene's chest hitched. Her heart stuttered with every careful movement as his palm slipped from the side of her face to the back of her neck and her hands found their way into his hair. She kissed him like that until time fell away and it was only them and the stars and the warm Kentucky night.

When she finally pulled away, she found the ground around

their quilt covered in butterflies. A startled laugh escaped Kaden's lips.

"It's called a kaleidoscope," Irene said, a little breathless. "The swarm."

"I like that," he said as one landed on his shoulder. "This happens a lot, then?"

"This many?" Irene asked. "Not in a long time."

"I guess we'll just have to change that." His easy smile almost undid her as he leaned in and kissed her again.

Chapter 21

Kaden

Kaden had not returned to Yarrow looking to fall for a woman, yet here he was, on Irene's couch, wrapped in a quilt from her bed as she slept only a few rooms away, the memory of her lips on his still fresh as he wondered at this thing growing between them. He'd never been one for omens and fortunes, but he found himself going back to the leaves in his cup. That fern, the sign of magic he'd been so sure would bring him answers—yet in the end, it hadn't been magic that brought him home at all, but a stranger who'd had a little too much to drink.

Irene had said the reading suggested a chance at love. All his life it had been hard for Kaden to let anyone in. He didn't want to become his father or his mother, and that's why, he always tried to tell himself, it was better if he didn't have a family at all. It was easier to avoid romance than take the chance at messing someone up the way his family had ruined one another.

But Irene had seen through him. She'd risked losing a memory to help him. Even after all that, he still couldn't calm his racing thoughts. He needed fresh air, so he stood from the couch. He slowed at the sound of a creaking floorboard overhead. After a few seconds of silence, he continued toward the back door and out into the night.

The moon bathed the shadow garden in silver light. Kaden followed the path away from the house, bricks warm and rough against his feet. Eventually, he stepped onto soil and found himself beneath a row of sunflowers, blooms turned toward him as though he shone like the sun.

He blinked, rubbed at his eyes. He'd thought one of the hollyhock plants had done that earlier. He wondered if this, too, was part of the shadow garden magic.

He lay back on a cleared patch of earth and stared at the moon overhead, letting his mind wander to Irene. Her hair like a slant of sunlight. Her freckles like a scattering of soil. Her eyes the green-gold of new spring leaves. She was a garden come to life.

He wondered if he could make a home in Yarrow. With his father gone, there might, finally, be a place for him here. But he didn't know if he wanted to live anywhere near his mother and brother.

As he turned the thought over in his mind, something tickled his skin. He glanced down expecting another beetle, but instead a strawberry vine had crept across the dirt toward him. He sat up and blinked, not sure if he was seeing clearly.

When he opened his eyes, the vine had wound around his wrist and deposited a small black berry in the palm of his hand.

He touched a fingertip to the piece of fruit. Then he looked around him. "You want me to eat this?"

Wind rustled through the leaves. The heavy black blossoms looked down at him. With a shrug, Kaden popped the strawberry into his mouth. He bit down, and it hit his tongue with a hint of chocolate. He smiled in wonder.

Then all at once, his vision went black. The soil fell out from under him, and he was standing in his own body, staring at Irene.

We sat together on the patchwork couch in the Haywood guesthouse. Irene had claimed it when she and Nate first started dating. Now, sitting with her over a pot of lavender-and-lemon-balm tea and watching her sort through the tatters of her heart, I felt like I was breaking.

"I don't get it," Irene said. "I should've seen it. A year, Kaden. A fucking year!" She shook her head. "I shouldn't burden you with this. He's your brother."

"And you're my best friend," I said, my throat raw.

"How did I miss it?"

"Maybe you didn't," I said. "Maybe..."

The world shifted. Kaden blinked but still saw only darkness as his own words played over and over in his head. He tried to stand, but his body wouldn't listen. The darkness faded, and he found himself standing face-to-face with his brother.

"You're just like him. You may not have raised a hand to her, but she loved you, Nate."

"And she'll love me again," Nate said. "Give it a couple weeks, she'll be back on our bourbon, and I can make all of this go away."

"You didn't," I said, stunned.

Nate laughed.

"She deserves better than you," I said.

Nate's eyes widened. "You love her."

*   *   *

Nate's face disappeared.

Kaden stood in a room he didn't recognize.

A shelf of barrels lined one wall; bottles—all carefully labeled—lined the other. My mom lounged on a plush leather couch, her hair only just threaded with white. I sat across from her, elbows on my knees and head in my hands.

"We have to put a stop to this, Mom," I said. "If he was willing to do this to Irene, for a year..."

My mom sighed and shook her head. "Sometimes we do what we have to do, Kaden. I'm sure your brother had his reasons, even if he's made a mess of things. Family comes first."

"Irene was going to be family."

"You think I don't know that?" Sylvia said.

What had his brother done? Before he could land on an answer, everything shifted again.

Irene pressed her forehead to mine, our lips inches apart. My chest hitched.

"Why did you keep this from me?" she said.

"I didn't want to risk what we had," I said. "Your friendship means everything to me."

"If it had been you instead of Nate..." She shook her head. Tears filled her eyes. "I'd never have learned the truth about your family."

"I'd have told you," I said. "I'm sure of it." But the only thing I was sure of in that moment was that I wanted to kiss her tears away.

He was sitting in the Haywoods' kitchen.

*   *   *

A little girl ran, laughing, through the room, followed by a stream of dragonflies. Nolan scooped her up from the ground and peppered her forehead with kisses before he sat beside Taylor.

"You should've told us sooner," he said.

"I know. I thought…" I shook my head. "I don't know what I thought. That we weren't all that different from your family?"

Maura planted her hands on the table. "I made this possible. I have to stop it."

"How?" Irene asked. "The bourbon's already out there in the world. It's not like we can just recall it."

There was only one option.

"We must expose my family," I said.

Maura nodded slowly. "I'll kick them off my land. Without the dark corn, without the soil, everything will go back to how it was before."

"It's not enough," I said.

"What other choice do we have?" Irene said.

"I could try to take it from them."

"You can do that?" Clem asked.

"I don't know," I said. "But I have to try."

Kaden's mind whirled through flashes of dark and light until he stood in the VIP tent at the bourbon festival with Irene and Yarrow's mayor, Tim Stokes.

A young, pregnant Indian woman stood beside us, head tilted. Her long dark hair fell past her shoulders, and she wore a white tank top, a pair of jeans, and dark sunglasses. Susheila Das Baker—Casey Baker's wife and a staff writer for the Yarrow Gazette.

She pulled her shades down enough to look at Kaden and Irene over the top of her lenses. "I have to be honest. When I married Casey and took a job out here, I didn't expect to uncover something like... this." She popped a bourbon ball into her mouth. "I'm off today, so I didn't bring my steno, which means I'm going to need a full interview later to get it right."

"And you'll let us read the article before you publish?" Irene asked.

She nodded, eyes gleaming. "This is one hell of a story."

Kaden stood staring out at the bourbon festival, his mother at his side.

I held my hand out for the mic as the crowd parted. Cicadas swarmed overhead so heavy the sky seemed black. Irene gripped her niece tight against her chest. Blood stained her shirt. Her eyes locked on mine.

Kaden came back to himself gasping for breath. He planted his hands on the dirt and glanced around. But he was alone. The strawberry vine had disappeared. The flowers faced east, waiting on sunrise.

He blinked and stumbled to his feet.

He hurried back into the house.

He slipped into bed.

Come morning, he would wake to warm light streaming in from the windows, his back sore from a night on the couch, and one hell of a headache. Except for the dirt on his feet, he would barely recall his walk through the garden. It was all flashes of various memories he didn't have, but it felt more like a dream.

What else could it have been?

Chapter 22

Sylvia

Beyond the barbed wire–topped fence at the edge of the Haywood property lay fields and fields of deep gray cornstalks that stretched toward the sky. In the predawn light, Sylvia Bonner stood in their midst. She pulled an ear from one plant, and it shuddered. The movement rippled down the row as though a gust of wind blew through it, but the night was still.

She peeled back the husk. Beneath, the black kernels were half the size they should've been. Some parts of the cob hadn't even formed seeds at all. It wasn't the first time it had happened, but more and more, the yield was turning out all wrong—ever since they stopped rotating the fields that spring and began using every last scrap of soil.

The corn slipped from Sylvia's hand and hit the ground with a thud. With a heavy sigh, she hopped onto her golf cart and made her way back to the Bonner estate.

Chapter 23

Quinn

As usual, Quinn's tea leaves that morning showed nothing. What she wouldn't give for a morsel from the universe, some small assurance that she was on the right path with her nightmares or her memories or whatever they were.

Meanwhile, her cousin's reading revealed a clear sprig of rosemary, an ear of corn, and that single curling fern. Again. She'd made three mugs of tea that morning and each one showed the same thing.

Addison looked down into her cup, then up at Quinn, and groaned. "I don't get it. I really thought this was a sign to sell to Sylvia."

"Maybe it was," Quinn said. "But there's obviously something more to it."

"Normally I'd take it to Grams for her thoughts, but after yesterday..."

"Blaming you for the problems with the rosemary was a real bitch move," Quinn said. "Even for Grams. Maybe Irene can help you figure it out."

Addison shook her head. "It wasn't just Grams. You heard them. They both blamed me." She rested her forehead against the counter. "What if they're right?"

"They didn't *blame* you for it," Quinn said as she rubbed at the black lipstick stain she'd left on her teacup.

"They kind of did," Harper said. She leaned her elbows on the countertop, her hands wrapped around a steaming cup of coffee.

"I should've told them about the vision sooner," Addison said.

"Probably," Quinn said. "But it's not your fault. The Haywoods don't control the magic in the garden. You give it pain, it gives you fruit. It's a symbiotic relationship. And this time that fruit had a bit of a different effect."

"It wasn't just a little bit different."

If word got out about what had happened last night, Quinn would be the one fielding questions from their buyers. But she'd deal with that when the time came.

"What if it really is all my fault?"

"Addy..." Quinn warned.

"No, I mean it," Addison said. "My broken magic means I can't give the garden the sorrow it needs."

"We don't choose how the Haywood gift works," Quinn said.

"So, what, the universe decided the garden is going to starve and there's nothing we can do about it?" Addison asked. "Either way, the problem is the same. My magic."

As much as Quinn loved Addison, this line of self-blame wasn't going to get them anywhere. She stood from her barstool and pulled Addison up. Then she pushed her toward the bathroom. "You need to get cleaned up, and then you need to go into the tea shop and talk to your mother. You can't solve this problem on your own."

Addison dug her feet in. "Absolutely not."

"Let's say the garden *is* starving," Quinn said. "You need to figure out how your magic plays into that. You need to figure out who you are. Not as Irene's daughter. Not as Maura's grand-daughter. But as you. You'll be the one who carries all this on when they're done. And if it's going to be different from here on out, then so be it. You have to embrace that. Now go."

"Fine," Addison said. Then she slipped off down the hallway.

Quinn turned back to find Harper smiling at her.

"Well done," Harper said.

"I'm trying." Quinn closed her eyes and sighed. "Sorry about her needing to crash here last night. Especially after the way you reacted to the rosemary..."

Harper hid her face behind her cup of coffee. "God, that was embarrassing, and I *like* PDA."

"I mean, I do look excellent in a suit."

"Hot, I think I said hot, but excellent works, too," Harper laughed. "If only Addison could also figure out your night-mares along the way."

"Sorry about last night." Quinn cringed as she remembered how she'd bolted upright in bed muttering about blood, thrown the covers off both of them, and stood up on the mattress, ready to tackle whoever or whatever was haunting her dream in that moment, before Harper managed to shake her awake.

"Don't be." Harper wrapped her arms around Quinn.

Quinn pressed her forehead to Harper's and closed her eyes. "What if they never go away?"

"Then they never go away," Harper said.

That was not the answer Quinn had been looking for. "If I knew what happened that day, what happened that summer, maybe I could put them to rest. It's the not knowing that's caus-ing them, I think."

Harper pulled back. Her eyes were soft when they met Quinn's. "I want to support you in this, but that summer is gone. I don't think those memories are coming back, and maybe with good reason. I don't want you to hold out hope for something that might be impossible."

"It's no coincidence Kaden left the same summer my dad died," Quinn said.

"But it could be."

"Fine," Quinn said. "Then it's no coincidence he's back now."

Harper nodded—even she couldn't deny the tea leaves.

"He was in my nightmare last night," Quinn said.

But the problem with Kaden ran deeper than his face in her dreams. There were certain things Quinn knew about the Bonners, things that reinforced her belief they'd been involved in her father's death, and one of them was that needling sensation in the space between her eyebrows every time she interacted with one of them—until Kaden showed up. Seeing Kaden at her grams's kitchen table had thrown her. He hadn't prickled her at all. Instead, he'd felt as soft as a sage leaf.

"He really was the man you didn't recognize?" Harper asked, taking Quinn's hands in hers.

Quinn nodded emphatically.

"I know how much you want the truth." Harper paused as she brushed a loose curl from Quinn's face.

"But?" Quinn asked.

"Is it possible your mind put his face on that man?" she asked gently.

She'd had the same thought herself, but it didn't line up. "It wasn't the Kaden we know. He was younger. How would I know what he looked like at that age?"

"Let's say it really is him in your dreams," Harper said. "How does that help you find out what happened that summer?"

"I haven't figured that out yet," Quinn admitted. "But if we could get closer to the Bonners..."

"After what happened last night?" Harper asked. "We both know it's going to be a long time before we have anything to do with Nate and Sylvia again."

"I could...I could go over there," she said. "Try to negotiate a refund."

"You really think Maura will be on board with that?"

"There's got to be something I can do," Quinn said. "It's all connected. It has to be."

"All right," Harper relented.

Quinn grinned and let out a triumphant laugh before she wrapped her arms around Harper and spun them both in a circle.

"What if you talked to Kaden about it?" Harper suggested.

Quinn shook her head. "If it turns out he really was the one who did it, I don't know if I want to be responsible for bringing back those memories."

"Which leaves us with Sylvia or Nate," Harper said. "Maybe we could use the bourbon festival. Baker's is one of the biggest sponsors. I'm sure I could come up with a reason I need to talk to Sylvia. Then you could join me and...do whatever it is you want to do."

Just then, Addison appeared from the bathroom, wet hair dripping onto one of Quinn's T-shirts, her phone pressed to her ear. "I'll let you know either way," she said. "Talk to you soon, Sylvia."

Quinn and Harper shared a look.

"You and Sylvia Bonner are talking?" Quinn asked.

"Apparently," Addison said as she grabbed her abandoned teacup and rinsed it in the sink. "She had my number from the delivery this week. She wants to invite our family over for dinner."

Quinn arched an eyebrow. "What was that about coincidences?" she said to Harper with a gleam in her eye.

Chapter 24

Addison

Every summer, for years, Sylvia Bonner would invite the Haywoods to her estate for the annual founders' dinner, a sort of end to the first day of the Yarrow festival, and every summer, Maura Haywood would decline. Eventually, Sylvia stopped asking. So when she extended the invitation to Addison directly, it seemed like she was making an attempt to apologize—somewhat publicly—for Nate's accusations. Though Addison knew the shadow garden was to blame for the chaos at the funeral, with this invitation, Sylvia had managed to ease at least some of what Addison was starting to think was permanent self-doubt.

"Out of everyone, a Bonner was the last person I expected to take my side." Even saying it out loud, it didn't feel real.

"Excuse me. *I* took your side." Though Quinn crossed her arms and had a slight huff in her voice, the softness in her eyes betrayed her.

"All I'm saying is that I've yet to see this awful person Grams warned us about our whole lives," Addison said. "I should be the one apologizing to Sylvia for the rosemary. I don't get it."

"The tea leaves literally told you this was coming," Quinn said.

"Three times," Harper added.

"There's no way in hell Grams is going to agree to join the Bonners for dinner."

"That's where you're wrong," Quinn said. She raised her index finger. "One, Grams would *never* pass up a public apology from Sylvia."

Addison started to interrupt, but Quinn held up a second finger. "And two, sure, the tea leaves may be somewhat responsible for getting us into this mess in the first place, but it's pretty clear they're not done with the Bonners yet, so neither are we, and not even Grams will be able to argue against that."

"But—"

Quinn barreled on. "Three, it's a founders' dinner. That means the Bakers will be there. That means *River* will be there."

Sometimes, Addison wondered if Quinn really *was* an empath, and she'd been lying to them about her lack of the family gift for all these years. "I have no interest in seeing River again," Addison said.

"You were both in tears yesterday," Quinn said.

"Because of the *shadow garden*," Addison said.

"Yeah, and the shadow garden only amplifies what you're already feeling," Quinn replied.

"It might surprise you to know that I've convinced myself the tea leaves led me to connect with the Bonners so I could finally let River go," Addison said. "I'm ready to move on."

"That's not at all surprising," Quinn said. "Wrong, but not surprising."

Addison threw up her hands. "Fine," she said. "I'll convince Mom and Grams to attend the dinner. Somehow."

∾☙∾

"I cannot believe I let you talk me into this," Addison said as she and Quinn stood in the alley behind the tea shop. Both her mother's truck and Kaden's white Audi sports car that looked like it had been dropped there right out of the '90s were parked out back.

Addison braced herself as Quinn pushed her up the back stairs and into the shop.

Clem called from the front room, "Irene, is that you?"

Addison and Quinn shared a look.

"It's me and Addison!" Quinn replied for them both.

They found Clem packing up four-ounce jars with Lavender & Lemon Balm's signature recipe teas to sell during the festival. She stood and wrapped them each in a hug. Then she abandoned her task, pulled a tea from the shelf, and spooned several heaping portions into a jar.

"I take it Mom isn't here?" Addison asked.

"I haven't heard from her or Kaden after I dropped him off over there with takeout last night," Clem said. "But I promised her I'd make sure she had her hangover cure when she woke up today, and I forgot to grab it for her last night," Clem said. "Will you run it over to the house for me?"

"You heard what she said to me yesterday," Addison said. "I'm not going over there. She doesn't deserve it."

"It's not about what she deserves," Clem said. "It's about what she needs. And yes, she was not herself, but she was also pissed at Maura on your behalf."

Addison arched an eyebrow. "You're not just saying that?"

Clem shook her head. "She doesn't blame you. If anything, she's likely thrilled the rosemary made such a ruckus. No one's going to realize she showed up intoxicated. Honestly, the shadow garden did her a favor."

Addison accepted the jar of tea. "Fine," she said. "I'll take it to her. But only because you promised and because I need to check on the garden anyway."

☙

When Addison pulled into the driveway, she was relieved to see that Maura's car wasn't parked in front of the old Victorian home. She wasn't quite ready to tackle her mother and grandmother at the same time.

But first, she needed to see to the garden.

Once she reached the familiar brick path, she slipped out of her sandals, and with her first step onto shadow garden soil, something inside her uncoiled. Had she been less stubborn, she'd have come home last night just to let the garden ease the ache in her heart.

There were very few places where Addison felt like she belonged, and kneeling in the shadow garden up to her elbows in dirt was one of them. Here, Addison felt connected to a magic deeper than her family gift. Here, it didn't matter that the power in her was unpredictable, that her unwillingness to own up to that wildness within her had lost her the love of her life.

In the heart of the garden, it was only Addison and the black and gray plants, their roots prodding at her fingertips, their leaves whispering their thanks for each insect she pulled free from their stems and each weed she tugged loose from the earth.

Though she still felt a sense of peace, she worried at her lip. She sat in front of the hedge of rosemary that served as a barrier between the rows of cabbages, brussels sprouts, and broccoli as though the shadow garden itself knew the herb would repel the cabbage moths that could obliterate a crop. The darkness had faded from the rosemary's leaves, the tips almost white beneath the morning sun.

"What happened?" she asked the garden around her.

Though the plants shifted, they offered no answers. She wormed her fingers beneath the soil. The roots were slow to greet her. When they finally brushed her fingertips, they felt tired, like they'd pulled all the nutrients from the soil in one quick burst and it left them weak and wanting. Just like what she'd seen in her vision.

She stood, brushing the dirt from her hands, and started for the house. She eased the back door open and set the kettle on in the kitchen. After the water started boiling, she poured two cups of tea.

"Good morning." Kaden's voice came from behind her.

Addison startled. She turned, eyes wide. She knew Kaden's car had been at the tea shop, but she hadn't really expected to find him in her grandmother's house. "Good morning?"

Kaden laughed softly and pointed behind him, toward the living room. "I slept on the couch."

Addison nodded slowly. "I'm going to wake Sleeping Beauty. There's tea on the counter."

She slipped past Kaden and padded down the hallway to her mom's room. She raised her fist and knocked. When there was no answer, she tried again. "Mom?" she called, knocking louder.

"Oh god." Her mother's voice came through the door, muffled. "Make it stop."

Addison cracked the door open to find her mom sitting up at the edge of her bed, head in her hands. She glanced at Addison between the gaps in her fingers.

"Clem sent me with your hangover tea," Addison said.

"Bless you," Irene said. "Would you put some water on to boil?"

"Already did," Addison said.

"You are a goddess," Irene said.

"Kaden is in our kitchen," Addison said.

A smile flitted across her mother's face as she pulled on her overalls. "Neither of us had our cars last night after...everything."

Addison did her best to keep from grinning. It had been a long time since she'd seen her mother this happy, and she was thrilled, even if she was still mad at her. Irene followed her down the hallway to where Kaden already stood drinking tea in the kitchen. Her mom stepped up to him, and he wrapped an arm around her waist. She stood on her toes and pressed a kiss to his cheek.

"So, this is a thing, then?" Addison asked.

Irene and Kaden shared a look. Irene arched an eyebrow and he laughed.

"Definitely a thing," he said.

Addison pushed a mug into her mother's hands. She took a sip and let out a long sigh.

Kaden did the same and said, "This tea is delicious."

"Of course it is," Irene said.

"You'll quickly learn my mom expects praise for all of her teas," Addison said.

"Well-deserved praise," Irene said.

"Chamomile?" Kaden asked.

"And rose and ginger," Addison said. "A little bergamot."

Her mother beamed. Addison wanted to soak up that small bit of her mother's approval, but then she reminded herself that even if Clem claimed Irene had gotten on Maura's case about everything, it was still Irene who'd pointed the finger at Addison.

"I'm sorry about yesterday, at the funeral," Irene said.

"You reading my aura?"

The Haywoods had an unspoken rule: you may not attempt to read another Haywood's emotional state without permission. None of them followed it.

"Maybe," Irene said. "The point is, I'm sorry."

"Then you can make it up to me by accepting an invitation from Sylvia Bonner to the founders' dinner tomorrow night."

Her mother coughed, almost choking on her tea. "Excuse me?"

"She wants to apologize. Also, I saw rosemary and corn in my leaves again this morning."

Her mom opened her mouth, and Addison saw the doubt in her aura.

"You owe me," Addison said. "After yesterday."

"Maybe this will be good," Kaden said to Irene. "If we're going to . . . keep this up," he coughed, "we could at least try to repair some of what's happened between our families."

Irene crossed her arms. "There is no repairing what your brother did to me."

"I meant between our mothers."

"God, you would think that at some point you get over the havoc that your mother wreaks on your life," Irene said.

"You'd think," Kaden grunted.

Addison arched an eyebrow.

"I have *not* wreaked havoc on your life," Irene said.

"No," Addison agreed. "But you still owe me this, and you know there's no way I'm going to convince Grams on my own."

Irene threw up her hands. "Fine," she said. "If it means I get you and Grams talking again so we can figure out what's happening to the garden, then I'll make it happen."

Chapter 25

Maura

As a child, Maura Haywood spent every summer looking forward to the first day of the Yarrow festival. Back then, it was a celebration of the summer solstice, and the Haywoods treated it accordingly. Her family would sell baskets of fresh produce: Stalks of basil to keep the evil eye at bay. A head of broccoli to heal the body. A bunch of cilantro to mend the soul. Three tomatoes for passion in the bedroom. A cucumber to keep that passion from burning a relationship to the ground. The finishing touch—one piece of fruit from the shadow garden to amplify it all. People went to the festival and came home with prosperity, protection, and good luck.

It wasn't until that first dark-corn mash had been distilled that bourbon had slipped its way into the festival, and the Bonners claimed the day for their own. Now, Maura only made the baskets to order, and the number of orders got smaller every year. She tied a ribbon and shot a look at the cup of tea steaming on her workshop table. Her leaves hadn't held anything good on a festival morning since the summer her son, Nolan, died.

She doubted today would be any different, but Maura was a creature of habit.

How her daughter and granddaughter had managed to talk her into a dinner with the Bonners, she would never understand. Maura trusted Sylvia Bonner as much as she trusted a vine borer moth to skip over her pumpkin patch and choose another garden altogether, which is to say she didn't trust the woman at all.

But Maura was a woman of principles. She couldn't just ignore the leaves.

Unless those leaves ended up contradicting her granddaughter's.

She drained the last bit of tea and flipped the cup onto her saucer.

"Well, hell," she murmured. She'd wanted an easy way out of dinner, not a host of bad omens.

A snake—treachery and disloyalty. Hidden danger.

A mirror facing a comet—the use of truth as a weapon.

A dragon—great and sudden changes.

And right at the bottom of the cup, a ladybug perched on a fern.

She tapped her fingertips against the wood.

"Anything interesting in your leaves this morning?"

She hadn't even heard Irene's footsteps. With a deep sigh, she turned to face her daughter. Irene wore an old T-shirt over a pair of leggings, and in the soft morning light she almost looked Addison's age.

"This and that." Maura tucked her cup and saucer closer, out of Irene's sight. They read their tea leaves every morning, but symbols like these were unusual. Unexpected readings, it seemed, were becoming a trend.

"We've lived together long enough that I know when you're hiding something from me," Irene said.

"Then we've also lived together long enough that you should remember that if you need to know something, I'll share." Maura pushed back from the table. "I'll put on the kettle for you."

"You want to see what's in my leaves."

Maura only shrugged and watched as her daughter spooned her own mixture of tea and herbs into a mug.

"I know you're worried," Irene said.

"Reading my aura without my permission is rude," Maura said.

The kettle whistled, and Maura poured the water into Irene's cup.

"This is about the founders' dinner," Irene said.

Again, Maura said nothing. She didn't want to influence Irene's reading. "Drink," she said.

Irene sighed but brought her cup to her lips. "Having you watch me is far from the morning ritual I was going for."

"If you'd drink faster, we could get this over with," Maura said.

Irene sipped slowly. Maura tapped her foot against the tile floor. When Irene finally flipped her mug, Maura peered over her shoulder and took a sharp breath. She grabbed her own cup, glanced from its contents to her daughter's and back again. Maura gripped the countertop and shook her head slowly.

"Well this isn't good," Irene said. "Not that truth or change are necessarily bad, but I don't like the snakes one bit. Or the comet, and all with Addison at the center."

She glanced up at her mother and her eyes went wide. "You knew it was going to be about Addison."

Maura pressed her mug into her daughter's hands. "They're the same."

"Again?" Irene held her cup next to Maura's.

"Twice in one week," Maura murmured as she sat down at the kitchen table. She was supposed to be the one with the answers, the one who guided her daughter and her granddaughter, who taught them to pull the sorrow out of Yarrow's heart and bury it deep in the soil just like Maura's mother and grandmother had done before her.

"I...I don't know what it means." Maura's voice was uncharacteristically shaky.

"It means we need to be wary," Irene said.

"Obviously," Maura snapped, but she let her daughter take her hand. "Can't we just skip this dinner?"

Irene shook her head. "Maybe, if there was something here that pointed to the Bonners. But there isn't. You need to make peace with Addison."

Maura rolled her eyes.

"Whatever this"—Irene gestured to the teacups with the matching signs—"is, if we're seeing it here, the wheels are already turning. We can't stop it now. We can only hope to guide our response to whatever is to come."

Tears pricked at Maura's eyes. "You sound like me."

Irene laughed softly. "I learned from you."

Despite Maura's worry, a honeybee found its way into the kitchen and landed on the table.

"Do you want to tell Addison?" Maura asked. Her granddaughter still hadn't spoken to her since the funeral. Addison might live in the guesthouse near the shadow garden, but she'd managed to make herself scarce over the past two days.

Irene pressed her lips together. "Not particularly," she said. "But..."

The leaves had given her and Irene the same message. They knew better than to ignore it.

"She doesn't think we take her seriously," Maura said.

"We *did* relegate her to the garden after what happened with River, and you laid it on pretty thick the other night," Irene said.

"I apologized," Maura said.

"You agreed to go to the dinner, and you did it through me," Irene said. "That's not exactly an apology."

Maura crossed her arms and tapped her foot.

With a sigh, Irene said, "If we keep this from her, it will only make things worse."

Maura knew her daughter was right, but she hated admitting it. She considered brushing it off, but as soon as she had the thought, the back door opened and Addison stepped into the kitchen, mug in hand.

She looked from Irene to Maura.

"You've been avoiding me," Maura said.

"Good morning to you, too," Addison said with a yawn. To Irene she said, "Do you both want to go to the festival with me? Sylvia says she has seats for all of us in the VIP tent—even if *some* of us aren't going to stay."

"I'm going to dinner," Maura said. "What more do you want from me?"

Irene elbowed her gently.

Maura closed her eyes, pressed her fingertips to her temples, and tilted her head back. "I'm sorry I blamed what happened at the funeral on you," Maura said. "Even if your interpretation of the tea leaves was what led us there in the first place."

"That's half an apology at best," Addison said.

"The other half will be my presence at dinner tonight," Maura said. "Speaking of which, I want you to be careful tonight, and in any situation that involves a single Bonner."

"Even Kaden?" Addison asked, and glanced at her mom.

"I'm still undecided about him," Maura said as she gently grabbed Addison's elbow and led her to the table where the tea-cups sat side by side.

Addison looked first at Maura's, then at Irene's. Then she set her own cup on the table and turned it over. It matched the first two, leaf for leaf.

"Are things with my magic ever going to stop getting worse?" Addison asked.

Maura wondered the same, though she didn't speak it aloud.

"What if the shadow garden isn't able to recover?" Addison asked.

"Then the universe has something else in store for us," Maura said, trying to believe the words herself. "Still, maybe we'd be better off skipping the dinner tonight and getting started on trying to fix the garden."

But Addison shook her head. "You're not getting out of it that easy, Grams."

Maura sighed. It'd been worth a shot.

Chapter 26

Kaden

The fireflies arrived with the sun. They floated through air thick with humidity and anticipation, their flashing only just visible against the morning gloom as people filled the streets of downtown from the square to the distillery. Booths lined the sidewalks, each offering a little piece of Yarrow for the tourists to take home. Children followed after their parents, sucking on bourbon-flavored lollypops or picking at bags full of smoky kettle corn.

"You know," Kaden said as he walked, his fingers threaded through Irene's, "I actually missed this."

"That's because the festival is amazing," Addison said.

"Is this the same daughter I raised?" Irene asked.

"Don't pretend you don't love it," Addison said. "You give me money to buy you a funnel cake every year."

She held her plate out to both of them, and Kaden pinched off a piece. It hit his tongue the way only grease and cinnamon could.

"It's not just the food," Kaden said. "When I was younger, I loved the memory harvest. It felt like my family was doing something more than just making and selling bourbon."

"Are you going to participate?" Addison asked.

Kaden shook his head. "It's going to be a long time before I touch bourbon again."

Irene laughed and tore off a chunk of the funnel cake. "Fine," she admitted. "The festival isn't all bad. I mean, other than the gloom. And the Bonners."

Kaden pointed at himself and mouthed, *Me?*

Irene rolled her eyes. "The *other* Bonners. I can't believe I let the two of you talk me into this."

After rescuing them with Irene's hangover cure yesterday, Addison had suggested they all attend the festival together. Though Kaden still felt uncomfortable around his mother, he hadn't been able to resist the nostalgia.

"If your new boyfriend—"

"He is *not* my boyfriend," Irene said, though she gripped Kaden's hand tighter and grinned at him.

"—is planning to get to know Yarrow again, then the festival is the perfect place to start." Addison popped a piece of funnel cake in her mouth and said, "Come on, lovebirds."

The distillery gates had been thrown wide. People packed the space from road to stage, and everything smelled of sweat and yeast and anticipation.

Children with chocolate-smeared faces ran through the crowds, carrying old pickle jars filled with fireflies. Teens poured bourbon into empty soda bottles when their parents weren't looking and slunk away behind the tents and booths to drink. Older women in elaborate hats waved paper fans to fight the summer heat while their husbands, dressed in thin, light-colored blazers, cast offended looks at all the twenty-somethings in their too-short denim and loose shirts.

A section to the right of the stage had been roped off and

covered with an open-air tent and a sign labeling it the VIP area. They found Clem and Taylor waiting for them there, along with Sylvia.

Kaden's stomach twisted at the sight of his mother. Maybe one day, with enough therapy, he'd be able to disassociate her from his father's abuse. For now, he had to remind himself that she was a victim, too. And, whether he liked it or not, she was family.

Sylvia wrapped her thin arms around him, forcing him to drop his grip on Irene. Then she pulled back, clasping his shoulders.

"You look much better than you did at the funeral," she said.

He took a steadying breath. "I showered this morning," he said.

Clem snorted behind her hand, and Taylor cleared her throat.

"Not that it will do you much good in this heat." Sylvia waved a paper fan emblazoned with the Bonner's logo. To Addison and Irene she said, "I'm so glad the two of you made it. Maura not feeling well?"

"She's well enough," Irene said. She looked like she was trying not to bite his mother.

"Maybe that's for the best," Sylvia said. "You know, it means so much to see the two of you here. None of this"—she gestured around her—"would've been possible without your garden. It really is something."

"If you invited us here to blame us for the other night—" Irene started.

"No, no, not at all," Sylvia said.

Taylor and Clem quietly backed away from them.

"It's just, there's something wrong with the corn. The plants aren't yielding like they used to, and the past few months the white dog has been off—weaker. The nostalgia doesn't really settle into the bourbon until it's been in the barrels for a while. I'm afraid for what it will all mean once it's ready to be bottled," Sylvia said.

Irene crossed her arms. Kaden rested a hand on the small of her back, and she leaned into his touch.

"With the increase in demand, Nate's had our farmers using every bit of that field since this spring. We used to rotate planting, to give different parts of the soil a chance to recover, but that just wasn't an option this year."

"Sounds to me like this is a problem you've created for yourselves," Irene said.

Sylvia's eyes gleamed in the light. "The memory harvest means a lot to this town. I'd hate for them to lose it. Even your family has benefited from it."

"Do *not* bring my brother's death into this," Irene said.

Sylvia shook her head. "No, no. Of course not. I was simply hoping maybe you could provide us with some fresh seeds."

"So now we get to the real reason why we were invited," Irene said.

"It's been decades since Maura gave us the corn. I thought..." She paused. "Perhaps it's grown weaker on our land. Maybe it's time for a new crop."

Kaden rubbed at the space between his eyebrows as flashes from his dream the other night resurfaced. Before he could grab onto anything, Irene said, "Let me guess, if I wasn't here, you'd have had this conversation with my daughter and tried to broker a deal like you did for the rosemary."

Addison didn't challenge her mother.

"I thought…" Sylvia said, her eyes darting from Kaden to Irene. She sighed and shook her head. "Just think about it. I hope you enjoy the festival, and I look forward to seeing you tonight."

With that, she turned to go.

"The nerve," Irene said.

Kaden shook his head. She was exactly the woman he remembered.

"Mom," Addison started to say.

"Don't even think about it," Irene said. "You saw the rosemary and corn in your leaves. Maybe it's a sign that it's time for their harvest to end."

She stalked away, farther into the VIP tent, leaving Kaden and Addison behind.

"She can be just like my grams sometimes," Addison said, shaking her head.

"I don't want to see the harvest go," Kaden said. "But my mother was absolutely inappropriate. She should've set a meeting with your family, not brought it up here. Especially when she knows what a big deal it is that Irene showed up to the festival at all."

"Right," Addison said. "Well, it's clear that you don't like your mom."

"She's a complicated woman," Kaden said. "I'm still trying to figure out who she is without my dad in the picture."

"And?"

He laughed and shook his head. "And I think it might take the rest of my life."

Quinn and Harper stepped out from the VIP tent. Quinn wore a plain gray tee tucked into denim cutoffs, paired with not-fully-laced black boots. Harper's burnt-orange short-sleeve blouse hung loose over her high-waisted jeans and flashed her midriff with every breeze.

"Something happen with Irene?" Quinn asked. "She's running a little hotter than usual."

"Sylvia," Addison said.

"Say no more," Quinn said. "That woman gets under my skin, too." She looked Kaden over, eyes narrowed. "Yet, somehow, you don't."

"I guess it's a good thing we don't all have to grow up to become our parents," he said.

"Our seats are this way." Quinn nodded toward a bartender who stood serving glasses of Bonner's. "Bourbon's over there."

"I'll pass," Kaden said.

"It's ten-year," Harper said.

"That doesn't make it any more appealing," Kaden said.

"I don't blame you," Quinn said. "That shit makes me feel weird."

Clem and Taylor were headed their way with Irene in tow.

"Nice of you to bail on us out there," Kaden said.

"You had it handled," Clem said with a shrug.

"Mostly," Taylor said with a quick glance at Irene.

"It's fine," Irene said. "I just need another funnel cake and I'll be over it."

Taylor held up a bourbon ball. "How about one of these?"

Irene shook her head. "No bourbon."

"You can't even feel it," Clem said. "It's for flavor more than anything."

"It's Bonner's," Irene said, as if that was that. "I'm going to go try to find a bathroom and get that second funnel cake."

"Oh, me too," Quinn said.

"Come on," Addison said to Kaden. "Let's find a place to sit."

He followed her to a row of folding chairs plusher than the ones in his apartment back in Ohio. He wasn't entirely surprised. Except for their group and the Bakers, the tent was filled with politicians and Kentucky celebrities in suits and dresses fit for derby. Kaden glanced down at his V-neck T-shirt and shrugged.

Before Kaden reached his seat, a Black man in his midsixties approached him.

"Kaden Bonner?" he said.

Kaden's heart lifted. Someone who knew him by name.

"Mayor Stokes?" Kaden said.

He chuckled and offered Kaden his hand. "It's just Tim these days. Haven't been mayor for a couple of decades."

"You remember me?"

"I saw you at the funeral," Tim said.

Kaden deflated. "Right," he said, and even though his stomach had long since settled, it churned at the memory.

"It's all right," he said. "My wife and I got into a shouting match over where we were going for dinner before the funeral was even over. It was a weird night."

"It sure was," Kaden said.

"I just wanted to welcome you back to Yarrow." He clapped Kaden on the back. "You planning to stick around?"

Kaden glanced the way Irene had gone. "I just might."

"Well, if you need anyone to help get you connected, I'm your man," he said.

"Thank you, sir," Kaden said.

Tim laughed, clapped Kaden on the back again, and took a seat a few rows over.

Kaden settled in next to Addison.

"You make friends fast," she said.

"Pays to be a Bonner, I guess."

The voice of the current mayor of Yarrow came over the speakers, cutting their conversation short.

"Welcome to the Annual Yarrow Bourbon Festival!" Cheers rang out across the grounds as people raised their plastic cups. "For those of you who are attending for the first time, the fireflies come out in droves this time of year. Tomorrow morning, the high school marching band will kick off our firefly parade."

On cue, two elementary-school children—a white boy and a Black girl—ran across the stage in homemade firefly costumes, beaming as people erupted in applause. Once they'd made it to the other side, the mayor held up a hand. Sylvia ascended the steps while Nate took up a spot next to the old still. River crossed to a large whiskey barrel, drill in hand.

"She's letting *River* tap the barrel?" Addison whispered, just loud enough for Kaden to hear.

"Don't worry," he said. "It's not hard."

She laughed, and her look of gratitude set something in him at ease.

Sylvia held out her arms. Her gauzy, goldenrod-yellow sundress fluttered in the breeze.

"Hello, Yarrow!" she called. "It's an honor to kick off another festival! Before we begin, let's give a round of applause for the Haywoods, who made the bourbon you drink today possible."

She was laying it on thick, Kaden thought.

Once the applause died down, Sylvia said, "For those of you visiting, we start things off by tapping our latest batch of bourbon." She gestured to the barrel on the far side of the stage. "For the rest of you, you know what to do."

All across the crowd, people pulled slips of paper from their pockets. "Today, we say goodbye to what we want to leave behind," Sylvia said. She gave them a few moments to read what they'd penned before they handed over the written memories to the person beside them—the one they'd entrusted with their darkest moment of the year, should they ever need it back.

"Most of you know our master distiller, my youngest son, Nate. With us today we also have our newest apprentice, River Baker."

River held the drill up over his head in a wave. His family erupted in applause. Casey Baker put two fingers between his lips and whistled, while Susheila snapped a photo with her phone.

Harper shouted, "That's my brother!"

Addison sank deeper into the seat next to Kaden.

Sylvia pulled the mic from the stand and crossed over toward River as he pressed the drill bit to the wood. Once he'd tapped the barrel, she offered him her glass, and he filled it. He held it under his nose.

Kaden mouthed, *Smells like a good one*, at the same time that River spoke the words into the mic. The crowd lost it.

Sylvia held up her glass. A wave of arms rose across the grounds, clear plastic glinting in the sun. Fireflies descended on the lawn, their flashing only just visible in the midday sun.

"Now," Sylvia said, her voice echoing out over the speakers. "To another year as the best bourbon in Kentucky."

She took a sip. The crowd mirrored her motion, though many of the younger people swallowed their full glass in one quick shot. "Let's forget what holds us back, leave behind all that darkness, and look forward to another year!"

The town's applause could've been an explosion. And as the cries left their lips, so too did a dark haze. Almost exactly like what Kaden had seen at the bar. His pulse ratcheted up as the darkness descended around them like a fog—much thicker than Kaden remembered. It was as if a cloud had passed over the sun, but the golden orb still hung unobscured in the sky. The shadows swirled, rising above them.

Kaden blinked and rubbed at his eyes.

"Did you see that?" he asked Addison.

"See what?"

"The gloom..."

Addison shook her head and took another sip. "There's always more of it this time of year," she said. "Probably what brings the fireflies out."

Kaden stared at her, stunned. "You didn't see it appear?"

"What do you mean *appear?*" Addison asked. "It comes from the angel's share of the bourbon. Wait, did you forget that?"

Kaden shook his head slowly.

"Are you all right?"

"I...I'm fine," he said, brow furrowed. "I think the heat's getting to me."

He rubbed at his eyes. When he opened them again, the gloom was still there, but the swirling he'd seen had faded, leaving him uncertain if he'd seen anything at all.

Chapter 27

Irene

Irene hadn't stepped foot on the front lawn of the Bonner mansion in twenty-five years, but as far as she could tell the house hadn't aged a day. The paint still held its brilliant peach hue, and the white porch railing was immaculate, not a single chip or stain in sight. It was as if the gloom didn't touch the place. More likely, Sylvia Bonner paid a pretty penny to make it appear that way.

She thought, after all this time, that the memory of Nate in the alley with that woman would've faded, but the sickeningly sweet scent of the hydrangeas and the familiar walk up the drive brought her time with him back in one unwelcome rush.

It had Irene reeling.

She was glad she and Kaden had arrived separately to the founders' dinner. She wasn't ready for him to see her like this. She rested her cheek against Clem's shoulder, her throat tight. She felt like she was twenty-one all over again.

"How does this still hurt so much?"

"You were going to have a life together," Clem said.

Taylor wrapped Irene in a gentle hug. "Of course it hurts."

"It's been decades," Irene said. "I'm seeing someone else. I should be over this by now." But even after all this time, Nate's betrayal still stung.

"You—more than anyone—know how long healing takes," Clem said.

It was a slow, messy, lifelong process of starving the roots of the pain, and even then, the grief didn't always die. That's what her family was there for, to pull those feelings free and ease that heartache. It was too bad a Haywood couldn't take another Haywood's suffering. Yes, Irene could've given up the worst moment of her relationship with Nate to the memory harvest, but she wanted to remember—needed to remember—not only what happened, but how that betrayal felt, so that she wouldn't ever make the same mistake again.

"You lost a life with someone you loved," Taylor said as she rubbed a hand against Irene's upper back. "That kind of thing doesn't go away on its own."

Taylor might not have remembered how Nolan died, but it hadn't made her any less a widow. In all that time, she'd never once asked Irene or Maura to take away her pain.

Irene shook her head as if that could get her out of her own feelings, and instead focused on her magic. Hyacinths bloomed in Taylor's eyes, a clear picture of sorrow and grief, and it left Irene feeling even worse than before.

"Here I am complaining about having to spend an evening with Nate, and it's twenty-five years since we lost Nolan," Irene said, another pain she'd never gotten over. "How are you holding up?"

"I've got a lot of love in my life. It helps." Taylor pressed a kiss to Clem's cheek, and lavender sprouted up to join the pale blue blossoms. "But I had a lot of love then, too. My grief is a loss, not a betrayal. Don't worry about me."

"That wouldn't be very empathetic of me." Irene gave a half-hearted laugh.

"Tonight, you get a pass," Taylor said.

"What a mess this whole thing is," Irene groaned. She'd much rather be back at the shop, curled up in one of the armchairs with a cup of lemon-balm tea and a book.

"Remember," Clem said, "you're doing this for Addison."

"My mother would've never done something like this for me," Irene said.

"Pretty sure she let you bring Nate to family dinner more than once," Clem said.

"Nate, yes," Irene said. "But to willingly eat at Sylvia's house?"

"And yet now she's here for your daughter," Clem said. "Addison has made you both better people."

"She may be the only good thing that came out of that summer," Irene said.

Taylor looped one arm through Irene's and looked up at the mansion. Fireflies hovered lazily. Taylor caught one with her free hand and offered it to Irene.

"To chase away the darkness," she said with a sad smile.

"To chase away the darkness," Irene echoed.

Clem bumped her shoulder against Irene's. "Now let's go eat some expensive food on the Bonners' dime."

◦◦◦

They were the last three to walk through the Bonners' front door, and with their arrival, staff members served the first course alongside glasses of bourbon that accented each place setting. Irene found herself immediately searching out Kaden, who'd saved her a seat next to him.

"We were wondering if you three were going to join us," Sylvia said with a bless-your-heart smile and a honey-sweet voice, bringing the chatter around the table to a halt.

Irene steeled herself, focusing instead on Addison, who sat next to Sylvia. She could feel her daughter's nerves. After everything, the least she could do was support Addison.

"Wouldn't miss it," she said a little too brightly.

Thank you, her daughter mouthed.

Unlike Irene's forced happiness, Maura was scowling a few chairs down. Elena Baker whispered something to her, which put a hint of a smile on Maura's lips.

As Irene settled in, conversation started up again.

She ducked her head toward Kaden and dropped her voice to a whisper. "How are you doing with all of this?"

"Not great," he said.

She grabbed his hand under the table and gave it a squeeze.

Nate sat across from Kaden. Irene did her best to avoid eye contact as she picked at her food.

"Irene," Nate said with a nod.

She set her fork down on the side of her plate and glared at him. She glanced up and down the long dining table, leaned in, and lowered her voice.

"Don't think for one second I've forgotten what you said to me at the funeral."

"Then why are you here?" Nate asked.

She didn't answer him as she sat back, avoiding the glass of bourbon that had been poured for her. Instead, she tore chunks off a biscuit and popped them into her mouth, waiting for Nate to turn his attention elsewhere.

It didn't take long.

He tapped a fork against his glass. The table quieted down.

"I know Mom already thanked you all for coming and shared her gratitude with the Haywoods for their contribution to my father's funeral, but that's not the only reason we're here. I've been working with the mayor's office on a special project."

Mayor Thomas—a white man in his fifties who'd been invited to the dinner despite not being from one of Yarrow's founding families—sputtered, face red. "I didn't know we were going to be talking about this here." He rubbed his hands against his napkin and glanced first at Maura, then Irene.

"What's this about, Nate?" Sylvia asked. "This is a celebration. For the first time in *decades*, all the founders are together." She raised her glass in Maura's direction, and Irene almost laughed at the look on her mother's face.

"Which is exactly why I wanted to bring this up," he pressed. "As we all know, the magic of Yarrow was here long before any of us were alive. It's Yarrow's special brand of magic that has made our success possible."

Irene planted her elbows on the table. "You're talking about the shadow garden."

"I am," Nate said. "The magic in Yarrow's soil has made our five-star restaurants the best in the state. It saved the bourbon industry, and it's allowed our economy to flourish, providing for everyone in this town."

The words almost sounded like a compliment, but Irene didn't like the way Nate was giving credit to the land alone and not to her family's relationship with it. It made her wary. Tansy bloomed and fell from his shoulders. It felt like the moment you hear a hornets' nest but haven't quite pinpointed where the buzzing is coming from.

Sylvia cut in. "We're grateful for everything your family has done for the distillery over the years."

Nate sighed and pinched the bridge of his nose. "Yes, we're grateful, but we're also concerned. Something is wrong with our dark corn."

"What's this?" Maura asked.

"It's nothing we need to worry about," Irene said to her mother. "At the festival, Sylvia mentioned their crop is growing weaker. I handled it."

"You turned her down," Nate said.

Irene saw the pride in her mother's aura, and she indulged in a small smile.

"So, now you're bringing it up here in the hope that we'll say yes?" Irene asked. "You trying to broker a deal in front of everyone isn't going to make a difference."

"The Bakers also have a vested interest in Yarrow's prosperity," Nate said.

"And we'll make our concerns known if we have any," Elena said.

"This dinner was never meant to be an apology, was it?" Kaden interrupted.

"Kaden—" Sylvia said.

"No, Mom," Kaden said. "I'd really hoped that my memories of you had blown your manipulation out of proportion, but this?"

"What exactly is it that you want?" Elena asked. "For the Haywoods to give you more corn?"

"Actually," Sylvia said, "we were hoping Maura might lease us some of her garden. Perhaps if the corn grew on their soil, we'd have a stronger crop."

Before the first dark-corn mash, shadow plants wouldn't grow outside of the Haywood land, but, miraculously, those seeds had, as if the garden had willed it so. If the corn would no longer grow in the Bonner fields, then that was as the garden willed, too. Simple as that.

"The land?" Kaden whispered, so soft Irene almost didn't hear it.

He planted his hands on the table. Irene stole a glance at him. Dead leaves swirled about his shoulders, and bindweed bloomed in his eyes—uncertainty and disappointment rolled into one.

"And cut into the rest of the garden's harvest?" Elena asked. "Yarrow has become known for more than just its bourbon."

"Even if we did lease you the land, it might make no difference," Addison said. "You saw what happened with the rosemary."

"So, you admit it!" Nate said.

Irene winced.

"No, that's not..." Addison blanched and drained the glass of bourbon that sat in front of her. A server swooped in to refill it.

"We *need* your soil to try to fix whatever has gone wrong with the corn," Nate said. "But if something's wrong with your garden, don't you think that's something we should all know?"

Irene bristled. The garden may have been struggling, but that was her family's business. And they would deal with it as a family, not with the Bonners' interference. "The fruit is unpredictable, you know that," she said. "Everyone who eats from it knows that and signs a waiver. You partake of it at your own risk."

"Something this monumental affects all of Yarrow, whether you like it or not," Nate said. "Since I had a feeling this would be your reaction, the mayor and I have started working with the city manager to put a motion before the council to make all soil infused with Yarrow's magic commissionable by the town."

Irene blinked. Then she laughed. She felt that familiar Haywood anger start to churn inside of her, and the telltale sound of cicadas started up outside.

It wasn't the soil alone that was magic—it was the synergy between the earth and those who lived and cared for it that brought forth its power. Sorrow transformed into new life. Irene had no intention of pouring the town's pain into the Bonners' pockets.

"You son of a bitch." She planted her hands on the table and leaned toward him. "You're trying to take the garden from us."

Maura stood, and as she did a cicada landed right in the middle of Sylvia's dinner plate. It rubbed its wings, filling the room with its song. "I should've known," Maura said.

Sylvia waved a hand at the bug, but it held its ground. "I would never try to take your garden from you," Sylvia said, ever the diplomat. "Yes, I wanted Irene to sell me some seeds, but I'd never just *take* them, much less your land. The only reason our distillery has survived was because of your family's help. Because your family wants our town to flourish just as much as I do."

"A likely story," Maura growled.

"Mom," Nate said. "I thought this is what you wanted."

"If you'd told me what you were planning, I never would've given it my blessing," Sylvia said. Nate started to object, but she rolled right over him. "What does it matter if our bourbon is weaker? Our brand is so well-known, a little change in the magic isn't going to stop what we've built."

"But—" Nate started.

"I wanted to have a *conversation* with Maura, not try to steal her garden publicly," Sylvia said.

Irene shook her head. She couldn't believe this was happening. Kaden rested his hand on top of hers.

"Maura, I'm so sorry about all this," Sylvia said.

"I doubt that," Maura said. "You knew as well as Nate did that I wouldn't give you a single kernel, so now you're trying to make yourself look the victim."

"This is why the town should have the rights to that garden—" Nate said, but Sylvia cut him short.

"What our bourbon does isn't all that different from what you do." Sylvia looked to Maura, and then Irene. "We take people's darkest memories, the same way you take away their pain."

Maura narrowed her eyes. "That's not the same thing. There is no healing in forgetting."

"The town seems to think there is," Sylvia said, and as much as Irene hated to admit it, her own business had seen the proof of it. "It's your choice if you want to take that away from them. But we won't force you to give up your garden."

"Can you even do that?" Addison asked. Irene couldn't help but see the flowers that sprouted in her hair like weeds.

The mayor cleared his throat. "If it's for the good of the town..."

"But you can put a stop to this," Kaden said to the mayor. "Just don't put the motion forward."

"I'm afraid I can't do that," the mayor said. "The entire city council was at the funeral. They won't stand for inaction, not when the distillery needs the corn."

"That's assuming there's something wrong with the garden," Elena said. "The Haywoods have cared for it for generations. One bad batch of rosemary doesn't give the council grounds to act."

Addison buried her face in her hands. Brilliant orange marigolds sprouted in her hair. Maura's eyes met Irene's and they both saw the same thing: despair.

"It wasn't just one bad batch of rosemary," Addison said. She clapped a hand over her mouth, horror in her eyes.

Kaden grabbed Irene's hand under the table.

"What does she mean?" Elena asked Maura.

Maura looked up at the ceiling, then back at Elena. "The garden might be changing."

"Why didn't you tell me?" Elena asked.

"It was too soon to say anything," Maura said. "We'd planned to sort through it all after the festival."

"And if there really is something wrong?" Nate asked. "It doesn't just affect our bourbon. It affects Baker's, the restaurants, everyone."

"You don't speak for Baker's," Elena said, eyes narrowed.

"And we don't control how the garden acts or why it does what it does," Irene said. "If the garden is changing, making our land commissionable won't make any difference."

Maura shook her head. "If I hadn't agreed to sell that rosemary in the first place, none of this would be happening."

Addison flinched.

Maura pushed her chair back and tossed her napkin on the table. "Enough," she said. She turned her attention to the mayor. "When you decided to work with Nate Bonner to steal my family's land, did you remember the grief I helped you with after your daughter died? You couldn't bring yourself to give up even a single memory of her, but the pain itself was too much. Our family has helped everyone in this town, and this is how you repay us."

A shadow fell over the room as cicadas hovered at the windows.

"Maura—" Sylvia started.

"Not another word," Maura said. She stepped back from the table, her thick braid swinging with the movement. Her eyes met Irene's, and there was no question as to whether Irene would walk out that door with her.

"You'll regret this," Irene said, her eyes locked on Nate.

"Is that a threat?" Nate asked.

"You better hope it isn't," Irene said. Though Addison sat rooted in her seat, Irene turned and followed her mother out the front door.

Chapter 28

Kaden

Kaden stood so quickly he toppled his chair, but he didn't even bother to right it. He met his mother's wounded gaze and shook his head in disappointment.

"I expected more from you," he said. "But I really don't know why I did."

The entire conversation had felt too familiar to be a coincidence. Maura's outrage, Irene's look of betrayal. He'd convinced himself he'd been mistaken about stealing memories from that woman in the bar. He'd let himself believe his fever dream in the shadow garden had been the result of too much bourbon and too many fears. He'd told himself he'd imagined seeing the gloom rise from the townsfolk's lips without them having any recollection that it happened.

Now, he heard his brother threatening to take the Haywoods' garden out from under them, and all those flashes played on repeat in his mind—snippets of conversation, feelings of conviction.

The words from his mouth: *"We must expose my family."*

The words from Maura's: *"I'll kick them off my land. Without the dark corn, without the soil, everything will go back to how it was before."*

The cicadas left as quickly as they'd come. Quinn and her

moms pushed back from the table without a word. Harper and her family followed, though River stayed.

"The town's going to hear about this," Susheila said. She pointed a finger at the mayor as she started for the door. "Don't think the paper doesn't sway votes."

Finally, Addison, too, started to stand.

"Kaden," Sylvia said. "Don't go. This is all a big misunder-standing."

He shook his head and followed the Bakers out the front door. When he made it out to the driveway, he found Maura fuming. "At least one Bonner has his head on straight," she said. Were he not so rattled by the whole evening, he might have thanked her for the compliment.

"Sorry about what happened in there, Maura," Elena said. "That wasn't right."

Maura grumbled a thanks.

"Still, I wish you'd told me about the garden," she said. "I might've been more help in there if I'd known."

"I didn't know myself until the funeral," Maura said.

Quinn grabbed her grandmother in a hug. "We'll figure this out."

"I don't need you to comfort me," Maura said. "But thank you."

Clem and Taylor hugged Maura in turn, and she relaxed vis-ibly, but as soon as they pulled back, she was pacing. The Bak-ers started for their cars, and Quinn followed.

"I'm going home and taking a bath and reading a book and drinking chamomile tea until I fall asleep," Maura said. "Then tomorrow, I'm going to find a way to tear that distillery to the ground."

"We're with you, Mom," Irene said as Maura climbed into the driver's seat of her truck.

Maura glanced back at the house. "Where's Addison?"

"She was on her way out," Kaden said.

"Probably not ready to face you after she let the truth slip," Quinn said.

Maura turned her key in the ignition. "She'll have to sooner or later."

"See you back at the house, Mom," Irene said.

"Don't bother rushing home on my account," Maura said. Then she shut the door hard and had the truck started and out the driveway before they could say goodbye.

Kaden rested a hand on Irene's shoulder and whispered in her ear, "We need to talk."

She narrowed her eyes. "Don't tell me you're on her side."

"What?" He shook his head. "Of course not." With all these conversations swirling around in his mind, he felt like he was on the verge of something, like he only needed a few more pieces to put the puzzle together into at least a semblance of a picture that might make sense. "It's just...can we get out of here?" He looked back at the house.

"What are we whispering about?" Clem asked.

Irene looked him over. "You're really freaking out."

"My aura?" he asked.

She grabbed his hand and held it up. "You're picking at your nails. Keep doing that and you might start bleeding."

"I need to talk to you." He looked from Irene to Clem to Taylor. "All of you."

"Tea shop?" Clem suggested.

"Tea shop," Irene said. Then to Kaden, "Are you okay to drive?"

"I haven't been drinking," he said. "Not that I couldn't use something to take the edge off."

"No more bourbon," Irene said.

"I was thinking tea," he said.

"A man after my own heart."

∽◉∾

When they got to Lavender & Lemon Balm, Irene put the kettle on while Kaden paced the length of the shop. After his third turn, Clem said, "For fuck's sake, please sit down."

He stopped where he stood, shoved his hands into his pockets, then curled up on one of the armchairs. He wrapped his arms around his legs and buried his head between his knees.

Irene crouched in front of him with a steaming mug of tea and offered it to him. "This should help."

"Thanks," he murmured, staying as compact as possible as he sipped.

Irene settled into the other chair.

"What happened in there?" Taylor asked. "I know your family threatened to take the Haywoods' garden, but there's no way they're going to be able to pull that off. The city council doesn't have that kind of power, even with the city manager on board. The Haywoods have a deed for the land. The town could make it some kind of historic site, but they can't just take it."

He looked up at her. "What if they can?" Then, "What if they have already?"

Clem said, "If my Google search on the way over has anything to say about it, they don't have a legal leg to stand on."

"I'm not talking about the law," Kaden said. "I'm talking about magic."

The room fell silent.

Clem was the first to speak. "Short of mind control, Sylvia can't really do that."

Irene's words came out as a whisper. "Unless she made us forget that it was ever ours to begin with."

"I thought you and Kaden put that whole theory to rest," Clem said.

"You told her?" Kaden asked.

Clem laughed. "Sound carries at the rope swing." At the hurt look on his face, she said, "It's not like I told anyone else."

Irene reached across the space between their chairs and rested a hand on his forearm. "What's happened since we last spoke?"

He set the tea down beside him and uncurled just enough to rub his temples. "The other night when I stayed over, I couldn't sleep."

"Not something a woman wants to hear," Clem said.

Kaden glared at her, but even that back-and-forth was starting to feel comfortably familiar, and he knew that a week in Yarrow was not long enough to account for such a strong sensation.

"I went out to the garden to clear my head," he said. "I sat down, and all of a sudden there was a vine tickling my hand. It wrapped around my wrist and gave me a strawberry. So I ate it."

"It *gave* you a berry?" Irene's eyes were wide.

He nodded. "Then I had these...flashes. Snippets of conversations. Memories. They were mine, but I didn't remember having lived any of the moments, which is why the next morning I thought it was all just a dream. I've been spending a lot of time with your family, working through my own shit..."

"Visions," Irene said. "Like what Addison said the other day."

"I guess," Kaden said. "Yeah."

"What was in them?" Irene prodded.

"You," Kaden said. "Me. The two of you," he said to Clem and Taylor. "Your family, my family. But we were all younger. I think..." He addressed Clem specifically, "I think that you and I were friends once—good friends. And you, too, Irene, we all knew each other before. Really well." He didn't tell them the other feeling he'd had in the dream, the aching sensation of wanting nothing more than to kiss away Irene's tears. "You were telling me about Nate cheating on you, then I was yelling at Nate, and he said he could make it all go away. Then I was talking to my mom about putting a stop to him. Then we were with your family, Irene, in your kitchen—all of us—talking about mine. You were worried about the bourbon, and Maura said she wanted to expose my family, to kick my mom off your land."

"The cornfield?" Irene asked.

Kaden shook his head. "I don't know. I only have pieces to put together, but after what happened tonight..." He took a deep breath. "In my vision, we went to tell the mayor about what was happening, and Susheila was talking about running an article in the paper. And then... then I saw you, Irene, holding a child. Quinn, I think. You were both covered in blood."

As much as Kaden wanted to close his eyes and bury his head, he looked Taylor in the eye as he said it. He knew he owed her that much. She tilted her head back and pressed her palms against her eyes, then she said, "Did you kill him?"

"I don't know," Kaden said.

"Tell us exactly what you saw," Clem said.

"I had a hand on the mic stand. There were cicadas, so many cicadas. Then Irene was there holding Quinn and looking at me."

"That's not proof you killed Nolan," Clem said.

"But you heard Quinn," Taylor said. "She dreamed about him."

"How did you feel?" Irene asked.

"Terrified."

"Not guilty?" Irene asked.

Kaden opened his mouth, then closed it. The sense of dread had been so heavy, almost like he'd been defeated. But it hadn't been guilt. He shook his head.

"And if you did kill him?" She looked at Kaden, eyes brimming with tears, but cold with resolve.

"Then I'll pay the price," Kaden said.

Taylor rubbed at her eyes. "I really hope it wasn't you."

"You and me both," he said.

"It doesn't make sense," Clem said. "If it really happened that way, we would've been there. Why would we all give those memories up?"

"That's what I've been trying to say," Kaden said. "What if you didn't? What if those memories were taken from you?"

Irene shook her head. "We've been over this. It isn't possible. You tried to do it to me, and it didn't work. And my mom never gave the Bonners our land to begin with," Irene said.

"Are you sure?" Kaden asked, thinking back to his childhood. "When I was younger, I remember we came to visit your mom to get the corn seeds."

Irene tilted her head to the side. "That was you? I...I guess I always assumed it was Nate and a friend of his."

Which meant more of Kaden lost from her mind. Days ago, Kaden would have thought she'd wanted to surrender those memories. Now, he wondered if Nate had taken them from her.

"From what I remember, we walked out to the garden, just the two of us," Kaden said.

Irene tilted her head to the side.

"It seemed to go on and on forever."

"We were so small," Irene said. "Of course it did."

"We walked all the way out to the edge of the cornfield," Kaden said. "But there was no barbed-wire fence."

Irene's eyes widened. "I mean, not for at least a mile until the yard meets the distillery." She leaned forward in her seat and rested her hands on her knees. "But I did always wonder how the dark corn grew on distillery land. Anywhere else other than the shadow garden, the dark seeds come up green and bright."

"You said Irene was worried about the bourbon, in your vision," Clem said. "But as far as we know, the only memory magic in Yarrow happens at the annual festival."

"You think it's in the bourbon," Taylor whispered.

Kaden nodded slowly. "I was drinking it at the bar that night, when I took that girl's memories."

"So, what, you drink it and it gives you the ability to take a person's memory?" Taylor asked.

"Maybe?" Kaden said.

"You weren't drinking Bonner's when we were at the rope swing," Irene said.

Clem ducked behind the cash register and pulled out a bottle.

"I thought I told you to get rid of that," Irene said.

"It's family reserve," Clem said. She unscrewed the cap and

took a sip, smacked her lips, and sighed. "That is a damn fine bourbon."

Irene rolled her eyes.

Clem grabbed one of the stools and set it in front of Kaden's chair. She handed him the bottle and threw back her shoulders. "Try it on me."

Kaden stared at her outstretched hand. "You're serious."

"I thought you wanted the truth."

"Not if it means hurting you," he said.

"So, don't hurt me," Clem said. "Make me forget about something that doesn't matter. Like coming over here to sit in front of you."

Part of Kaden was terrified this would work, but he was more scared about what would happen if it didn't. Then he'd have no answers, no way to help fix this problem his brother had created. He reached for the bottle and took a sip. It hit his tongue sharp with dark notes of oak, butterscotch, and cloves. It went down smooth, and he hated how good it tasted.

With a deep breath, he said, "You were sitting over at the table. Then you walked over here and told me you wanted me to take one of your memories," he said. "Forget it all happened."

As the words left his mouth, his chest warmed. Like he'd taken another sip of bourbon. Clem blinked. Her lips parted. A puff of dark smoke—gloom—rose into the air and hovered above them before it dissipated. Kaden's heart lurched.

"Did you see that?" he asked Irene.

She nodded slowly, eyes wide.

"How did I...?" Clem looked down at herself and back at Taylor, then shrugged and said, "Try your magic on me. Make me forget about something that doesn't matter."

Taylor clapped a hand over her mouth.

Clem narrowed her eyes. "Why are you looking at me like that?"

"Please tell me you're joking," Kaden said. But he'd watched it happen. The gloom was no angel's share. It was the town's memories lost on the wind.

"I'm serious," she said. "Try to take my memories."

"Babe," Taylor said as she stood and planted her hands on Clem's shoulders. "He already did."

The reality of it crashed into Kaden. He'd stolen one of Clem's memories. He'd stolen that stranger's memories. If Kaden could do this, then it was likely his brother could, too. He took a ragged breath. His *mother* could do this.

Sylvia had lied to him when he confronted her about his magic, and if she'd lied about that, then there was no telling what else she'd twisted. Her words echoed in his mind.

Something horrible happened that summer. Bad enough the whole town let it go. A month after you left, Nolan Haywood's body was found in the river. Maybe if the town chose to forget you, there was a reason for that.

"My mom wants me to believe that you all surrendered your memories of me." His throat felt thick. His eyes stung. "She wants me to think I murdered Nolan."

"Why?" Clem asked. "I know Sylvia's a bitch, but she's your *mother.*"

He brushed away a tear, but another replaced it just as quickly. "Because she's hiding something, and she doesn't want me to go looking for the truth."

Irene shook her head slowly. "Your family stole our land."

Then her eyes widened. "You said in one of the visions the garden gave you that you were confronting Nate."

"Yes, you'd caught him cheating on you," Kaden said. "It wasn't the first time. And he said he'd take care of it."

"He took my memories." Irene shook her head. "Over and over again. But if we were friends, then why didn't you tell me?"

"Apparently"—Kaden's face flushed—"I had a crush on you." *I loved you; I think I've always loved you* was what he really wanted to say, but he was scared. Why didn't he tell her that his brother was cheating on her? "That doesn't excuse it, but maybe I was scared of my brother? Or maybe... he was stealing memories from me, too? Irene, I don't know. I only remember snippets of things."

"What does the shadow garden have to do with any of this?" Clem asked. "That's what I don't understand."

Kaden hadn't thought it possible for his heart to drop further into his stomach. "It made the bourbon—and our magic—stronger."

"So, you're saying that there is some kind of inherent Bonner magic?" Irene asked. "That you could take someone's memories if the conditions were right?"

"And since the shadow garden magic is an amplifier, when it's combined with Bonner magic, it makes it stronger," Clem said.

"Strong enough for even a memory harvest," Taylor said. "All those people in one place..."

"So, what do we do now?" Irene said.

"What *can* we do?" Taylor replied.

"We could expose them," Clem suggested.

"If what the garden showed Kaden is true, we tried that already and it failed, miserably." Irene shook her head.

"And whatever it was that we tried to do, it got Nolan killed," Taylor said.

"We didn't get anyone killed," Clem said. "But I do think Quinn's been right all along. Nolan was murdered. But I don't think Kaden did it."

Kaden held a hand over his mouth. "What if someone was trying to shut him up?"

Irene's eyes widened. "Maybe he was immune."

Something about that idea felt familiar to Kaden.

"Like Quinn?" Clem asked.

"It would explain why she recognized Kaden," Irene said.

"She would've been so young," Taylor said. "How could she even remember?"

"Trauma like that leaves a mark," Irene said.

"You've lost me completely," Kaden said.

"Not every Haywood is born with the power to heal," Irene said. "Those who can't heal also can't be healed by one of us. We can't read their auras. The shadow magic doesn't affect them. It's like they're immune. Nolan was resistant to our magic like Quinn is—maybe he was resistant to your family's magic, too."

"And you think someone in my family either killed him or arranged to have him killed because they couldn't take that summer from him." Kaden's stomach twisted. Who knew what else his family had covered up over the years? What else *he* might have been party to without even knowing it.

"We can't know for sure." Irene pressed her hands together and held them over her mouth. "We're working off flashes of memories that you thought were a dream."

"And the fact that he literally took my memories just now," Clem said.

Irene held up one hand. "The garden," she said. "It gave you those memories."

"As far as I can tell," Kaden said.

"It must've recognized you. The hollyhock. I saw it move, but I just thought it was the wind, or me, or the bourbon," Irene said. "If it sought you out, maybe it wants to give you all of the memories, but it only gave you what it had."

"But how did it get them in the first place?" Taylor asked.

Irene shook her head.

"Maybe they seeped into the garden from the gloom," Kaden said. "Like the pain."

Irene narrowed her eyes. "Your mom said what you do with the memories isn't all that different from my family's magic."

"I thought someone had to give up their pain willingly," Taylor said. "Wasn't that the whole issue with Addison's magic?"

"Just go with me here," Irene said. "The pain a Haywood takes, it doesn't just disappear, and we can't hold on to it ourselves. We have to put it somewhere. What if the memories you take work that way, too?"

"Great, so they're lost to the cloud over Yarrow," Clem said.

"Unless someone could bottle them..." Irene whispered.

Kaden nodded slowly. "It would be just like my mother, to keep those memories, in case she ever needed them."

"So what, she's literally stashed them in a bottle?" Clem asked. "One sip, and we'll all be riding the train to memory town?"

Everyone turned to look at her. She pointed finger guns at them. When they didn't laugh, she said, "That was a joke."

"The memory harvest," Taylor said.

Kaden was nodding. "What better place to hide them than in the bourbon?"

"Then wouldn't we be drinking memories in every bottle?" Clem asked.

"You get the feeling of them," Kaden said. "The nostalgia."

"Refined memories," Clem said with a glance at the family reserve. "This is the best of the best. They should be in here."

But Kaden shook his head. "The family reserve is good. But it's not the honey barrels. Mom bottles those special, and she doesn't sell them."

Irene had a gleam in her eye. "Do you happen to know where she keeps the ones from the summer of 1997?"

Chapter 29

Addison

Addison knew she should've followed her family when they'd walked out of the Bonners' dining room, but something compelled her to stay. She sat frozen at the table, heart hammering and hands cold with despair. If she'd listened to her grandmother's warning, maybe she could've avoided all of this. Now her family might lose the garden completely. She pushed up from her chair, limbs heavy, mind thick with the bourbon she'd helped herself to throughout dinner.

Too bad the memory harvest had already happened—she would've given anything to forget this night altogether.

Sylvia reached up and clasped bony fingers around her wrist. "Wait," she said. "Please."

Addison didn't have the energy to shake her off. "My grams was right. I never should've agreed to sell you that rosemary."

"This is all a big misunderstanding," Sylvia said.

River pushed back from the table as well. "I can't keep working at the distillery if this is how your family does business." His eyes met Addison's. "This is wrong."

"I hate to see you go," Nate said. "But that's your decision."

"I'll clear out my things." Then, River was gone, too.

"I should leave," Addison said.

"Of course." Sylvia's eyes glistened with unshed tears. "I'll walk you out."

"Mom—" Nate started, but she shook her head.

Addison allowed Sylvia to guide her to the front door.

As she reached for the doorknob, Sylvia placed a hand on the crook of Addison's arm. "I must tell you that I didn't want any of this. I'd hoped tonight's dinner was going to be a chance to bring our families closer together, not tear them further apart."

"My grams will never see it that way," Addison said. Maybe her family had been right about the Bonners, but that still didn't explain why the leaves had led her here. Over and over again.

"I'd planned to share a glass of our family reserve with all of you tonight," Sylvia said. "It was supposed to be a way of thanking you for making this dinner happen. Will you stay long enough to have one with me now? We can make a pact— that together we will find a way to stop my son."

"Do you even think that's possible at this point?" Addison said.

"I'm sure the council will listen to me," Sylvia said. "And if there really is something wrong with your family's garden, I just know that you'll be the one to find a way to fix it."

"I'm not so sure about that," Addison said.

"That garden belongs in *your* hands," Sylvia said.

"I'm glad you think so," Addison said, "but I don't think my family agrees." Even if they put a stop to Nate, she doubted she'd be trusted with the garden again. The rosemary reacting all wrong, the emptiness in the soil, it had happened under her watch. With her unable to give the garden the pain it needed to thrive, it was starving. After what she'd taken from River, what she'd almost taken from the woman in the shop last week, she'd never be able to support the shadow garden on her own.

"Come on," Sylvia said, gently tugging on her arm. "Why don't you forget about leaving so soon?"

Addison's chest warmed, and when she exhaled, the air grew just a tinge darker. She glanced at the still-open door. It wasn't like this night could possibly get any worse.

"One glass," Addison relented. If any of them could put a stop to what Nate had already set in motion, it was Sylvia. Maybe Addison could do some good after all. Find a way to fix this mess.

"This way," Sylvia said.

She led Addison down a long hallway lined with portraits. Sylvia, Christian, Nate, and . . . Kaden was noticeably absent.

"My father," Sylvia said with a nod to the next painting. "My grandfather. All the way back to the Bonners who set up the first still."

Though Addison didn't recognize their faces, they all had the same dark hair. The same strong posture, heads held high, brown eyes full of secrets.

Sylvia stopped short at the end of the line and pulled open a thick wooden door with a metal handle. It led to a set of concrete steps that descended into darkness. Sylvia flipped a switch.

"This way," she said as she started down.

Once they reached the bottom, Addison found herself surrounded by bourbon. One large row of barrels ran down the center of the room, stacked three barrels high. On the closest wall she saw bottles upon bottles, complete with a sliding ladder—like some sort of library. The floor was a rich wood, and it glowed golden in the warm yellow light.

In the center of the room, framed by all that oak, sat a plush leather couch and two chairs. A barrel had been sawed in half and fitted out as a small, circular coffee table, and two end tables.

"This is beautiful," Addison said, a little breathless.

"My own private cellar," Sylvia said. "The Bonners who built this house had it custom made. Of course, I updated it a few decades back."

"You can keep bourbon like this?"

"For a time," Sylvia said. "After ten years in the barrel it starts to taste more like wood than anything. But I keep some of the honey barrels here and a few bottles from our best years." Sylvia stepped up to the shelf and trailed her fingers over the glass. "Norabel and Webb were some of my favorites."

"I've always loved that you named the bourbon," Addison said as she turned around to watch Sylvia over the back of the couch. "It felt to me like I was having a conversation with someone while I drank."

"All part of the Bonner's charm." She pulled a bottle from the bottom-right corner. It refracted the overhead lights in a rainbow of amber. "This one's from the year that Kaden left. Feels appropriate, with everything that's been going on. I hoped he'd stay the night tonight instead of going with your mother, but he has new loyalties, I suppose."

She sighed sadly as she broke the wax around the top and poured two glasses. Then she carefully capped the bottle and slid it back into place. She offered one glass to Addison before settling into one of the armchairs with the other.

"Nate laughs at me for keeping the best bottles," Sylvia said as she held the glass up to the light. "Christian would get mad and tell me we could sell these for a pretty penny. But what's the point if we can't enjoy it ourselves?"

Addison stared into her own glass. "I should've realized something was wrong with the garden sooner," she said. "Kaden mentioned your husband wasn't...a great dad. But I didn't mean to ruin his funeral. I feel like this is all my fault."

"It's not your fault," Sylvia said. "It's our corn, too, remember?"

"I don't know if that's any better," Addison said.

Sylvia held out a hand, and Addison accepted it.

"So, what do we toast to?" Addison asked, wanting to talk about anything but the garden.

Sylvia smiled sadly over the rim of her glass. "I'm not sure this is a night for toasting. Not anymore. Let's just drink."

When Addison lifted her glass to savor the scent, she didn't smell the bourbon as much as she felt it—in her nose, on the roof of her mouth, tickling the back of her throat. It hit her tongue, too sharp to distinguish much of anything at first, and her eyes spotted over. She took another sip. It warmed the back of her throat when she swallowed. The heat lingered, then spread until her whole head felt the burn.

She closed her eyes to savor it, but when she did, the world fell out from under her.

Chapter 30

Irene, 1997

*T*he sunset lit the sky on fire, casting an orange glow over every leaf and flower in the shadow garden. Kaden and I had gone out beyond the far edge of my family's property, where the distillery was out of sight and out of mind and the tilled earth gave way to tall grass and the forest beyond.

We sat on an old quilt I dug out of the attic after deeming the one at the foot of my bed too tainted to sleep under. Kaden wrapped his arms around his knees as he stared out into the night. The fireflies dotted the darkening sky like stars.

I could do this for the rest of my life and be perfectly happy.

The thought hit me like the heat of the sun coming out from behind a cloud. It soaked into my skin and warmed me all over. It had only been a month since I found Nate in the back alley, and while part of me was afraid people would think I was bouncing from one brother to the next, using Kaden to try and move on, I knew it wasn't like that. This was at once something new and something that had been growing inside us both long before this moment. I'd loved Kaden for so long, I just hadn't realized I'd been falling in love with him.

Maybe this summer hadn't been all bad.

I moved closer to Kaden and rested my head against his shoulder.

I'd done it a hundred times before, as friends, but this time, with my cheek pressed against his flannel, everything felt different. More alive.

"You know, my mom told me that if you were just a rebound, I needed to stop all this foolishness right now," I said. "That you don't deserve a broken heart simply because I gave mine to the wrong man."

Kaden laughed softly. "I'd happily be your rebound." He threaded his fingers through mine and tilted his head back. "I've wanted to do this for so long."

"What? To stare up at the sky and hold my hand?" I asked.

He gave me a half smile, then leaned closer, his lips brushing the shell of my ear as he whispered, "You have very nice hands."

I let out a laugh. "Sure, if you like calluses."

"I do, in fact, like calluses."

I had to admit that I'd thought about going out with Kaden long before then, but I'd been too scared to lose my best friend. When Nate had asked me out, I'd mentioned the idea of dating him to Kaden to see how he'd react. He'd been nothing but supportive. I'd decided I'd made the right choice. I could have the best of both worlds—Nate as my husband, and Kaden, his brother, my best friend.

"I wish you'd told me sooner," I said.

"That I like calluses?" he asked.

I smacked him on the shoulder, and his answering grin dug its roots into my heart. Kaden stood and offered me a hand up. Then he grabbed the quilt and walked me back through the rows and rows of plants until we reached my mother's guesthouse, which I'd moved into a couple of years ago.

Kaden brushed the back of his knuckles over my cheek. As desperate as I was to read his aura, I resisted the urge. I wanted him to tell me his feelings directly, rather than use magic to see for myself.

After a few seconds, I asked, "Want to come in for a cup of tea?"

Kaden ducked his head. "That sounds nice."

I pushed open the door.

He dropped the quilt on the couch.

We both glanced at it, then at each other. I bit my lip and crossed to the kitchen, where I set the kettle on to boil. Then I planted my hands on the counter, leaned forward, and Kaden came up behind me and wrapped his arms around my waist.

I let out a soft gasp and relaxed against his hold. A monarch butterfly found its way through an open window and landed on the countertop.

"This okay?" he asked.

"More than okay," I answered.

He pulled my braided hair over one shoulder and kissed the back of my neck, lips so soft they sent tingles down my spine. My knees went weak, and I gripped the hand he held tight to my waist.

Kaden turned me to face him. His eyes drank me in.

He planted his hands on my hips, and heat seeped through the fabric of my overalls. It spread along my sides. Up and down my legs. He lifted me onto the countertop.

I reached a hand up and held it inches from his cheek. I touched his jawline, traced the shape of his face. When he shivered, I wrapped one leg around him, pulling him closer. His breath came in shallow gasps.

I cupped the other side of his face. I pressed my lips to his. Opened my mouth, just slightly. My back arched, and he took a step closer until he stood between my legs.

The guesthouse melted away. Time stretched between our mouths.

I ran my hands along the hem of his T-shirt. He trailed his hands up the sides of my overalls. He grazed the bare skin at my waist, just beneath my crop top. I dragged my teeth against his lower lip.

"Shit, Irene," he murmured into my mouth.

I reached for his jeans, undid his belt. Then I stood and pulled his shirt up as I backed him toward the stairs that led to my lofted bedroom. We took a step, and he unbuckled my overalls. Another, I unbuttoned his pants. Another, the denim fell at our feet.

Until we were at my bed, having left a trail of clothes in our wake.

Chapter 31

Addison

Addison blinked once. Twice. Three times. Sylvia's sipping room came back into focus. Her vision swam. The taste of the bourbon was still heavy on her tongue. She'd seen... What had she seen?

Kaden Bonner. Her mother.

Together.

Younger than she was now.

The weight of that moment settled into her. As far as anyone could remember, her mother had no history with Kaden other than what had started growing between them over the past few days, but Sylvia had told her the date on the bottle before she poured their glasses. If her mom had slept with Kaden that summer, then as far as Addison knew... there was a very good chance that Kaden Bonner was her father.

She sucked in a breath at the revelation, her teeth cold and her fingertips numb. She braced herself with a hand on the armrest as the glass of bourbon slipped from her grip and crashed to the floor.

She winced, the sound forcing her back to the present.

"Kaden..." Sylvia whispered.

Addison glanced up, her dark eyes meeting Sylvia's. She took in the lines in the older woman's cheeks. The sharp nose, so different from the Haywood button nose, but so much like Addison's.

How had she not recognized herself in this woman before? Addison was a Bonner.

"You saw it, too?" The words almost stuck in her throat.

Sylvia looked at the bourbon in her trembling hand. She set it down on the table carefully, then pushed herself up from her chair, sidestepping the shattered glass. She took Addison's hand in hers. Though her skin was thin and spotted with age, her fingers were strong and long and lean. She pressed them to Addison's hands—tip to tip—and a small cry escaped Addison's throat.

"How?" Addison managed through tears she didn't realize she was shedding.

"The memories must've gotten trapped in the bourbon," Sylvia said.

"That's possible?" Addison asked.

"You saw what I saw."

"They were from *that* summer?" Addison asked.

"The bourbon was," Sylvia said.

"That means they gave up those memories," Addison said. "They let them go, willingly."

It didn't make sense. *Why would they do that?*

"Your family has never seen eye-to-eye with mine," Sylvia said.

"Your family *is* my family," Addison breathed.

"Only if you want us to be." Sylvia tucked a curl behind Addison's ear, trailed the tip of her finger along her cheek.

Addison leaned into her touch for a second before pushing

back. "I need to think." She stood, her head a mess of memories and alcohol.

They could've had a full life together. They could've been a *family*.

But they'd given it all up. Her mother, her grandmother, even Kaden—her father—had handed over those memories. Why?

She shook her head. It wasn't like Addison could just go running to her mother with what she'd seen. Irene's relationship with Kaden was so new and so young, like a seedling that could wither without warning. If Addison brought this news to them now, she could very well destroy the roots of something real before they ever had a chance to develop.

"Please don't tell anyone what you saw," Addison said.

"You're upset." The hurt was clear on Sylvia's face.

"It's a lot to take in," Addison said.

"I'm sorry. If I'd known what was hiding in that bottle..."

"No," Addison said. "I'm glad I know the truth."

"I'm here if you need me," Sylvia said. "We will fix this mess my son started... My other son, I mean, of course."

Addison nodded as she backed toward the door. Part of her wanted to stay, but there was a lifetime of hate built up inside her against what might be her own family. This was all too much, too fast. She hurried up the stairs and down the hallway, her head spinning.

She burst through the front door.

The night air hit her face, thick and warm. Rays of blue clung to the horizon. Crickets and frogs sang as if this was any ordinary night. As if Addison's world hadn't just turned itself upside down. She stumbled toward her Bronco, her mind racing too fast for her to keep up.

Her eyes widened as she remembered the omen in her tea leaves that morning. Memories in the bourbon, a family stolen from her. Truth as a weapon.

She'd thought it was a warning about the sickness in the shadow garden. But it was so much worse. Could she just pretend she hadn't seen any of it?

Would Sylvia let her?

Did she even want that?

When she reached her car, the bourbon still had its claws in the edges of her mind. She fumbled for her keys. Steel scraped against the lock as she tried, unsuccessfully, to fit it into the hole. Her keys slipped from her hands and hit the ground with a tinkling of metal.

"Fuck," she murmured through a voice thick with tears. She needed to get out of there, but she was much too drunk to drive. She stared at the door and considered her options. She wanted to call Quinn, but that meant explaining why she'd stayed after everyone else had left. And she couldn't answer those questions yet. She wasn't ready.

"Addison?"

The sound of River's voice almost broke her. As if this night couldn't get any worse. She leaned her forehead against the window. She couldn't face him. Not now.

"Come to gloat?" she asked.

His voice came out quiet, almost impossible to hear over the loud sounds of the Kentucky night. "I don't want to see this happen to your family."

"Still, it must feel like some sort of justice, right? After what I did to you." She knew her words were slurred, but she was beyond caring.

"That's not justice," he said. "I'm not the monster you think I am."

"No," she agreed. "That's me." Her shoulders shook as she cried against the glass, and she felt him move closer, heard him pick up her keys from the ground.

"Why are you still here?" he asked.

"Sylvia asked me to stay and . . ." A sob escaped her lips.

"Hey," he said, voice soft as he rested a hand on her shoulder. "Are you okay? She didn't hurt you, did she?"

Addison turned to face him, the world spinning with each step. She tried to catch herself, but she missed and pitched forward right into River.

"Damn it," she murmured into his chest.

His grip was gentle as she tried to right herself.

"You shouldn't be driving." He looked down into her eyes, hands on her shoulders. "Let me drive you home."

"Why are you being so nice to me?" Addison said, the tone of her voice uneven. "You hate me."

"I don't hate you," River said. "And I certainly don't want you to end up dead somewhere in a ditch."

She could feel heat rolling off him. She wanted more than anything to collapse into him. But he pulled back and lifted a cardboard box full of his things. He really was leaving the distillery. He steered her away from her Bronco and toward his car. After putting the box in the back seat, he pulled open the passenger door and helped her in.

"Are you sure? Maybe you should call someone to come get me. Or just leave me here," she said. "I know what I did to you . . ."

"What's done is done." He started up the car. "Let me get you home."

"Why? So my family can remind me I ruined everything?"

"They won't stay mad at you forever."

"But you will," Addison said.

He glanced at her in the dark. "I'm not mad," he said. "It hurts to be with you." He shook his head. "I don't want to get into this right now."

River rolled down the windows as he followed the Old Yarrow Highway. Fireflies flashed in the darkness, winking like stars. Tonight, they reminded her of the gloom, which reminded her of the Bonners, which reminded her of herself.

Addison couldn't handle the silence.

"If I were a real Haywood, we'd probably still be together. You'd be working at the grocery. The shadow garden would be fine."

"You're not making any sense," he said.

Haywoods could take away pain. But a Haywood mixed with a Bonner? What did that make her?

River pulled into the driveway and killed the engine. "Let me walk you to your door."

Addison stopped him with a hand on his forearm.

"Wait," she said. "What I took from you. Do you remember what it felt like?"

"Don't make me go into this right now," River said. "You've had a rough enough night as it is. This is only going to hurt us both."

"Please," she begged. An idea had started to take form in Addison's mind.

River sighed, but he dropped his hold on the door handle and leaned back against the headrest.

"I don't remember," he said. "That's why it hurts. When I

think of my grandfather and try to remember how he made me feel, there's just this big hole."

"Like the memory harvest," Addison pressed.

"I guess," River replied. "It's been a long time since I've given anything up to it. After what happened..." He shrugged.

"The memories weren't gone, though," she said, her words getting faster as the realization hit her.

"But—"

She barreled on, eyes wide. "They were right there in the bottle, even after all these years." Addison didn't know how the memories her mother had offered up had made their way into the bourbon, how the Bonner distillery had managed to capture them. But it made sense that they'd gone somewhere. Pain didn't disappear when the Haywoods took it; why would memories disappear when the bourbon took them?

"What if..." She thought of that blackberry vine offering her its fruit, the garden's own feelings hiding inside of it. "I think there might be a way to get back what I took from you," she said.

"You already tried," River said. "And it didn't work."

"This is different. This is..." She pressed her lips together. "I don't know what this is. But I'd like to give it a shot... if it's okay with you."

River shook his head sadly, but Addison tugged him out of the car.

"Come on," she said. "Let me get at least one thing right tonight."

"I'm only entertaining this because you're upset," he said as Addison dragged him around the Haywood home, past the guesthouse.

"Trust me," Addison said.

"I did that before and look where it got us."

The words stung, but she didn't let them stop her as she dropped to her knees in the dirt, her skirt fanning out around her. The plants shifted, turning to face her.

"Did they just..." River knelt beside her, so close their arms almost touched.

"Yeah." Addison grinned. "They did." She ran her thumb over a nearby leaf, and she felt it press back at her, almost like it was comforted by her presence, like it had been waiting for her return.

"Are you sure this is a good idea?" River asked.

She glanced up at him. With her own emotions on overdrive, it was impossible not to pick up on his. Fear, curiosity, doubt. But beneath it all, there was hope.

She rested her palm on the ground and took a deep breath. "I need your help."

Sunflowers tilted their heavy heads toward her, their stalks bending in an arc. Black hollyhock blossoms curved around their stems until all the bell-shaped flowers faced her. When she shoved her hands beneath the earth, the roots met her eagerly. They wrapped themselves around her fingers and her wrists, crawled up her forearms.

Something pulsed beneath the surface, like the garden itself was suffering.

She felt along tendrils that turned into taproots that led into stalks and stems and leaves in search of River's pain, and everything she'd taken along with it.

"It has to be here," she murmured. "Come on, show me..."

Addison closed her eyes and remembered that night beneath

the snow and ash, the rush as River's joy had filled her, as she felt his grandfather's love as if it were her own—full and strong and true. The pure adrenaline of it before she realized what she'd done. The things she'd taken. The plants guided her, their energy an outstretched hand in the dark until she found that familiar ache that was all River.

"It's here," she whispered.

"You found it?" River rested a hand on her back.

Addison glanced up at him. The wonder in his eyes took her breath away.

"Please," she whispered to the garden.

A vine snaked its way across the earth in front of them. It rose up from the ground, facing her, and as it did, the plants around them edged closer.

"Give it to me," she said.

The garden shifted. Roots pushed against her fingertips. Those that had snaked around her hands tightened their grip, as if searching for the sorrow she didn't have to offer. The shoots closed in around her and River, like a cocoon of shadow in the night.

But the garden listened.

At the tip of the vine, a bud formed, bloomed, and fell. A blackberry ripened on the stem. Addison reached for River's hand, and to her surprise, he let her take it, let her guide it to the berry. The plant released the fruit into his palm.

"What now?" River asked as he looked up at her.

"Now," Addison said, "you eat it."

Chapter 32

Addison

Darkness enclosed them. Sunflowers looked down on them from above, only just letting the moonlight through as more buds burst into blooms along their long, black stalks. Addison had known the shadow garden all her life. She'd thought she'd seen all the plants had to offer, but over the past couple of weeks they'd been surprising her at every turn. The vines around her forearms crawled higher, up her shoulders, toward her face, desperation in their gentle movements.

"What's happening?" River asked, still cupping the berry.

Addison stretched out her arms as she looked down at the vines. "I don't know. I thought the garden was starving, but this much growth..." She shook her head. "It gave us what we asked for."

"Are you sure this is a good idea?" River poked the black-berry. "After what happened at the funeral..."

"It's going to hurt," Addison said. "It's not just the good in there. All the grief, the guilt. You're going to feel that, too."

River nodded slowly and brought the fruit to his lips. He closed his eyes as he set it on his tongue. Then, he bit in. All at once his body went rigid, and a soft cry escaped his mouth.

Sorrow rolled off him. His shoulders hunched forward, and he started to shake. Tears splashed onto the soil at his feet.

"I...forgot," he managed after a few moments. Then he laughed, voice thick. "It's like I'm living that night all over again."

"I'm sorry. I wanted to save you from this," Addison whispered. "That was all I was trying to do."

"I never wanted to be saved. I just didn't want to be alone." He brushed the back of his hand across his face and let out a choked sob. But when he looked up at her, he had light in his eyes. "It's here," he said. "My grandfather—he was so proud of me, of the man I was becoming." He splayed a hand over his heart. "He loved me," he whispered. Then, louder, "He *loved* me."

He pressed his palms over his eyes and shook his head, his tears at once sorrow and joy. "I'd forgotten."

"I know," Addison whispered. "I'm sorry."

She started to stand, but River grabbed her hand before she could.

"I never should've pushed you away," he said. "I didn't know who I was anymore. I had to find myself. To *remake* myself."

"I get it." Addison shook her head. "But I realized how broken I was that night, and there was no one on the other side to help me put myself back together again. I love Quinn like a sister, but you were more than just a boyfriend. You were my best friend; I didn't know how to function in a world without you."

"It's been so hard without you, too," he said. "I looked for you at my graduation. I know I asked you not to come, but I found myself searching for you anyway."

"I look for you every time I go to Baker's," Addison said, "even though I know you won't be there."

"I hated myself after I left you like I did. That's why I stayed away. I knew you needed me, but it was too hard, too much. I couldn't look myself in the mirror, and anger was easier than confronting that."

Addison's eyes stung. Her voice caught in her throat. "I never stopped loving you. I tried so hard to move on..."

River rested his forehead against hers. They sat like that for a few seconds in silence until his eyes met hers, his pupils dark and deep. His aura exploded in ambrosia, like a field blooming all at once.

And then, he kissed her.

Her mouth came alive beneath his. She slid a hand around the back of his neck, fingers in his hair.

"We've both said a lot of horrible things to each other," he whispered against her lips. "I'm sorry, Addison."

"I'm sorry for taking more than you were willing to give. For using my magic on you when it wasn't welcome." She brushed his hair back gently.

River kissed her again. "Your magic is beautiful," he whispered. "Just look." He nodded his head to the garden around them, as if Addison was the one who'd coaxed the petals from their buds, before he started crying all over again.

Addison brushed the pads of her thumbs across his cheeks.

"Sorry," he said, voice heavy. "The grief..."

"It comes in waves," Addison said. "It will, for a long time."

He nodded slowly.

"I can make you some tea to help," she offered.

He smiled sadly. "I'd like that."

Addison got to her feet and offered him a hand up until they both stood in the circle of plants.

"Do you think they'll let us out?" he asked, fingers entwined with hers.

Addison took a step forward, and the sunflower stalks parted. Maybe, she thought, the garden wasn't in as much trouble as she'd feared.

∽

After she led River back to the guesthouse and prepared a cup of tea with chamomile, lavender, and Saint-John's-wort, they settled in on her patchwork couch. River sipped slowly as he took in the space. The nearby floor lamp cast the room in a soft yellow light. The ground floor included a great room that was the kitchen, living room, and eating area all in one. The loft at the back held her bedroom. It had been her mother's, once, before Irene moved back into the main house so Maura could help her raise Addison. After high school graduation, Addison had made it her own.

"You haven't changed it much," River said.

Addison shrugged. "I spend most of my time outside." She held her mug tighter. "I didn't think I'd ever see you in here again."

River watched her over the rim of his cup. "I'd like to think we'd have forgiven each other eventually."

Addison wondered what had made her mom and Kaden choose to give each other up—if they'd discovered Irene was pregnant and decided it would be easier that way. She knew the entire town had handed over that summer, but why hadn't her parents kept that one part of their memories?

"Would it have been easier to forget what we had?" she asked River.

"At the memory harvest?"

She nodded.

"I thought about it," he admitted. "But there was so much good even with all the pain. It would've been like losing a part of myself."

She knew the feeling.

"Where do we go from here?" she whispered, almost afraid to ask. They clearly couldn't just pick up where they'd left off.

"We have a lot of catching up to do," he said. "Maybe we start there."

"You have dinner plans tomorrow night?"

"Seeing as I am now unemployed, my schedule is wide open."

"It's a date," Addison said.

River set his cup on the coffee table and started to stand. "I should probably get going."

"Stay," Addison said, reaching for his forearm. "I'll make us more tea. We can...we can just binge-watch some Netflix."

River grinned. "Like old times."

"Yeah." Addison smiled softly. "Like old times."

Chapter 33

Addison

Addison woke before the sun to find herself pressed against River on the couch, his arm draped over her. Though still on, the TV had paused their show at some point to ask if they were still watching. Addison settled into the feeling of waking up with River, something she thought she'd never experience again. They may not have done anything more than kiss last night, but he was here, in her living room.

But before the smile could finish forming on her lips, the reality of what had happened the night before came crashing down. Not only did Nate Bonner intend to take her family's garden from them, but Addison had learned the truth of where she'd come from. She knew she should talk to Maura and Irene, but she wasn't ready to share what she'd discovered inside that glass of bourbon. Her mother had let go of that moment with Kaden. She'd chosen to forget Addison was a Bonner. Addison was terrified what would happen if her family discovered the truth.

At least one thing had gone right. Despite everything she'd seen in the soil, the garden had listened to her. More, it had *grown*. Fast and strong and all at once. That had to be a good sign.

She wriggled out from under River's arm. Cold crept

through the room and pricked at her skin. The lofted ceiling had never been the best at keeping warmth in—except during the hottest part of the day, exactly when you didn't want it. She grabbed a sweater from a hook by the door before slipping outside.

The plants turned toward her as she stepped onto the brick-lined patio. Gladiolas tilted their blooms. Vines shook off the night. The air was thick with gloom. She stepped off the path, bare skin meeting earth still damp with morning dew, and made her way to the enclosure the garden had created the night before.

But the closer she got, the stranger the plants looked. Rather than arcing around the circle they'd formed, lithe and pliable, they bowed as if their blooms were too heavy to hold. The once turgid stems bent over on themselves, close to breaking.

Overnight the new blossoms had wilted. Rot had set in among the petals and crawled along their stalks. All around, fireflies hung in the air, far too early in the day. As the insects made contact with the curling leaves, the plants crumbled to dust.

Addison's eyes widened in horror.

The garden had been starving. Even when she went searching for River's pain, she'd felt its need, yet she'd asked it to give back what she'd poured into its soil, the very heartache it relied on to survive. Without it, the plants had flowered quickly, set seed, and died.

"No..." she whispered, turning in a circle. All around her, the garden that had once stood so tall drooped like it would during a heavy rain. The rot hadn't spread from the sunflowers, but Addison feared it was only a matter of time.

"There has to be something I can do," she said. "Show me. Please, show me."

A nearby row of cherry tomatoes tilted toward her, their highest stalks leaning under the weight of a single purple fruit. It dropped off the branch and fell at her feet. Addison crouched to retrieve it. She looked down at the fruit in her hand, and back up at the garden to find that the tomato plant, too, had begun to wither, as if the energy it put into creating just that one fruit had been all it had left to give.

"Another vision?"

The garden leaned closer, waiting.

With a deep breath, she rooted herself in the soil. She buried one hand beneath the earth. The roots met her immediately, eager and hungry, like the night before, but the only pain Addison had to offer them was her own, and that was something a Haywood couldn't give. Unless...

She popped the tomato between her teeth. The juice sprayed into her mouth with just a hint of dill and garlic. Addison became unmoored. Tears streamed down her face, every dark thought about her family, about herself, multiplied until she thought she might burst.

Addison focused on her own heartache. "Take it," she said. "I took from you; it's only fair."

Black ivy and honeysuckle crawled along the ground and up her ankles. Roots sprouted from the vines and pressed into her like thorns.

One prick.

Another.

Blood dotted her forearms.

Red trailed down her wrists.

Addison gasped and cried out. She tried to pull back, but before she could, her vision went dark, and the garden showed her what it had revealed before. Those hungry roots sinking deeper and deeper, tangling beneath the earth with the Bonners' corn. As Addison watched the plants struggle, she realized there was only one place she could make sense of this, and the only way she could get there was with Sylvia Bonner's permission.

She surfaced from the darkness to River's voice.

"Addison? Addison!"

She blinked her eyes open to find him tearing at the vines that had spiraled up toward her throat, his hair mussed from sleep and his aura bright with panic. The roots-turned-thorns held firm, but try as they might, they couldn't get to Addison's pain.

"Stop," she said, first to him. Then, to the garden, "Stop!"

The vines hesitated. Roots retracted, pulled away, before they buried themselves beneath the soil once more.

"It's okay," she said, reaching for River's hand. "I'm okay."

"You're bleeding," he said as he touched her bare arm gently and stepped away from a nearby plant. "The garden attacked you."

"I wanted to give it my pain."

"You can do that?" River asked.

She shook her head. "But I had to try."

"Saving the garden isn't worth risking your life," River said.

"The garden is like a part of my family," Addison said. "I can't just let it die." She held out her arms, and River stepped back as he took in the wilted sunflowers.

"I don't understand," he whispered.

"It's starving," Addison said. "But I think it's trying to show me how to fix things."

She pushed herself to her feet. "I have to talk to Sylvia,"

she said. "The garden is pointing me to her cornfield. I need to
see it for myself." But talking to Sylvia meant facing what she'd
seen in the bourbon head-on, and for that, she needed strength.

She led River back to the guesthouse, where she put the kettle on. Mason jars of her mother's teas lined the countertop.
She selected one labeled, *For courage*. Green tea, thyme, fennel,
Saint-John's-wort, and lemon balm. She unscrewed the jar and
breathed in the earthy aroma, then sprinkled a few pinches
into two cups before setting the water to boil.

"I don't know if you should talk to Sylvia again," River said
as the water started to boil. "You were pretty shaken last night,
and after the stunt with Nate trying to take your family's land, I
don't think you can trust her."

"I had another vision that led to the Bonners' cornfield,"
Addison said. "I have to follow it. The garden is sick, and nothing will be right in Yarrow until we figure out what's wrong."

River nodded slowly. "How can I help?"

"Will you take me to Quinn and Harper's?"

"Isn't it a little early?" he said.

Addison shook her head. "This can't wait, and my car is still
at the Bonners'."

"Whatever you need," he said, and started to push back
from the table.

"Wait," Addison said.

She drained her tea, flipped the cup, and examined the contents. She saw the same things, over and over again: rosemary
and corn, the fern and the ladybug. But this time they were surrounded by small leaves, a sign that she had a choice to make.

"Anything helpful?" His eyes searched hers.

"The same symbols that led me to the Bonners in the first place," Addison said. "Let me see yours."

River swirled his cup and tipped it, just as Addison had taught him years ago.

"You remember," she said.

"When you fall in love with a Haywood, there are some things you never forget." He held out the mug to her, and they both leaned over it. Small leaves dotted his cup, just like the leaves around hers. At the bottom, she saw a fruit basket and several ears of corn.

"Well?" he asked.

"There's lots of corn. Corn on its own can be a sign of success," Addison said as she pressed a finger to the symbol, showing him. "Same with the fruit basket. But both of them together, combined with the leaves, it looks to me like you may have to make a choice between the distillery and the grocery."

River furrowed his brow. "But I already made a choice. I left the distillery. With what the Bonners want to do to your family, why would I ever choose them?"

Addison pressed her lips together. "For the same reason I might."

"What?" River said.

Addison closed her eyes and leaned her head back. She hadn't planned to tell him—she hadn't planned to tell anyone except Quinn—but if she and River were going to move forward from here together, she wanted him to know the truth.

"I think Kaden Bonner is my father."

"He...what?" River shook his head. "How could you possibly know that?"

"It's why you found me like you did last night. Sylvia shared a glass of bourbon with me, a bottle from the summer of '97, and there was a memory trapped inside. We both saw it when she cracked open the bottle and we took a sip."

His eyes widened. "That's what made you think my pain would still be in the garden, because your mom's memories were in the bourbon."

Addison nodded.

"And since Sylvia is likely your grandmother, you think she'll let you into the cornfield so you can figure out what the garden was trying to show you in your vision."

She nodded again.

"Then what are we waiting for?" He was up out of his seat and putting on his shoes before Addison had even set his mug down. Together they started across the yard toward the driveway, just as the back door opened and Maura stepped onto the porch.

"Addison?" she said. "*River?*"

"Grams," Addison said, knowing there was no chance she was getting out of there without Maura realizing something was wrong.

"Well, this was the last thing I expected to see this morning."

River grabbed Addison's hand and gave it a squeeze. She had to tell her grandmother something, but she wasn't sure where to start. The truth would be easiest, even if she didn't tell it all. But she knew Maura, and it was always best to begin with an apology.

"I shouldn't have mentioned that there was something wrong with the garden at dinner last night," Addison said.

"No," Maura agreed. "You shouldn't have."

"I'm sorry," Addison said.

Maura nodded, but still, her eyes were narrowed.

"I found River's pain in there," Addison said, pointing behind her.

"Impossible," Maura said.

"It's true," River said, his aura rife with mourning, as if the fire had taken his grandfather the night before, rather than two years ago.

"How..." Maura stared out at the garden, and Addison's stomach twisted.

The wilting had spread, and even from where they stood, the plants looked all wrong. Maura looked her granddaughter over from head to toe, her eyes landing on the scratches along her arms and wrists. Addison released her grip on River's hand.

"What happened?"

"Nothing," Addison replied, too quickly. "I just got stuck in some brambles."

Maura arched an eyebrow. "We don't have any brambles."

"I...It's not as bad as it looks."

"What aren't you telling me, Addison? Did the *garden* do this to you?"

The color drained from Addison's face. "I tried to offer it my pain."

"You know it can't take from our hearts," Maura said. When Addison didn't respond, Maura walked to the edge of the patio and dug a hand into the soil.

"It's getting worse," she said, brow furrowed. "There's not enough sorrow in the dirt to keep them alive much longer. Not only that—the garden itself is in pain." She sat on the ground. "I knew stepping back from healing would put more on Irene's shoulders, but I didn't think..."

She was talking more to herself than to Addison, but that didn't stop Addison from saying, "You didn't think I would be a problem—that I wouldn't be able to feed it."

"No," Maura said. "It's not that…It's…" But her grandmother didn't finish the sentence, and Addison's throat grew hot with shame. "There has to be a way to fix it," Maura said.

This, Addison realized, was her chance.

"The leaves pointed me to the Bonners," she said. "What if we can get the answers we need from them? My vision had their cornfield in it. If Sylvia will let me behind the gate, maybe we'll be able to sort this all out."

"The Bonners," Maura scoffed. "They made it perfectly clear that if we give them the chance, they'll swoop in and take the garden right out from under us."

Maybe if Maura knew what Addison had seen, she'd understand. Addison wasn't ready to share the truth, but if it meant saving the garden, she'd do it. "After dinner I had a drink with Sylvia and—"

Maura cut her short. "I'm not letting a Bonner step foot onto our soil. The leaves showed you the Bonners as a warning. Mark my words, whatever is wrong with those plants started with them, and we don't need their help to fix it."

Addison let her hands fall to her sides and tried not to let the tears come.

"This is a family matter," Maura said. "And we will solve it together, as a family."

Chapter 34

Maura

After spending sixty-nine years on this earth, there were few things that surprised Maura, but her granddaughter's magic was one of them. It was new at every turn. She'd never understood how Addison had taken what she had from River in the first place, much less how she'd now managed to pull it back from the garden. She'd always thought the plants broke down the pain that the Haywoods poured into their soil, and though she wanted to sit and think and sort through the possibilities, in that moment she was more concerned by Addison storming off and climbing into River's car.

Granted, Maura might've come off a bit too harsh, but the Bonners had threatened to take her land. That was reason enough to crush any idea Addison might have about working with them. If they really did need to get into the Bonners' cornfield for answers, Maura had a pair of wire cutters that would do the job just fine.

She rubbed at her temples as River's tires rumbled over the gravel. What she hadn't admitted to her granddaughter was her disappointment in herself at having missed what was happening in the garden. Somewhere along the line she'd stopped listening to the plants, and now she was paying the price.

She leaned her head back and groaned.

"I'm getting too old for this." She pulled her phone from her pocket and started searching for Addison's number when Irene's face appeared on the screen.

"Irene?" she asked. "You didn't come home last night."

"I need you to come to the tea shop," Irene said. "And for the love of all that is good in the universe, please get us some coffee."

"*Coffee?*" Maura asked. She wasn't opposed to coffee, but her daughter rarely drank it. "Did you get any sleep last night?"

"As a matter of fact, no," Irene said. "We've been here all night talking about the Bonners."

It seemed Maura couldn't escape that damn family.

"Speaking of them—"

But Irene cut her off. "We can talk about it when you get here. Please come, and bring Addison."

Irene hung up before Maura could tell her that Addison was already gone.

৩৶

Maura took her time getting to Lavender & Lemon Balm. She hadn't even finished her morning tea before she'd found Addison sneaking out.

Only after her leaves informed her of what she already knew—the trouble all stemmed from the Bonners and her granddaughter's magic—and she'd watered the front-yard vegetable patch, did she wash up and head into town.

Yarrow was still crawling with tourists as the second day of the festival was in full swing. She navigated around the blocked-off town square before making it to the tiny lot behind the tea shop and trudging up the back steps. Inside she found Irene, Kaden, Clem, and Taylor sitting around the table, with boxes of takeout scattered throughout the room and the shop sign flipped to Closed.

For the first time in decades, Maura was glad she only made her harvest baskets to order. Otherwise, there'd be no one to sell them, since her entire family was here. She set a traveler box of coffee on the table along with a stack of paper cups.

"My hero," Clem said.

"Thanks, Mom," Irene echoed.

Kaden was the first to the box. Maura crossed her arms as she looked him over. She'd been warming up to him, but watching him help himself rankled her.

He handed the first cup to Irene, and Maura flushed. She caught Irene's look, wondered what her daughter saw in her aura, and sat down as Kaden filled two more cups—one for each of the women at the table—before looking up at Maura. "You want one?"

She shook her head. "I had tea."

"Where's Addison?" Irene asked.

"I am not your daughter's keeper."

Irene narrowed her eyes as the distinct sound of a cicada's hum started up outside the window. "What happened?"

"She went digging around in the shadow garden and it attacked her," Maura said.

"It did *what*?" Irene asked.

"And now it's even worse than before," Maura said. "The plants are hurting. They're *dying*."

"Why didn't you call me?" Irene asked.

"I was going to tell you on the phone, but you hung up."

Irene held her face in her hand. "This is not a time to be petty, Mom."

Maura shook her head. "We'll figure it out. Addison found what she stole from River in the soil. And apparently the garden gave it back to her. Then it started wilting. So she tried to give it her own pain."

Irene's aura bloomed from begonia (worry) to amaryllis (pride) to marjoram (happiness) all faster than Maura could blink.

"She's finally coming into her magic," Irene said.

"That's your takeaway from all this?" Maura said. "If the Bonners find out, it'll be one more thing they can use against us."

"That's why I wanted you to come in." Irene sighed. "Addison should really be here for this."

"You can try calling her, but she might not pick up. She left in a state."

"Do not tell me you blamed her again for what happened in the garden," Irene said.

"She took something from it. The garden reacted. It's cause and effect, Irene."

"You sound like...like..."

"Like my mother?" Kaden offered.

Clem and Taylor both studied their coffee.

Maura settled deeper into her chair. "I am nothing like Sylvia Bonner."

"Seems to me like you want to be able to control Addison," Kaden said.

"Sounds familiar," Irene said.

"Well, you've been a bit too distracted," Maura said to her daughter, and looked pointedly at Kaden.

"Do you even hear yourself?" Irene said.

Maura did hear herself, and she knew Irene was right. She crossed her arms and sighed. "Fine," she said. "Maybe I took things too far with Addison."

"And?" Irene asked.

"And I'm glad to see you so happy," she said. "I'm on edge, and I'm just trying to protect Addison, but she won't listen."

"She would if she were here," Irene said. "This thing with the shadow garden goes a lot deeper than Nate working with the mayor and the city manager."

Maura leaned forward. "You found something?"

"Why else do you think we've been up all night?" Irene asked.

"You've been working on this all night and didn't think to call? Why does everyone in this family insist on keeping things from me?"

"We're telling you now," Irene said.

"You sound like your daughter."

"If you weren't so convinced you were right all the time, maybe we'd pull you into things sooner," Irene said.

"But I *am* right all the time."

Irene arched an eyebrow.

Maura sighed. "Most of the time. I taught you and Addison everything you know!"

"And I've grown a lot and learned a lot on my own since then."

"Like Addison," Taylor added.

Irene tilted her head back and closed her eyes briefly. "We've been so focused on trying to be the ones to fix things *for* her that when the universe gave her a tea-leaf reading we didn't like, we did everything we could to blame it on her. But it seems pretty clear to me that those leaves brought us to this point."

"And what, exactly, is this point?" Maura challenged.

Irene looked to Kaden.

"People haven't just been giving up their worst memories at the bourbon festival. We think that my family has been stealing whatever memories suit them," Kaden said. "And they've been doing so for years."

Maura narrowed her eyes.

"Mom," Irene said. "The cornfields don't belong to the Bonners. That's shadow garden land. They took it from us. Then they made us forget that it was ever ours. Now they're trying to do it again."

Maura let her daughter's words sink in. She'd long thought the Bonners had a magic of their own. Her eyes landed on Kaden. "Why didn't you tell us right away?"

He shook his head. "Whatever memories I had of it, my family took from me."

That was exactly the sort of thing Sylvia would do.

"How does it work?" she asked.

"It's in the bourbon," Kaden said. "When I drink it, I can steal your memories."

"And the shadow garden..." Maura started.

"Amplifies it, yes," Irene said.

"That bitch," Maura said.

"You don't seem surprised," Kaden said.

"The gloom hung over Yarrow long before the memory harvest began," Maura said. "It was always the heaviest near the distillery. But after that first dark-corn batch was tapped, it just grew and grew and grew. The town chalked it up to an increase in bourbon production, but I knew there was something else to it. I just didn't know what it was." She started to stand. "If the cornfields are on our land, there has to be a record of it somewhere."

"It won't be that easy," Kaden said. "My mother would've taken precautions. She probably got her hands on whatever documents proved it was yours and had them destroyed a long time ago."

"Then what do we do?"

"That's why we called you here," Irene said. "We thought you might have some ideas."

"I'm going to need a cup of tea."

Clem jumped from her chair. "On it."

Maura started to pace, long braid swishing at her back. "You said your mother took your memories away."

He nodded slowly.

"Which means you can do this to each other."

"I think so." Kaden gulped.

"Well, it seems to me," Maura said, "that it's time for you to repay the favor."

Chapter 35

Addison

Addison let herself relax into Quinn's hug as every accusation her grams had hurled at her melted away.

"You did it," Quinn said. "You *actually* did it."

"I've got to be honest," Harper said. "I never thought I'd see the two of you in our house at the same time again. Does this mean you're back together?"

Addison glanced at River.

He gave his sister a wry smile. "I slept at her place last night."

Harper's eyes widened. "That was *fast*."

Addison rolled her eyes. "We fell asleep on the couch watching TV."

"Are you going to come back and work at the grocery?" Harper asked.

"I quit my job last night, so..."

"Good," she said. "I can't wait to tell Dad. We need you, especially now, with the festival and all."

"Wait, if you found River's pain in the garden, does this mean you can stop my nightmares?" Quinn asked.

Addison bounced on her toes. One good thing had come out of that bottle of bourbon. Addison didn't think she could stop Quinn's dreams, but she knew where Quinn might be able to find some answers.

"I know you asked me to take away your nightmares," Addison said. "And I'm willing to try again, but the memories from that summer aren't gone. They're in the bourbon."

"They're *what?*"

"I need you to come with me to the distillery," Addison said. "I'll tell you everything on the way."

Quinn glanced at Harper. "I was going to help out at the Baker's festival booth."

"I've got extra hands, remember?" Harper said as she grabbed her brother in a side hug and rested her head against his shoulder. "Thank you, Addison."

Addison smiled. "Don't thank me," she said. "Thank the leaves."

"You're the one who followed the leaves," River said, "despite your family's hatred for the Bonners." He wrapped his arms around Addison. "Come find us at the festival when you're done."

He dipped his head and kissed her softly.

Quinn let out a wolf whistle.

Addison kissed him deeper.

When they broke apart, she was flushed and happier than she'd been in ages. A ladybug landed on River's shoulder, and she scooped it up.

"Let's go get those memories and fix the shadow garden," Addison said to Quinn.

"I still have a lot of questions," Quinn said as she pushed Addison out the door. "Spill."

Addison let the ladybug escape into the early morning sun,

then gave Sylvia a quick call. She invited Addison to meet her up at the house. So Addison hoisted herself into Quinn's truck, and then she told Quinn everything as they pulled onto the Old Yarrow Highway—from the memories trapped in the bourbon to what she thought was the truth of her lineage, how she got back together with River, the wilted shadow garden, and her attempt to give it her own pain. It was the one time a year that the two-lane road was ever backed up, which meant Addison had time to tell all.

Quinn sat tapping her hands against the steering wheel.

"What if we find out something we don't like in the bourbon?" Quinn said. "Something we don't want to know?"

"You still think Kaden might be responsible somehow?" It was one thing when Quinn had suggested it at dinner, but now that Addison had started to get to know Kaden, the idea of it seemed even more improbable.

Quinn shook her head. "If Kaden and your mom were together that summer, it makes sense he'd be in my dream. Maybe I misunderstood what I saw."

"I hope so," Addison said.

Quinn adjusted the rearview mirror as they edged closer to the distillery. "Do you really think Sylvia can get us the answers we're looking for?"

"I don't know, but she clearly wants to be in my life. I've always defined myself by our family. My magic was wild, different, but I was still a *Haywood*—it was still Haywood magic. I thought that taking over the garden would help me find my place, but I was wrong, because I didn't know my whole story. My magic *is* different, and that's okay. I need to let it guide me, not try to dampen it."

Quinn glanced at her. "So, what, now you're going to hard pivot and call yourself a Bonner?"

"No," Addison said. "But at least Sylvia doesn't blame me for everything."

"Maybe Grams was right. She always thought there was something magical about the Bonners," Quinn said. "Maybe you're a hybrid!"

"That's even worse. Can you imagine me telling Grams I have *Bonner* magic? She'll never let me touch the garden again. I hoped fixing what I broke with River would help me understand the garden, or at least heal something in me," Addison said. "But the garden and I are worse off than before."

"Seems to me like the closer you get to figuring out who you are, the more things will become clear."

"Easy for you to say," Addison grumbled.

"What? Because I wasn't born with the ability to heal?" Quinn shook her head and held one arm out the window as they inched along. "Don't think I didn't wish I had Haywood magic in me—some sort of clear path to follow. Instead, I grew up watching my mom try to pick up the pieces of her grief without any memories to understand what had happened and why, while I woke up screaming every night with nightmares of blood."

"Why didn't you ever say anything to me?" Addison asked.

"I didn't want to talk about it," Quinn said. "I felt like an outsider. Like there was something wrong with me. Then when your magic didn't work right...I don't know. I didn't want to make things worse for you."

"Maybe we would've both felt less alone," Addison said. "Thank you for letting me in."

Quinn only nodded as the highway became Main Street, and she took the turn that would lead them around to the back entrance of the distillery. The staff lot was roped off from the general public, but when they pulled up, the parking lot attendant recognized them and waved them through.

"What's that for?" Addison asked as Quinn shoved a beach towel into her oversize bag.

"The bourbon," Quinn said, as if it were obvious.

"We're not *stealing* it," Addison said. "Sylvia shared it with me willingly, remember?"

"I'm not taking any chances."

Addison shook her head. It would take years for her family to get over their deep-seated distrust of the Bonners.

"Fine," Addison said. "Just don't be weird about it."

They made their way up the front steps of the mansion. When she knocked at the door, Sylvia greeted them almost instantly, arms open wide for a hug. Addison let herself relax. The Bonner matriarch smelled like gardenias and the smoky scent of bourbon.

"I'm so glad you came." Sylvia welcomed them both inside. "After what we learned last night…" She trailed off and glanced at Quinn. Pink oleander bloomed in her aura, but Sylvia had no reason to distrust Addison's cousin.

"She knows," Addison said, hoping to ease Sylvia's fears. "But I haven't told the rest of the family yet."

Sylvia took one of Quinn's hands in hers. "Any of Addison's family is family to me," she said. "Why don't the two of you head to my sipping room, and I'll get us some lemonade. You remember where it is?"

Addison nodded before she led Quinn down the long

hallway to the thick wooden door at the end. They left the day-light behind and descended the stairs. At the bottom, Quinn turned a circle in the middle of the room before making a bee-line for the shelf full of bottles.

"Maybe we should wait for Sylvia?" Addison suggested, but her cousin opened the center cabinet wide.

Tumblers of various shapes lined the shelves—heavy bot-toms with thin sides, goblet-shaped vessels, square cups where the glass twisted around on itself. Quinn abandoned the glass-ware and ran her fingers along the bottles.

"Which one was it?" Quinn asked.

"Bottom-right corner."

Quinn dropped into a crouch.

"I see you have an eye for vintage," Sylvia said as she stepped into the room, a hint of a smile at her lips.

"Addison mentioned the memories," Quinn said. "I thought I might find something about what happened to my father in there..."

"Of course." Sylvia set a tray of lemonade down on the table. She took a sip from the only full glass, then poured the others. "I thought we could start with something a bit more refreshing."

Addison took the seat across from Sylvia—her grand-mother; she still hadn't fully wrapped her head around that—and accepted a glass of lemonade. The first sip hit her mouth with a bit of a burn.

"Is this spiked?" Addison asked.

Sylvia gave her a sly smile. "We *are* in the middle of the bour-bon festival. I hope that's all right. It's Bonner's, of course."

Quinn grimaced.

"Please," Sylvia said. "I insist."

"Sure," Quinn said. She pressed the glass to her lips with a look at Addison that said, quite clearly, *I'm doing this for you.*

Addison proceeded to explain what the plants had shown her, careful not to mention the wilting and the garden's attack. She and Sylvia might be related, but as upset as Addison was with her grams, Maura was right. The Bonners were trying to steal their land, and while Sylvia might've claimed she'd stop her son, Addison didn't have any real reason to believe her.

"You say all of this happened after you pulled River's pain from the garden?" Sylvia asked.

"It started before that, when it showed me something similar—that was the first time I felt like the garden itself was in pain," Addison said. "But yeah, after what I did with River, I saw your cornfield again. I'd like to go out there myself, to see if I can find the spot from my vision. You said the corn was weak. It's got to be connected."

Sylvia shook her head. "It's weaker, but we haven't seen anything like what you're describing. It sounds to me like the problem is in the shadow garden itself."

"Then why would the garden show Addison the cornfield?" Quinn asked.

Addison set her cup down on the table. "Can we go out there right now? I want to get this figured out before things get any further with the city council."

Sylvia sipped her lemonade slowly. Addison bit her lip. Maybe this had been a mistake. Sylvia had her own interests as far as the shadow garden went. At the end of the day, the distillery was hers. Would discovering Addison was her granddaughter really trump all that?

Sylvia topped off Addison's drink. "Maybe we should forget about the cornfield for now, hmm?"

Addison blinked, her chest growing warm. She exhaled, softly, and tilted her head as a puff of air rose from her lips—dark, like smoke. She glanced down at the bourbon in her hand, then back up at Sylvia. "What were you saying?"

"Perhaps you could use your magic to heal the shadow garden," Sylvia suggested.

"Don't you have to find the root of the pain to heal it?" Quinn asked. "What if the root of whatever is wrong with the soil is in the cornfield?"

Sylvia glanced at Quinn with one eyebrow raised.

"Why would I go to the cornfield?" Addison asked. "Anyway, my healing magic doesn't work the same way as the other Haywoods'. They can take pain. I can take...whatever I want. Does your family have magic, too?" She turned to Sylvia.

"Only what the dark-corn mash has given our bourbon. Perhaps..." Sylvia paused, tilting her head to one side. "Have you considered testing what you did with River on the garden itself? Maybe it's not starving at all. Maybe there's something in the soil that's causing all of this. If you can pull out whatever that is, ask the garden to offer up its own pain the way one might offer up a memory, you might be able to ease its suffering."

Addison's mind went back to the rot on the sunflowers. She hadn't seen it anywhere else, but maybe she hadn't been looking closely enough. "It's worth a try," she said.

"I thought the garden needed the pain," Quinn said.

"It needs the pain we feed it," Addison said. "But it has its own pain now, too."

"What about the cornfield?" Quinn asked.

"What about it?" Addison said.

Quinn narrowed her eyes, glanced from Addison to Sylvia. "Your vision?"

Addison shook her head, unsure what Quinn was going on about.

Sylvia leaned forward, and the oleander Addison had seen in her aura was back in full bloom. She reached across the table and rested a hand on Quinn's shoulder. "I meant that we should *all* forget about the cornfield for now. Probably best you forget about that vintage bottle of Bonner's, too, just for now. We have more important things to deal with."

"Okay..." Quinn looked down at the drink in her hands, brow furrowed. She reached for the pitcher, but it was empty. "I'd love some more of this."

"Maybe another glass and then we can head over to the shadow garden together?" Sylvia said.

Chapter 36

Quinn

Out of everyone in the family, Quinn had internalized Maura's suspicions about the Bonners the most, but on the drive over, she'd put all that aside for a chance at the truth. If Sylvia had been somehow responsible for her father's death, she'd reasoned, then she wouldn't let Quinn anywhere near a bottle of bourbon that might hold the answers she sought.

Now, she wasn't so sure.

She dropped her bag behind the couch, then followed Addison and Sylvia as they started up the stairs, trying to think past the pounding in her head. One minute she'd been sitting there with that familiar warm-soil feel of Addison and the uncomfortable but not unbearable prickling sensation the Bonner family gave her; the next it was as though Sylvia had taken a gardening fork and shoved it right between her eyes.

Addison had forgotten about the cornfield, about her vision, about all of it except what Sylvia wanted to talk about. Quinn didn't understand it, but she'd watched it happen. And then she'd felt the moment Sylvia had tried to do the same to her. But it didn't work. It only gave her a splitting headache.

She stumbled and caught herself on the banister.

Addison turned. "Are you all right?"

She shook her head. "All of a sudden I'm not feeling so well."

Addison offered her a hand and helped her the rest of the way up the stairs. Sylvia watched the exchange between them, and Quinn did her best not to look terrified.

"What's wrong?" Addison asked.

For once, Quinn was glad she had no aura. The last thing she wanted right now was for Addison to start asking questions. "I have a migraine coming on, I think." She rubbed at the space between her eyebrows. "Maybe I had too much to drink. I should go before it gets worse."

"You're not coming with us?" Addison said.

Quinn didn't want to leave her cousin alone with Sylvia, but Addison had made her plans clear.

"Would you like to lie down in one of my guest rooms?" Sylvia offered.

"Thanks," Quinn said. "But one of my moms gets migraines like this, and it puts her out for a day or more. I'd rather drive home before that happens."

Addison grabbed her into a hug, leaned in, and whispered in her ear. "Thanks for coming out here with me. I don't think I could've done it alone."

"That's what family's for." Quinn squeezed her cousin's shoulders, wishing she could pull her away from all this, but she knew how much Addison wanted to trust Sylvia—to find who she was as both a Haywood and a Bonner.

With what Sylvia had done in there, if Quinn came out against her now, she might lose Addison forever. So she headed outside and started for her car, slowly, keeping an eye on the house. As soon as Sylvia and Addison disappeared down the drive, she doubled back.

She reached the front door, took a quick look around, and ducked inside. Then she made her way down the hallway.

A woman in a branded polo stepped out of one of the rooms. Quinn stopped, eyes wide.

"Can I help you?" she asked. Quinn recognized her—they'd graduated the same year at Yarrow High. They hadn't been close, but they'd been friendly.

"Alexis?" Quinn asked. "I didn't realize you worked for the Bonners."

"Quinn!" she said. "I took the job earlier this summer." She lowered her voice. "I thought I'd be working the festival, but all I've been doing is running errands for Nate Bonner all day. What are you doing here?"

"I was having lemonade with Sylvia and Addison," she said. "I think I left my bag down there. I was just going to go grab it."

Alexis pressed her lips thin. "In the sipping room?"

Quinn nodded.

"I'm not supposed to allow anyone in there. *I'm* not even allowed in there."

"My keys are in my bag…" Quinn said.

Alexis glanced around them. "Go," she said. "But hurry."

Quinn flipped on the light and quietly shut the door. Her head still throbbed but not enough to stop her from taking the stairs in twos.

She went straight for the bottom-right corner of the shelf, searching for the bottle marked *1997*. There was more than one, but only one that looked like it had recently been opened. She tugged it from its place and turned it over in her hands.

Below the year, the bottle was named, as all Bonner bourbons were.

It said, *Irene.*

Quinn's eyes widened. She picked up the one next to it. *Kaden.* And the next. *Maura.* There was one for each of her moms as well. She grabbed her bag and wrapped as many as she could in her towel to keep them from clinking. Then she fished her keys from her front pocket and started up the stairs.

Alexis stood keeping watch at the door. She eyed Quinn's bag.

"We're heading out to the river today," Quinn said. "Harper's going to kill me if I'm late. Thanks!"

Alexis nodded and said, "Have fun. I'd much rather have my feet in the water than be stuck here."

❧

By the time Quinn got back to her car, some of the pain in her head had subsided. She tried to sort through their conversation—Sylvia's insistence they forget about the cornfield, her desire to get Addison into the shadow garden. Quinn didn't know what had happened in there, but she had the most important thing of all: the memories Addison had promised her.

She considered all the bottles in her bag and ultimately chose Taylor's. She lifted the cap and took a sip. Her body tingled, like it was just waking up after falling asleep. It started on her tongue, then spread down her throat until it reached the tips of her fingers and toes.

Then it stopped.

Her heart sank.

She blinked her eyes open.

"Well, that didn't work," she murmured.

But Sylvia had steered her away from the bottles, tried to get her to forget about the bourbon—and there was no way the names were a coincidence. Quinn tapped her free hand against the steering wheel. The shadow garden magic had no effect on her. Maybe she was resistant to whatever had stored the memories in the bottle, too.

There was only one way to find out.

She dialed her mom and put the phone on speaker.

"Quinn?" Taylor said after the third ring.

"Mom!" Quinn said, as she pulled out of the lot. "Are you at the bed and breakfast?"

"I'm at the tea shop. We're all over here," she said. "Actually, I'm glad you called. We could use your help."

"My help?" Quinn asked.

"I'll explain when you get here."

With the town square blocked off for the festival, she had to cut through residential side streets until she could take the alley leading to the tea shop. As soon as she threw her truck into park, Quinn started up the back steps.

"Mom?" she called. "Mama?"

"In here!" Taylor and Clem answered from the front room.

Quinn gripped the bag tight as she ran down the hallway.

"Good," Maura said at the sight of her. "Now does anyone have some Bonner's so Kaden can test his magic on her?"

"Excuse me?" Quinn asked.

"We need to know if you're immune."

"If I'm immune..." Her eyes widened. "So your mom *did* try to do something to me."

"You were with Sylvia?" Maura asked.

"Addison wanted to get into the cornfield," Quinn said. "I told her I'd go with her, but Sylvia did something to her."

Everyone stood at once. "We have to stop her," Maura said.

"Wait," Quinn said. She set the bag on the table and started pulling out the bottles. She set each one in front of its respective owner and watched as they took in the labels.

"You found them," Clem said before grabbing her in a hug.

Taylor narrowed her eyes. "How did you get these?"

"I stole them from Sylvia's sipping room," Quinn said.

"That's my girl." Clem turned the bottle over in her hands.

"My mother has a sipping room?" Kaden asked.

"It's in the basement," Quinn said.

"I'm guessing she didn't want me to remember it for this exact reason," Kaden said. "How did you get in there?"

"I was with Addison," Quinn said. "We went to her because..." Her eyes strayed. Quinn should not be the one to tell Kaden or Irene. Better they find those memories in the bourbon themselves. "Last night, Addison shared a glass of that stuff with Sylvia. The *Irene* bottle. There are memories in the liquor. From that summer." Quinn tapped the date on Irene's already opened bottle.

Maura sat back down slowly. "She didn't tell us?"

"She tried to tell you this morning, but..."

Quinn never thought of her grandmother as a frail woman. She'd always been larger than life. Even at sixty-nine, her presence was like that of the shadow garden itself. But in that moment, she seemed so small as the realization hit her.

"I..." Maura's voice came out quiet. "Oh."

"Are there really memories in here?" Taylor asked.

"I drank some of yours," Quinn said to her mom. "But I

didn't see anything. I thought maybe...Dad..." Her voice cracked. "But it didn't work on me. Apparently nothing does."

Taylor took Quinn's hand, and Clem wrapped an arm around her shoulder. A lump formed in Quinn's throat. She swallowed and brushed back the tears welling in her eyes. "I was hoping you could try..."

Chapter 37

Maura

Maura stared at the bottle in front of her like it was a cotton-mouth preparing to strike. She didn't drink Bonner's on principle, but she had to know what Sylvia had taken from her.

With a shudder, she sipped enough to coat her tongue and hated how much she enjoyed the smoke-and-honey taste. As soon as she swallowed, the tea shop disappeared.

As long as the Bonners had been in Yarrow, it had been a bourbon town. But in 1982, people no longer wanted to drink what their fathers and grandfathers drank. They wanted new things, empty things. Most of Yarrow depended on the distillery for their livelihood, but at this rate, in a few years Bonner's would have to shut their doors, which was why, against my better judgment, I agreed to sit down with Sylvia and her husband while our children played in the yard.

I glanced out the window over the sink, reminded myself that I was doing this for them—for their future. My kids needed Yarrow just as much as every other person in this town. I wasn't going to let the town go down without a fight.

Still, at twenty-nine years old, this shouldn't have been my decision to make. But as the last remaining Haywood adult who had stayed in Yarrow, I was the only one who could make this decision.

"This really is the best thing for the town," Sylvia said. "Can you imagine? Our bourbon mixed with your shadow magic? That could never lose out to vodka and blue curaçao."

Christian Durant leaned across the table, hands splayed against the wood, knuckles white with the strain. My eyes flicked toward them. My heart stuttered, but I didn't lean back.

I wouldn't cower before this man.

I glanced at my attorney, Tim Stokes. My mother—may she rest in peace—had taught me not to trust the Bonners. The dog's-bane and snapdragons in their auras always hinted at falsehood and deception, and whenever they wanted something enough, things seemed to go their way. It wasn't natural. So I wasn't about to lease away the land without a witness. No doubt Mom would haunt me until the day I died if anything went awry.

Tim cleared his throat.

"Just hurry up and sign," Christian growled. "I've got a team waiting to clear that land."

Sylvia rested a hand on his forearm. When he shook her off, she flinched.

My eyes narrowed as I saw the fear blooming in her aura and, with it, resolve. Maybe we weren't that different after all. I recognized in Sylvia the same sort of survival instincts that had led me to leave my husband a few years earlier when he'd raised a hand to me.

I'd have to try to get Sylvia alone.

"I'm not going to hand over my land without reading the fine print," I said. I'd already had Tim read it—more than once—even had him amend it. And he said everything was sound. Fifteen years *for the Bonners to grow corn on shadow garden soil. Long enough for them to truly establish the new recipe.*

My tea leaves had warned me about signing any contracts...but Yarrow needed me, and when Yarrow called, the Haywoods answered.

I pressed my pen to paper.

As soon as I'd finished signing, Christian tried to snatch it up, but Tim beat him to it. "I'll have copies made. My office will deliver them."

Christian pushed up from the table and grabbed Sylvia's wrist. "Let's go."

She looked down at his hand on her. "I'm going to get the boys," she said. "I'll meet you in the car."

After a few seconds, he released her and stormed out.

I glanced at the red marks around Sylvia's forearm, then at Tim. "Thanks, Tim. I'll meet you out front with a check."

He gave me a slight nod. I knew he, too, had picked up on the dynamic between Sylvia and her husband.

As soon as Sylvia and I were alone, I said, "If Christian is hurting you, I can help."

Sylvia reared back. "Excuse me?"

"There's violence all over that man."

Sylvia shook her head. "I have the situation under control."

"You don't have to be alone in this," I said. "Once he starts on you, it won't be long until he goes after the boys."

"There's nothing Christian can do to me that I can't handle."

"Is this about his money?" I asked.

Sylvia crossed her arms and looked me over. "You're not hearing me. I'm the one who is leading this family. Not Christian. It's in both our best interests for you to stay out of it."

And with that, Sylvia stalked out of the kitchen.

*   *   *

The world shifted.

Maura was older, her children were older, Yarrow was older.

Kaden and Irene sat at my kitchen table—the same seats occupied by his parents all those years ago. Yarrow was booming again, and I had no intention of letting the Bonners continue farming my family's land.

Had Irene still been planning to marry Nate, things might've been different. I hadn't liked him from the start, but Irene had been smitten, and I wasn't going to throw away my relationship with my daughter because of a grudge.

But Nate had turned out to be just the kind of man I'd expected him to be. What I hadn't seen coming was Kaden's confession. The revelation of his family's memory magic. It didn't come as a shock.

More than anything, I felt vindicated.

I tapped my fingers against the table, wishing that if my daughter had to end up with a Bonner boy, she'd have chosen Kaden. I'd long sensed the boy's feelings for Irene. It didn't take an empath to see it, even if Irene had remained oblivious.

Maybe Nate had seen it, too. The thought made my blood boil as I started to piece things together.

"The lease is up on the land this year," I said.

"How is that related to Nate cheating on me and making me forget about it?" Irene asked.

Across the table, Clem held a hand over her mouth, then mumbled from beneath her fingers, "You don't think..."

Beside her, Kaden paled. "He went after Irene to make sure we didn't lose the land."

I nodded.

Petunias bloomed behind my daughter's eyes, and the hum of cicadas started up outside. "He used me?" *Irene asked.* "For the land?"

"Now I'm really going to f—" *Clem started.* "Mess him up," *she finished.*

Taylor winced, and Clem glanced at Quinn, who ran laughing through the room followed by a stream of dragonflies.

Nolan scooped Quinn up from the ground and settled her onto his lap.

"Not if I get to him first," *he said. He shook his head, and though his anger drew the cicadas, too, he spoke in soft tones and gently ran his fingers through Quinn's curls.* "I went to him when I found out he cheated on you."

"You didn't tell me," *Irene said.*

"He offered me a bottle of the family reserve as a sort of apology. Fifteen-year."

"And?" *Irene asked.*

"I mean, I took a drink," *he admitted.* "It was the best bourbon I've ever tasted."

"Nolan!" *Taylor said.* "After he cheated on your sister?"

"I told him to f—" *He glanced down at his daughter. She looked up at him, eyes wide and mouth full of giggles.* "I told him I did not accept his apology. He told me to forget about ever talking to him."

"But you remember," *Kaden said.*

Irene's eyes widened. "Your immunity."

"Guess it works on Bonner magic, too."

Clem leaned forward, hands on the table. "We can totally use that to our advantage."

Maura's memory changed, and once again she stood in the same kitchen, alone, a few weeks later, just days before the bourbon festival.

*   *   *

The table should've been covered in harvest baskets. The coming weekend would mark the first Yarrow festival since Irene and Clem had opened up shop, and they'd invited me to sell my wares from a table out front.

Instead, we had work to do.

I'd called Mayor Stokes to make sure we both had extra copies of my contract with the Bonners filed away should things go awry. That, and he deserved to hear the truth. My former attorney knew firsthand the town's dependence on bourbon. As soon as he took office, he'd made a point of trying to help new businesses—ones that were independent of the bourbon industry—flourish. Yet the Bonners always seemed able to convince him to funnel the city's money toward infrastructure that directly benefited the distillery.

It had seemed uncharacteristic of him, and I'd wondered if Christian had gone after him with threats of some sort. Now I knew the one behind his sudden change of heart had been Sylvia.

I had a few choice words I'd like to call her when this was all over.

I swirled my almost-empty teacup three times to the right, focused on what my family had to do. I tipped it over and flipped it back up.

An hourglass warned of imminent danger.

Hawks suggested enemies at the door.

And right at the top of the porcelain, near the handle, a kettle.

A slow smile spread across my face. The death of the Bonners' influence was close at hand. What else could the kettle possibly mean?

Chapter 38

Irene

Irene watched as her mother went slack and her eyes glazed over. Clem and Taylor followed. She lifted the bottle and glanced at Kaden.

He held his high. "Bottoms up."

One sip.

Another.

As the bourbon coated her tongue, her head went heavy, and the entire missing summer flashed before her eyes, along with other memories she hadn't realized she'd forgotten. Every day she and Kaden and Clem spent time at the rope swing. His cheers as she and Clem cut the ribbon in front of Lavender & Lemon Balm. His outrage when he learned what his brother had done. The first night she and Kaden spent together...

It all whirled around in her mind, coalescing into the morning of the bourbon festival.

Kaden and I met up with Nate at one of our favorite restaurants on the square—the same place I'd found Nate's car parked earlier that summer. He wore a pair of pressed khaki shorts complete with a belt, a tucked-in T-shirt, and a blazer that spoke more to his money than the weather. He'd arrived before us and was already deep in conversation with the bartender. He waved when he saw us. At the sight of his smile, that familiar itching of anger started up, but when the first cicada landed, I forced it away. There was too much to do today to let it get the best of me.

As I redirected him to an open booth, Kaden ordered a round of Bonner's, with a whisper to the bartender to fill ours with a different brand.

"I've got to be honest," Nate said. "I didn't expect your call."

"Well," I said. "If Kaden and I are going to do this thing, I was going to run into you eventually."

"Mom's happy anyway," Nate said.

The thought made my skin crawl.

The bartender brought our drinks to the table. I held up my shot, and we all clinked our glasses before throwing them back.

"We thought we could meet up with everyone at the tea shop after this, head over to the distillery together," Kaden said. "The bourbon festival's all about leaving the past behind us, right?"

Nate nodded slowly. "I'm happy for you both. Maybe it was never right, what we had."

"Obviously it wasn't," I said. "You cheated on me. For almost the entire relationship."

"We got engaged too young," he said, as if that had been the only problem.

I shook my head, glanced at Kaden. He gave me a short nod. I rested my elbows on the table and leaned toward Nate, relishing this moment, the chance to expose him for the bastard he was.

"I know what you did," I said, voice low.

"You caught me in the act," Nate said.

"Not that," I said. "You made me forget that you cheated on me."

He glanced at his brother. "Wow, I guess you're serious about her."

"How many times, Nate?" I asked.

He hesitated, but his eyes gleamed. "How many times did I cheat, or how many times did you catch me?"

"You disgust me," I said.

"I can fix that," he said. "Make you forget again." He nodded to my glass.

"This isn't Bonner's."

His eyes widened.

Kaden leaned forward. "I love you, Nate, but Irene's right. It's over. It's time for you to forget about our family's magic—every conversation we've ever had about it, every time you've used it, even the past few minutes."

Nate cupped his hand over his mouth as if he could keep the memories in. He stood, backed away from them. Then, he blinked. He looked down at himself, up at them, and slowly sat at the table again.

"What were you saying?"

The memory released its hold on Irene long enough for her to realize they'd been wrong about how Kaden's magic worked. The Bonners' power didn't come from drinking their own recipe; it was in their victim consuming it. As soon as she had the thought, she was back inside her own mind, standing outside the tea shop.

After we left the bar, we met up with Clem, Taylor, and Nolan outside Lavender & Lemon Balm. While Kaden had taken care of Nate's magic, we didn't think it was a good idea for Nate to be there when we exposed his mother. According to Kaden, his father didn't know about the family's magic, which left Sylvia as the last remaining threat.

"Nice outfit." Clem snickered as Nate adjusted his blazer.

He flipped her his middle finger.

"You're flipping me off?" she asked. "I've half a mind to finish the job Irene did on your nose."

I wished she would.

"I thought we were all good now," Nate said.

"We'll never be all good," Clem said.

"Fine," he said. "How about I treat you to one of the honey barrels, and we call it even?"

He was playing right into our hand.

"Count us in," Nolan said with one arm around Taylor's waist and the other holding Quinn up against his side. Kaden may have taken his brother's magic, but I still didn't trust Nate. Better to have someone we knew he couldn't charm keeping an eye on him.

"Irene?" Nate asked.

"I'm good," I said.

Nate shrugged. "Your loss."

Once we reached the entrance, we split up—half the group headed toward the warehouse to take Nate up on his offer of the honey barrel and the other half toward the VIP tent, where Mom had already pulled Mayor Stokes aside to explain the last few details of our plan to him. While she was doing that, we found Susheila and told her the whole story for a piece in the Yarrow Gazette. There was no way Yarrow was going to let the Bonners get out of this.

As we followed the mayor toward the massive stage near the visitor center, I caught sight of Clem and Taylor in the crowd.

"What are they doing back here?" I asked.

"And where are Nolan and Nate?" Kaden said.

"Let me go find out."

Before I could leave, Kaden grabbed my hand. He pulled me toward him and kissed me softly on the lips.

"It's almost over," he said. He rubbed his thumb against my knuckles before I slipped from his grasp and wove my way through the crowd toward our friends.

"I was wondering when you were going to show up!" Clem said.

I pressed my lips together. "What do you mean? This was always the plan. Did you leave Nolan with Nate?"

I stood on tiptoe to look over the mass of people.

Taylor glanced around. "I didn't even realize Nolan wasn't with us." Her cheeks reddened. "Or Quinn! All the work getting ready for the guests this week must be getting to me."

I rocked back on my heels, looking from Clem to Taylor, the confusion clear on their faces. Despite the heat, my whole body went cold.

"You don't remember." It was almost a whisper.

"Remember what?" Clem asked.

There was no time to explain. I took off at a run toward the warehouse.

The memory shifted again.

The first thing I heard when I threw open the warehouse doors was my niece's screams. The air smelled smoky and sweet, with just a tang of something metallic underneath. Gloom floated heavy in the room. Black smudged the shelves, the concrete floor.

I looked left, then right. But as far as I could see, no one else was there.

"Quinn?" I called. "Where are you, baby girl?"

The crying grew to a wail. My heart hammered as I ran down rows and rows of charred oak barrels toward the sound. I skidded to a stop at the back wall and slipped, falling to the ground. With a groan I pushed myself up to find my hands warm and wet and crimson.

I lifted my head slowly. What I saw took the wind out of me.

Nolan lay in a puddle of blood.

Quinn sat beside him, whimpering softly.

A sob tore from my throat. I held a hand over my mouth, staining my face red.

"No," I whispered, unable to fight back the tears. "This can't be happening."

"Daddy," Quinn said, her voice soft, so soft, as she pushed Nolan's shoulder.

I scrambled toward them. My brother's chest rose and fell, but just barely. He held his hands over his sternum, where red spilled from beneath his fingertips.

"Nolan?" I leaned toward him.

His eyelids fluttered. "Irene?" he sputtered.

I pressed my hands against the wound, but it did nothing to slow the bleeding. Nolan's face had lost most of its color. "I'm going to get help. We'll get you out of here. You're going to be okay."

"Nate—" He winced. "He couldn't...couldn't make me forget..."

Tears dripped from my chin, splashed against my brother's stained shirt.

"I love you," Nolan said. "Make sure that Taylor...that Quinn knows how much I loved her. Both of them."

"Don't you let go," I cried, my body shaking. "You're not dying on me."

"Tell Taylor..." Nolan rested his hand on mine.

He blinked once. Then he never blinked again.

I stared at him, unmoving. Blood pounded in my head, behind my eyes, raced through my veins.

Anger, rage, but more: my heart was breaking.

Cicadas descended from the sky. A swarm so big they covered the warehouse like a storm cloud. They made their way through the still-open doors, landed on barrels and concrete, filled every stretch of space save a circle around me and my family.

Quinn wailed. She crawled toward me. Blood soaked through her clothes. It dripped from her hands. I pulled her from all that red and stood.

My eyes burned. As much as I wanted to sit there and hold on to my brother, I had to warn the others. I was the only one who knew what Nate had done, the only one who might be able to stop him before it was too late.

I gripped Quinn tightly and took off at a run. With each footfall, the cicadas parted for me, then settled back in behind me. They followed as I burst through the doors and into the sunlight.

Chapter 39

Kaden

Kaden watched as Irene's pupils dilated. The bottle slipped from her grasp. Quinn grabbed it just before it could crash to the table and spill. The last thing Kaden saw before the memories pulled him under was Irene's face contorted in fear, her lips parted.

My heart raced with nervous energy as I crossed the stage. My mother stood on the other side. Her striped dress fell midcalf, and she wore it belted at the waist. The collar, which lay open like a men's shirt, gave her at once the appearance of authority and summer femininity. A woman who could be trusted. What a farce.

My father was nowhere to be seen.

Once I reached her, she looped her arm through mine.

"Where's Dad?" I asked.

But she shook her head. "Where's your brother?"

"He snuck off to give Nolan, Taylor, and Clem a taste of the honey barrels. We'll have to kick off the memory harvest without him."

"Typical," she grumbled. "At least you boys are playing nice again."

I ground my teeth. My mother knew what my brother had done, and when I'd confronted her, she'd shrugged it off like it was nothing.

"I'd like to kick things off today if that's okay with you," I said, trying to keep my voice steady. "I asked the mayor."

My mother arched her eyebrows, but she nodded. "By all means."

Already Mayor Stokes had stepped up to the mic and was introducing my family, reminding the town what they already knew—how every year they came together to let go of their worst memories.

It would be up to me to tell them the truth.

"Kaden Bonner, everyone," Tim said, and I slipped from my mother's grip.

I took the mic with a sense of triumph. After that moment, things in Yarrow would never be the same.

"I know you're all here for the tapping of this year's bourbon," I said.

Cheers erupted from the crowd as people lifted plastic cups into the air, then swallowed the bourbon down, and my mom stepped toward me.

"I hate to be the bearer of bad news," I said, "but there's not going to be a memory harvest this year."

My mother stopped short. The excitement in the air fizzled out.

"What's this about, Kaden?" she whispered, disappointment and anger clear on her face.

"Our family has been lying to this town for too long."

She crossed the space between us and grabbed my hands. "Don't do this."

I wanted to give some elaborate speech, to tell her what I'd learned, what I thought of her machinations, but there was only one thing to be done.

"It's time you forgot your magic."

As a soft cry escaped her lips, I turned back to the crowd. "My mother doesn't only take your worst moments; she takes whatever she wants. I don't know what she's stolen, but it's time you know the truth."

People looked around at one another. While some shook their heads in disbelief, others nodded slowly, mouths open as if trying to piece together gaps in their own memories.

"Are you quite finished?" my mother asked.

My stomach bottomed out. I gripped the microphone tighter and turned.

"I'm glad you came to me with your worries," she said. "But you should've known I'd do what was best for this family. Nate, please get your brother off the stage."

Nate stood at the base of the steps sneering. I hadn't seen him arrive.

"But..."

Before I could finish the thought, a heavy buzzing filled the air.

The crowd parted.

Irene ran toward me, surrounded by a winged swarm, a blood-drenched child in her arms. My heart froze at the sight of her. I blinked, tried to reconcile what I saw. A scream pierced the cacophony as Taylor ran for her.

Irene opened her mouth, and the sound ceased. She confronted Nate. "You killed my brother."

The silence that followed was thick with her pain.

My head went light. Nolan was dead?

"You didn't really think I'd drink Bonner's with you, did you?" Nate's laughter cut like a knife. "I talked to the bartender well before you showed up to make sure you had the family recipe, not me."

I brought a hand to my throat as I realized the implication.

I watched in horror as my father appeared behind Maura in the crowd. He grabbed her around the middle and shoved a bourbon ball into her mouth. She tried to push him off, but he was too big. No one helped. They were all too focused on the woman dripping blood.

My mother nodded to Nate, who hopped off the stage and started toward the antique still. Then, to the crowd, Sylvia said, "I'd hoped it wouldn't come to this, but it's time you all forget the Haywoods ever owned the land where we grow our corn. You can forget about this little conversation, too—this whole summer, in fact—and everything you know about my son Kaden beyond his name. Like none of it ever happened at all."

Lips parted. Smoke poured into the air, the gloom thicker than I'd ever seen it. Eyes glazed over as the dark mist swirled up and around and toward the old still.

My mother leaned in closer to me and whispered, "I think it would be best if you forgot your friendship with Irene, with her family and her friends—that she and Nate ever ended things."

The last sound I heard before the memory passed from my lips was Quinn's screams as Nate led a dazed Irene away from the festival.

Chapter 40

Addison

The shadow garden had transformed. Ebony vines overran once-neat rows of vegetables. Sunflower and sage reached up and up, higher than the roofline. Pumpkin and zucchini and cucumber crawled across the dirt, sinking roots between the cracks in the bricks to support them on their upward climb into darkness where the gloom hung cloud-like and heavy over it all. Addison had to stop their growth, to heal them like Sylvia had suggested, or at least calm them. At this rate, they'd drain what little sorrow remained in the soil before she had a chance to fix it.

Fireflies hovered in the unnatural darkness, flitting in between plants, their abdomens pulsing a greenish-yellow light. The festival always brought them out in droves, but never like this. They were meant to chase away the darkness. Instead, everywhere they landed, shadow trailed them like a fog, almost as if they were releasing the gloom they'd soaked up at the distillery the day before.

Addison stood with a family member whom, until yesterday, she hadn't known she had, in the one place she'd always felt safe. But now, with the garden in as much disarray as her own heart, she wasn't sure what to feel.

She wished River was with her and not working the festival, that Quinn hadn't succumbed to a migraine, that her mother and grandmother trusted her interpretation of the leaves.

But maybe they'd been right to doubt her.

Sylvia rested a hand on Addison's shoulder. "Are you sure you don't want to call Maura and Irene? I could call Kaden. Maybe we could all do this together."

Addison shook her head.

"You don't want them to know about your father," Sylvia said. Though her voice was soft and sad, Addison could tell she wasn't surprised.

"They gave up the memories from that summer," Addison said.

"The whole town did," Sylvia reminded her. "Maybe whatever happened was so hard, they had to sacrifice their love."

Addison hadn't considered that. "What if you give those memories back to them?" she asked.

"If they wanted them, I'd be happy to," Sylvia said. "But I wouldn't force it on them."

"I wish there wasn't all this hate between our families," Addison said.

"You're afraid to tell them the truth?" Sylvia asked.

Addison shrugged. Her grams had loved her all her life, but she'd hated the Bonners in what felt like equal measure. And after the way she'd responded that morning when Addison had almost told her what she'd learned, she feared Maura would disown her if she discovered the truth of her lineage, that her hatred for the Bonners ran so deep it would extend to Addison, too.

"If I know Irene, she's not going to stop loving you simply

because she realizes my son is your father," Sylvia said. "Especially not after what I saw between her and Kaden at dinner."

A firefly landed on Addison's shoulder. She cupped it gently with one hand. As it crawled along her palm, she held it close to her face and whispered, "It's not my mom I'm worried about."

"Ah," Sylvia said. "Maura."

At Addison's nod, Sylvia continued, "Who knows. Maybe loving yourself—loving me—would be easier if you forgot Maura's love altogether. Irene's, too. Then it wouldn't hurt so much."

Addison exhaled, and smoke passed from her lips into the hazy air. The lightning bug took flight, moving straight into the darkness until Addison wasn't sure if she'd seen anything at all. It flew off into the garden.

When she looked back at Sylvia, her grandmother extended her hand. "We don't know each other well, but I know I love you already."

Addison smiled softly, her chest growing warm at the words. As far as she could remember, she'd never known a grandmother's love. That must've been why the leaves led her here. As the two of them stood staring out at the garden, a familiar voice echoed across the yard.

"Mom? Are you out here?"

Addison turned, her heart sinking. "What's he doing here?"

Nate walked toward them, shoulders thrown back and forehead glistening in the heat.

"I thought if we could all work together to fix your garden, maybe we could put Nate's efforts with the city council to rest. I didn't realize it would be like...this." She gestured vaguely at the wild plants.

Nate rested his sunglasses on the top of his head and surveyed the garden. "This is a nightmare."

"You can't be here," Addison said, almost pleading. "He can't be here."

Sylvia rested a gentle hand on Addison's shoulder. "Let's forget your hatred toward Nate, too, hmm? Yes, he was working with the mayor and the city manager to get access to your family's land, but he only had Yarrow's best interests in mind. We both know Maura would've never allowed us to shore up the corn crop otherwise. But the garden is your domain, isn't it?"

Addison tilted her head to the side and blinked. "It is," she agreed. She glanced at Nate, who was now smiling at her, all teeth. "Thanks for coming to help. My family wouldn't understand."

"Wouldn't have missed it for the world," Nate said.

She knew this man had cheated on her mother, that he'd threatened to take their land, but she didn't feel any animosity toward him. Besides, there were more pressing matters at hand.

"The garden is hurting," Addison said. "Sylvia thought we might be able to heal it."

"Or make it forget whatever caused all this," Sylvia suggested.

Nate coughed, surprise clear in his aura. "Even if we could..." he said with a quick glance at Addison, "we don't have any bourbon."

Sylvia produced a bottle from her bag.

"These are plants. Not people." Nate narrowed his eyes. "It doesn't work that way."

"Not for us," Sylvia said. "But it might for Addison."

Nate furrowed his brow. "But—"

Sylvia held up a hand, cutting him short. "Trust me."

"Even if this works, the soil still won't have enough sorrow to feed them," Addison said. "But it'll be a start if we can get the plants to slow their growth."

Sylvia nodded. "Then maybe you can clear out some of the land, give it a chance to recover," she said. "Like we used to do with the cornfields."

"The cornfields?" Addison asked.

Sylvia pursed her lips. "Basic farming," she said.

Addison was familiar with the concept of crop rotation. The garden had never needed it, but that had been before Maura pulled back from healing, before they realized Addison wouldn't be able to pull her weight. It was certainly an idea.

Addison started down the brick path. "Come on."

With each step they took, the plants closed in around them.

"Is this safe?" Nate asked warily.

Addison wanted to believe it was, but she didn't know anymore, so she shrugged. "Let's hope so."

She stopped when she reached the small clearing where she'd shoved her hands beneath the earth that morning. The vines had lashed out at her here. They'd shown her their fear, the depleted soil.

But something had done that to them.

Something had drained them.

She pressed her eyes closed and tried to remember, but she came up empty.

Chapter 41

Irene

Irene came out of the haze of memory to find tears streaming down her face and a lump in her throat. A weight pressed against her chest. All around the table, the same pain echoed in her loved ones' faces.

Her brother had been murdered.

Her family betrayed.

Her love lost.

"I didn't do it," Kaden whispered. "I didn't kill him."

Irene didn't have to see his aura to hear the relief in his voice.

"It was Nate." Irene choked back her tears. Her brother's death was as fresh as if she'd just witnessed it. "He must've figured out his magic didn't work on Nolan. It was just like you saw in your dream," she said to Quinn. "I'm sorry we didn't believe you."

Quinn pressed her fist to her mouth and started to cry. Her curls got caught in her tears, and all at once Irene saw her infant niece and her adult niece as one. She felt the blood on Quinn's hands, watched the final breath leave her brother's lungs.

As Quinn fell apart, Taylor wrapped her arms around her and wept. They rocked back and forth on the bench, their wailing louder than the cicadas that had taken up outside. Clem stood behind them and held them both, rested their heads against her chest.

Beside Irene, Maura's entire body shook as she cried. Irene had never seen her mother so broken. Irene uncurled clenched fists to find nail marks in her palms and took a steadying breath before she reached for Maura's hand.

"Sylvia stole him from us," Maura said, her voice small as she looked up at Irene. "My son."

Irene pressed her lips to the top of her mother's head as Maura collapsed into her arms. She held her like that for a few moments before she looked up, and her eyes met Kaden's. Despite the shared heartache—or maybe because of it—he had ambrosia in his irises. That reciprocated love ran far deeper than only a week could account for.

A sob tore through Irene's throat.

She loved him then. She *still* loved him now, and Sylvia had taken that from them. Two decades, gone. A life they could've lived together. A family they never got to have.

Maura pulled back from Irene's hold and glanced between them. Then, she gave Irene a little push toward him.

"Irene." His eyes glistened, and the longing in his voice opened wide a crack in her heart.

"Kaden," she whispered.

For the first time since he'd returned to town, she saw him— really saw him. Though the furrow between his brows was now permanent and gray sprinkled his beard, he was still the young man she'd fallen for all those years ago. The young man Sylvia had ripped from her mind.

She brought her hand to his face, trailed her fingertips along his cheekbone, over his widow's peak, through his hair. Finally, her hand came to rest against his chest.

He leaned his forehead against hers.

"I've always loved you," he said, the words choked.

She threaded her fingers through his and let the tears fall, when the reality of what she'd seen hit her. She pulled back from him and saw the truth sink in for him at the same time.

"Addison," they whispered. The one beautiful thing to come out of all that pain.

Irene held a hand over her mouth and let out a small laugh. Teardrops landed on her knuckles. Kaden brushed a curl behind her ear. Butterfly weed blossomed. Hope from sorrow.

"I should've been here," he said.

"You didn't know," she whispered. "*I* didn't know."

"It doesn't matter. If I hadn't run from my family, if I'd looked back, even once, I know I would've found you. We might not have had the memories, but we could've had each other. You wouldn't have been alone."

She looked back at her family, at their heartache and pain, but more: their love.

"I've never been alone."

"You understand now?" Quinn asked. "About Addison?"

"You knew?" Irene and Kaden said at the same time.

"It's what she saw in the bourbon." Her eyes strayed to Maura. "Why she called me in the first place."

"She tried to tell me." Maura's voice broke. "And I pushed her away."

"It's not your fault," Irene said, gripping her mother's hand.

Maura pulled back from her. "I saw she was in pain, but I chose my hatred for the Bonners over her."

"You can't blame yourself," Irene said.

"There's no one else to blame." Maura squared her shoulders and sat up straighter. "And now she's with Sylvia. This is probably what that bitch wanted all along."

"Of course," Kaden said. Then to Irene, "Back then, my mother wanted you in the family to ensure she'd never lose access to the garden. But after the festival, she didn't need you as her daughter-in-law anymore. She had your land, and no one remembered otherwise."

"Then a few months later my pregnancy started showing," Irene said.

"A Bonner and a Haywood child," Kaden said.

"Our child," Irene whispered.

Kaden nodded, eyes gleaming. "She must've shown Addison those memories to gain her trust."

Irene stood. "We have to stop her."

Taylor looked up at them with red eyes and tear-stained cheeks. "But we drank the bourbon. If we go now, Sylvia can take it from us all over again."

"We can't wait," Irene said. "Addison's in danger. There's no telling what Sylvia will take from her, and with no one there to capture it, we'll never be able to get it back."

"We may already be too late," Maura breathed.

"I'm immune," Quinn said. "I'll go."

"It's too much of a risk," Taylor said. "Nolan tried to do the same thing."

Maura sat up taller and threw her thick braid over her shoulder. "We should have trusted Addison with her magic. We have to trust Quinn with hers."

"I don't have magic," Quinn said.

"Your immunity *is* magic," Maura said. "It's time you owned it."

Quinn's eyes widened, and her lips spread into a smile. A dragonfly fluttered down from a nearby shelf and landed on the table in front of her. "I'll do it. If Sylvia tries anything, I can pretend it worked on me, too...and...and...I'll find a way. But we have to hurry. Sylvia and Addison are headed to the shadow garden."

"Then there's no time to waste," Irene said.

"I'll go see if I can get in touch with Tim Stokes." Clem held up her bottle, which still contained plenty of bourbon. "I have a feeling he'll want to sample some."

Maura handed her own bottle over. "Show him mine, too. It won't give him his own memories back, but it might give him an idea of where to look for copies of my contract with Sylvia if they still exist."

"Show the Bakers, too," Quinn said.

Clem nodded.

"What if this doesn't work?" Irene asked. "Kaden tried taking the memories from Sylvia before, and we failed."

"Last time, I showed my cards. I told her what I'd learned about Nate. She knew I wanted to protect you—and without the engagement, there was no way your family would let her stay on your land," Kaden said. "She didn't have any bourbon in her system. She made sure of that."

"She drank the spiked lemonade at her house today," Quinn said.

Kaden nodded. "We have to take her memory of the magic away. Only this time, we make sure she doesn't see it coming."

Chapter 42

Kaden

The gloom had grown so thick it blocked out the sun. Kaden peered into the garden, but it was impossible to make out person or plant. He knew where the guesthouse should be—the memory still fresh from the bourbon—but even that was swallowed up in the fog.

"Does anyone see them?" Irene called out.

Kaden gripped her hand tightly, afraid she'd take one too many steps and disappear into the shadows. All around them, the others had gone as far as the edge of the patio, staring off in different directions.

"Why is there so much gloom?" Kaden asked.

Irene reached for a flash of yellow-green light and opened her hand to find the lightning bug crawling along her palm. A puff of shadow escaped onto her skin. "It almost looks like the fireflies brought it here."

"I thought they chased away the darkness," Taylor said.

"Maybe they haven't been chasing it away," Irene said. "What if they've been capturing it?"

"They're as much a part of Yarrow as these plants are," Maura said as she dropped into a crouch and pressed her hand to the dirt. She squinted into the shadow. "The soil's depleted. If the gloom really is the memories that didn't make it into the bottle—the angel's share of our town's sorrow—it's possible the garden is trying to call the fireflies here to make up for what the soil is lacking."

"Look!" Quinn pointed into the haze.

Yellow and green flashed in synchronicity, and in the glow of their light, Kaden could just make out three shadows moving through the darkness.

"That has to be them," he said.

They took off at a run. Vines crawled across the dirt after them until they reached a clear patch of land. Addison—his *daughter*—knelt in the dirt, her hands beneath the surface. From the dark hair that hung in tangled waves down her back to the freckles scattered across her skin to the gentle way she turned the soil in her hands, she was every bit him and Irene and so much more. How hadn't he seen it before?

She looked up at him, the whites of her eyes pale moons in the gloom. Kaden was no empath, but he saw desperation in her—his mother had always been an expert at cultivating it.

"Addison." He nearly choked on her name.

Nate stepped in front of her, right in Kaden's path. At the sight of his brother, rage spotted Kaden's vision.

"What are you doing here?" Addison asked Kaden.

"Saving you," Quinn said, appearing beside him.

Addison pushed herself up from the dirt. "I thought you were on my side."

Maura held out a hand. "Come here."

"I'm fine where I am," she said.

"I'm sure we can sort this all out," Sylvia said. "Addison

asked me to help her fix the garden. She seemed to think the rest of you weren't up to the task, but it's good that you're here."

Her smile felt like a knife in Kaden's heart.

"I don't know what you think you're doing—or what you've done since that summer—but I'm not letting you hurt my daughter," Irene said, as the cicadas took up her song. She clenched her fists.

Nate took a step back.

Taylor stepped up behind Irene. She'd rolled her sleeves up to her elbows, and she bounced on the balls of her feet. "You son of a bitch," she said. "You murdered my husband."

Nate's eyes widened a fraction, and he glanced at Sylvia. "I did what?"

Kaden felt no remorse as he looked his brother in the eye and said, "It's time you forget how to use our family's magic." Nate clapped a hand over his mouth, but not before darkness poured from his lips and went up into the gloom.

"How does it feel?" Taylor said, baring her teeth. "Knowing you're going to have to pay for what you did to my family? To my husband? My daughter? To me?"

"What are you talking about?" Addison said.

"I was right," Quinn said. "The Bonners murdered my father."

Addison shook her head. "That's not possible. They wouldn't." She looked at Sylvia, and Kaden followed her gaze.

His mother stood watching him impassively, almost resigned. There was so much he wanted to say, so much guilt he wanted to make her feel, but every second he waited was a chance that she'd beat him to the punch.

"You lied to me," he said.

She shook her head sadly. "Am I next, then? Has it really come to this? You want to take what is mine, just like every other man who's come into my life. You're just like your father."

For once, her words didn't cut the way she'd intended them to. Kaden thought he'd feel a little guilt, coming here to steal the one thing that had allowed his mother to get out from under her own father's control, but she made it too easy to hate her.

Irene rested a hand on his upper back.

"It seems you've found something to like about Yarrow," Sylvia said. "Maybe she'll be enough to keep you here."

He felt Irene stiffen beside him. He grabbed her hand. "She's always been enough, but you knew that. Yet you still took her from me. I have a daughter, mom. A daughter I never knew."

"I told you I'd do whatever I had to do to protect this family," Sylvia said.

"You did. And so will I," Kaden said. "It's time for you to forget how to use your magic."

She turned away from them.

"No…" A soft whimper escaped his mother's lips, but Kaden didn't comfort her. Instead, he wrapped an arm around Irene's waist and waited.

When Sylvia turned back toward him, her eyes gleamed with tears, and he felt a sick sort of satisfaction. He'd wanted to believe it would be hard, that stripping his mother of her magic would've broken something in him.

But after everything, he found betraying his mother was the easiest thing of all.

Chapter 43

Irene

"It's over," Irene said, breath rushing out of her. She slipped from Kaden's grip and started for Addison. "Please tell me you didn't do...whatever Sylvia was asking you to do to the garden."

Addison pushed herself up from the ground, brushing dirt from her hands. When Irene got close, she pulled back and wrapped an arm around Sylvia. She glared at Irene with barbs in her eyes, her aura a tangle of emotions. Doubt and abandonment strangled her love like kudzu in a forest.

"Get away from her, Addison," Irene said, but with each word that slipped from her lips, her daughter's gaze grew harder.

"Why? So you can hurt her more?" Addison asked. "She was only here to help us, and you...What did you do? Other than accuse her son of murder?"

Sylvia leaned against Addison for support.

Maura came to stand beside Irene. "We stopped her from hurting Yarrow, from hurting this family, ever again."

Addison shook her head. She turned to Quinn. Betrayal burned bright in her eyes. "I can't believe you told them. I trusted you."

"Listen to me," Quinn said. "I don't know what Sylvia told you, but it's not what you think. She took your memories. You had two visions of the cornfield draining the shadow garden dry. She stole that from you."

"I love you, Addison," Sylvia said.

Irene almost threw the older woman to the ground.

Addison worried at her lip, but ultimately she shook her head. "Sylvia's the only one here who showed me the truth. I've never been good enough for this family. I thought you'd understand that, Quinn."

"If I hadn't watched Sylvia mess with your head, I'd be really pissed at you for saying that," Quinn said. "Actually, I'm still a little pissed."

"Whatever Sylvia's asked you to do, it's not going to help the garden," Irene said. "She wants this land as much as Nate does."

"You've got it all wrong," Addison said. "I can fix this."

"You can't trust Sylvia," Maura said.

"Our family's hatred for the Bonners kept both of you from ever loving me. You gave up the truth of who I am because you couldn't put that hatred aside," Addison said. "Well I've finally found a family that loves me the way you never did."

Each word out of Addison's mouth cut right to Irene's core. Her daughter's aura faded until only chrysanthemums remained—their yellow blooms a sign of neglected love, their white petals a symbol of honesty. Addison believed every word she was saying.

"That's not true," Irene said. She'd been the best mother she knew how to be. "Everything I have is yours."

"Not everything," Addison said. "You could never reconcile my magic. And you know why? Because it wasn't yours."

Irene's eyes widened. Of course. What Addison had done with River, the way her magic had always taken more than should've been possible. She had more than just Haywood power in her. She was a Bonner, too.

"Baby, I know," she said. "And I'm sorry."

"We both understand better now," Kaden said. He took a step toward her.

Addison's eyes widened. "What?"

Irene pulled the bottle with her name on it out of the bag. "I saw it all in here."

"I see," Sylvia said, her eyes flicking to Quinn. "It seems my suspicions were right about you."

"I was wrong, and I'm sorry," Maura said to Addison. "I should've listened to you this morning. I should've listened to you from the beginning—your leaves led us all here. To the truth."

Addison shook her head. "Sylvia loves me."

"Sylvia lied to you," Irene said.

"I showed her where she comes from," Sylvia said.

"Something you could've done years ago, but you waited until it would have the most impact," Irene said. "When it would tear my family apart."

"Yet you let me think Irene and Nate were still together," Kaden said.

"I couldn't have you here before the time was right," Sylvia said.

"Why not just push them back together?" Kaden asked. "Make everyone forget about their breakup?"

"You loved Irene, and I loved you," Sylvia said. "I would never do something like that to you."

Kaden scoffed.

"Besides, it was only temporary. I knew one day your father would die, and you'd come back to me," Sylvia said.

Not to Irene, not to Addison—to *her*. Every word out of this woman's mouth made Irene hate her even more.

"What about me?" Nate asked.

Sylvia sighed. "You're my son, Nate, but you're too much like your father. I didn't know Irene was pregnant then, but if she'd married you, if she'd *stayed* with you...I couldn't trust you with any grandchild of mine."

"But you could've used your magic to make the town forget about Dad instead!" Kaden said. "Long before any of this happened."

Sylvia shook her head. "Our marriage was far too publicized. It wouldn't matter what I did; the evidence would be out there. Worse, someone might've learned the truth about us, and where would that have left our family?"

"And what about what he did to me?" Kaden asked.

"I tried to stop your father—more than once. But he was the kind of man who hurts people. I could make him forget his anger in the moment, but I can't change a person's nature," Sylvia said. "I couldn't be there every time he decided to hurt you all over again. Only you could do that."

"I...I don't understand what's happening here..." Addison said, shaking her head slowly.

Sylvia patted her arm gently. "It's okay, dear. Now that everyone has said their piece, I think it's time we set things right."

"By you and Nate confessing and going to jail for murder and obstruction of justice?" Quinn said. "Gladly."

Sylvia shook her head. "You're so much like your mothers."

"Thank you," Quinn said.

"It wasn't a compliment." Sylvia turned her focus on Kaden. "Do you really think I'd make it so easy for you to strip my power from me? Didn't you learn anything from the bourbon you stole?"

Fear blossomed in Kaden's aura. It gripped Irene's heart, clawed up her spine until the base of her neck prickled with it.

"Quinn saw you drink the lemonade," Kaden said.

"I haven't had a glass of Bonner's since you tried to turn my own magic against me that summer. I've put so many precautions in place to prevent you from doing exactly this."

"Thank God," Nate said. "So you can fix this?"

"Nate, using your magic is as simple as telling them to forget. See? No harm done." She tapped a finger against her lips. "Once this is over, we can raze some of these wilted plants and change the land over to corn, give my fields a time to rest. I admit we got a little too ambitious, planting all of them this year, but Addison can help the garden forget, and we'll all be better for it."

Addison released her hold on Sylvia and stumbled away from her. "Wait..."

"I suppose I should thank you all," Sylvia said. "Everyone's here. Now that we all know that Kaden and Irene are Addison's parents, I can pull just enough of these memories out to make us into the happy family I'd always hoped we could be."

"A happy family you can control?" Kaden said. "No thank you."

"Don't interrupt me," she said. "If you all know what happened, then you all have the bourbon in your system. Which means that all it will take is one word from me and everything you've uncovered will be gone. We'll have to do something about Quinn."

"Don't you dare touch her," Taylor said.

"Nate, I'm sure you'll be up to the task," she said.

"Me?" He blinked. His eyes widened.

"Don't worry," she said. "I'll take it from you, just like last time."

"No," Addison whispered. "It can't be true."

"It'll all be over soon," Sylvia said. "Only this time, we'll make sure you can't get the memories back."

"You...lied to me?" Addison said.

Irene watched her daughter's heart break before her eyes.

Addison dropped to her knees and shoved her hands into the soil. "Please," she whispered.

Sylvia let out an exasperated sigh. "Now's not the time to act the hero, dear. We'll take care of this, and then we can fix the garden together. It's time for you all to forget—"

Chapter 44

Addison

The ground around them began to shake. Soil shifted. Sylvia stumbled, her sentence left unfinished as Addison fell back into her mother.

The bottle of bourbon slipped from Irene's hands. Glass shattered as it hit the ground. Bourbon spilled into the soil, and with it, whatever memories of that summer that may have been left inside.

All at once, ferns sprouted from the dirt, encircling the Haywoods and Kaden right along with them. Massive black fronds unfurled, so thick it was impossible to see through to the other side. Sylvia's voice faded, inaudible through the foliage.

Maura turned in a circle. "What did you do, you beautiful girl?"

But Addison barely heard her. After a life without a parent's love, without a grandparent's love, she'd finally found a grandmother who wanted her, but it had been a mirage. She dropped to her knees and held a hand over her heart.

"It doesn't matter now," Addison said, voice thick with tears. "The memories are gone, and we all hate each other."

The ferns around them grew taller, so high they blocked

the bit of light the gloom hadn't stamped out. Addison's family stood in shadow, lit only by the flashing of a handful of fireflies.

"It's getting worse," Addison said.

"I don't think it is," Maura said. "Look."

At the center of the broken glass, where the soil was still damp with bourbon, a leaf had appeared. Another followed as a vine forced its way out from the earth. It coiled itself up and up until it faced Addison like a snake. A black bud sprouted, bloomed, and fell away, leaving a plump berry in its place. A firefly landed on it, and as it flashed, a puff of gloom rose from its wings and seeped into the fruit.

Addison blinked, then held out her hand. The blackberry fell into her palm. The message was clear. The garden wanted her to eat it.

She stared at the tiny fruit. Then, she dropped it into her mouth. When she sank her teeth in, it exploded with memory.

Irene.

Kaden.

Maura.

Clem.

Taylor.

Nolan.

Quinn.

Every moment her mother lived through that summer flashed before Addison's eyes. But the last thing Addison saw before the world came back into focus wasn't from that summer at all.

A torrent of memories from her own life—captured by a firefly and deposited into the shadow garden—came rushing back to her, and, with them, a warmth she hadn't realized she'd been missing settled into her chest.

A mother's love.

A grandmother's love.

A newfound father's love.

She gasped as she remembered Sylvia's words from that afternoon: *Maybe loving yourself—loving me—would be easier if you forgot Maura's love altogether. Irene's, too. Then it wouldn't hurt so much.*

Addison blinked back gossamer-like threads of memory as the reality of what she'd seen in the bourbon, of what Sylvia had said about that summer, became increasingly clear. Her mother had never given up the truth of Addison's lineage. It had been stolen from her. Then, it had been used against Addison.

Worse, Sylvia had used that same twisted method on Kaden—Addison's father—her own son. And then she turned on the shadow garden. She wanted to make it forget the harm she'd done by overworking the dark cornfield, as if forgetting could somehow erase the effects of trauma and her own culpability in bringing it to life.

Sylvia Bonner knew nothing of healing.

As Addison wiped away her tears, Maura knelt beside her.

"Grams," she hiccuped. "I'm so sorry."

Maura shook her head. "No," she said. "I'm sorry. I saw what she did to you. This wasn't your fault. If only I'd listened to you before..."

Addison looked up at her parents.

Kaden offered her a hand, and she took it. She found it pleasantly strong and callused, the knobs of his knuckles not unlike Addison's own.

Chapter 45

Kaden

Though Kaden stood surrounded by overgrown, shadow-dark ferns, he only had eyes for Addison. For his *daughter*. He couldn't believe that after everything he'd lost, he wasn't alone anymore.

He had a family.

He was a father.

He held open his arms. "Can I...can I hug you?"

Irene pressed a hand to his upper back, and he couldn't hold back his tears. Yes, his mother stood just on the other side of the leaves. She could still take it all away. She *would* take it all away from him. But not before Kaden let himself feel what it was like, just for a moment, to have a daughter.

He wouldn't waste this opportunity, even if he ended up losing it forever.

At Addison's tearful laugh, something in Kaden's heart crumbled. He'd built so many walls, so many ways to protect himself from his own trauma. How could one young woman's smile send them all tumbling down?

She stepped into his embrace.

He held a hand over the back of her head, her hair soft and dark and *his*.

"I'm so sorry," he said.

"None of this is your fault," she murmured into his chest.

He wanted this to last forever, to never let her go.

When he pulled back, he found her tears matched his own. He reached a hand forward, and when she nodded, he brushed them from her face.

"Is it too soon to say I love you?" he asked as Irene wrapped an arm around his waist.

Addison shook her head and bit her lip. "But it might be too soon for me to start calling you Dad."

He laughed with an ache right in the center of his chest. He wanted to say there'd be time for that, that they'd figure it out, but he couldn't make that sort of promise. Not now, not with what his mother could do. Maybe the best he could wish for was that she'd let them keep at least some of this newfound hope.

Chapter 46

Addison

Addison had always wondered what it might feel like to look into her father's eyes. Now that she stood face-to-face with him, she found it was everything she'd hoped it would be and more.

Her eyes were his eyes.

Her smile was his smile.

But her magic was her mother's—or was it?

Addison crouched low. She pressed a hand into the soil. "All right," she whispered to the plants. "I think I understand."

The ferns around them began to shift. Their fronds parted, opening a pathway to the rest of the shadow garden. On the other side, a similar barrier had trapped Sylvia and Nate, but the leaves had opened just enough that Addison could reach them.

"Where were we?" Sylvia asked.

Addison stepped up to her grandmother and took her hand.

"Addison?" Irene said.

"Good girl. If you could please deal with these fronds." Sylvia looked over Addison's shoulder at the other Haywoods. "A nice trick. I wasn't aware you all could control the garden."

"There's a lot you don't know about us," Quinn said. A cicada landed at her feet, and she gave Addison a short nod.

Addison closed her eyes and blocked out their conversation, prayed her cousin kept Sylvia distracted as she called to the magic in the older woman's heart, the way she might call to grief or loss.

It answered at once.

"Enough." Sylvia pulled a vial from her pocket with her free hand, uncorked it, and held it high.

Addison tugged up one root, then another, and another.

She lifted Sylvia's magic free.

And then she buried it in her own heart.

Sylvia gasped as Addison slipped from her grasp and wrapped her hand around Nate's wrist. Uprooting the magic from him was easy.

Addison stumbled back, heavy with the weight of their power.

"What...what have you done?" Sylvia asked, breathless.

Addison dropped to the ground.

She shoved her hands deep into the earth.

Then, she released the Bonner magic into the soil.

The roots pulled at it—all hunger and desperation. And as the power traveled up the stems and stalks, as it broke apart into leaves and flowers, the wilting plants straightened, the curled blooms opened their petals once more. The thick fog of gloom settled on the earth, seeping into the soil, and sunlight broke through the clouds.

Addison looked up at Sylvia, amazed that this woman had managed to capture her heart and then break it so easily.

She brushed back her tears and said, loud enough for everyone to hear, "There will be no more forgetting."

Chapter 47

Irene, One Year Later

Irene leaned against one of the columns on the front porch in a pair of faded overalls, arms crossed as she watched Kaden carry the last cardboard box from the U-Haul up the stairs. He grinned as he passed her. She could spend the rest of her life looking into those eyes.

She pushed herself up and followed him into the house, down the hallway, and up the stairs to the attic Maura had given up for the first-floor bedroom—claiming the stairs had become too much for her. But Irene knew her mother was as glad to have Kaden moving in as she was.

Once he dropped the box he was carrying in front of the closet, he turned and grabbed her around the waist, lifting her up and twirling her in a circle like they were the twenty-somethings they never got to be together. She kissed him, openmouthed and hungry. Kaden's hand found the hem of her tank top almost instantly and started its way up her side.

"Mom? Kaden? You up there?" Addison's voice came from down the stairs.

They broke apart in a breathless fit of laughter. Kaden leaned his head against Irene's.

"I could get used to this," he said.

"I already have," she replied. Then she slipped out from under him and started down the stairs, fixing her hair as she went. When she ran into Addison, her daughter arched her eyebrows and laughed before she smoothed down the side of Irene's bunched-up shirt.

"We were just..." Irene blushed.

Addison shook her head. "No," she said. "Don't tell me. He might be my father, but that doesn't make thinking about you two together any less weird, especially after having experienced that first time myself through your memories."

"You know I could've taken care of that for you," Kaden said with a wink as he came down the stairs behind Irene.

"A little late for that offer," Addison said.

After Addison uprooted Sylvia and Nate's magic, Kaden had given his up, too. With so much of their bourbon out in the world, he didn't want to risk taking another person's memories.

"Come on," Addison said. "Everyone's out back. Grams wants us all to celebrate the solstice together."

Though the festival continued another year, that summer brought no memory harvest. Most still rang in the celebration with a glass of Bonner's. Once a bourbon town, always a bourbon town. But Yarrow's people had seen for themselves what Sylvia and Nate had done. After Addison found the memories in the bourbon, it had given her an idea, and they'd poured the bottles hiding in Sylvia's sipping room into the soil, then invited the town to pick a piece of fruit, trusting the shadow garden to deliver all the right memories to all their rightful owners.

And while the Bonners had been stripped of their magic,

their money, the land they'd stolen, and their place in Yarrow, then put on trial for Nolan's murder thanks to both Clem's and Taylor's eyewitness testimonies, a semblance of their power still lived on in Addison. But now that she understood why she could uproot more than pain freely offered, she'd mastered the ability to leave behind those things people didn't want her to take. For the first time, she'd been trusted to handle her own magic, and more and more it was Addison who managed Lavender & Lemon Balm's healing sessions.

The distillery was turned over to the town—ownership shared among every citizen of Yarrow, with River splitting his time between the still and the grocery—while the cornfield was razed to the ground and the land was returned to its rightful caretakers, part of the shadow garden once more.

Now, the Haywoods set to making new traditions.

Irene and Kaden followed Addison into the backyard, where the garden stood as dark and beautiful as ever—healthy and strong and ready to accept whatever sorrow the people of Yarrow had to give. It had taken time for it to recover, but without the dark corn drawing more than its fair share, the roots found rest once more.

Addison and Quinn had spread out what appeared to be the Haywoods' entire collection of quilts right at the edge of the brick patio, and in the center sat a basket of ripe blackberries fresh from the shadow garden. Sure, the garden had all sorts of fruit to offer, but this was the vessel it had chosen to give the town back its memories a year ago, so this was how they would honor it.

On one side of the garden, Clem and Taylor sat hand in hand, staring out at the setting sun. Beside them, Quinn lay with a hand on her swollen belly and her head in Harper's lap, eyes closed as Harper ran her fingers through her hair. Addison ran to join River, sliding easily under his arm. Right in the middle, Maura sipped her julep, complete with muddled shadow mint—the amplified contentment clear on her face.

On the path in front of them, they'd lit a candle for Nolan. The loss of her brother still hit Irene sometimes, the memory only a year old even though he'd been gone for twenty-six. Kaden caught her staring at the flame and gave her hand a gentle squeeze before leading her to join the others.

Maura passed the basket of blackberries around, and they each took one, then placed that shadow fruit on their tongues and let both their happiness and their grief rise to the surface.

At the edge of the blanket, Irene blinked back tears. She rested a hand on the ground, then sank the tips of her fingers beneath the dirt. With the Bonner magic now in the earth, the garden had learned to ease her heartache—no longer only capable of taking the suffering the Haywoods had pulled from their neighbors' hearts, but able to cull the pain from the Haywoods, too. And as the garden eased Irene's grief, she knew that someday, her feelings would transform into something else entirely, something beautiful and strong, and the memories would still ache but with a sweet sort of sadness—the way sorrow often does, given enough time.

Chapter 48

The Shadow Garden

As the Haywoods pressed the blackberries to their lips, fireflies nestled among the petals and vines. No longer did they carry the gloom on their wings, keeping the sorrow in the town's memories from being lost forever. Still, they were drawn to the garden as they'd always been, as all magical things in Yarrow were.

The patch of land that once held the dark corn sat empty for months. Though the fence had been torn down, a line had been drawn between life and death—between a garden tended and a field abused. The husks and stalks had been cleared; the soil had been turned. To the casual observer, nothing had grown. Nothing might ever grow there again.

But beneath the earth, the garden was hard at work.

Roots that had once fought for nutrients stretched out and out and out, carrying the suffering they'd taken from the gloom, from the bourbon, from the town—and, now, from the Haywoods.

That evening, beneath the dying light of the setting sun, the first sprout emerged from razed earth. The seed split open and black leaves unfurled, as land that had been broken came to life once more.

Acknowledgments

This book would not exist without the heartfelt support and thoughtful critique of so many people: Rena Rossner for understanding this story from day one (and my writing for even longer) and for helping me find the magic in the bourbon. My editor at Forever, Leah Hultenschmidt, thank you for falling in love with the Haywoods, for helping me get the story just right, and for having the perfect vision for this book. Sabrina Flemming for your support throughout the process. Daniela Medina for a cover that is not only stunning but so perfectly captures this story. Luria Rittenberg for making sure the book is as beautiful on the inside as it is on the outside. Alayna Johnson for helping me keep things straight. Nicole Andress for getting *In the Shadow Garden* into the hands of readers. And to everyone else at Forever who had a hand in bringing this book to life.

To my Beez: Sara Biren, Rebekah Faubion, Tracey Neithercott. It's wild to think I was trying to fix the very first draft of this story the same weekend when I met you all in person for the first time. For your friendship, for your critique, and for the T. J. Oshie and BTS GIFs, thank you.

Lola Sharp, it was that writing workshop we attended together where I first had the idea for this book. Alison Ames, thank you for your notes and for always being open to my anxiety texts. Our friendship bloomed at the same time this story did, and I couldn't have asked for better fruit. Amber McBride, my fellow '88 forest witch! Your critique was pure magic. I never would've finished these edits if not for our writing sprints and your encouragement. Ally Malinenko, thank you for shouting about this book almost as loudly as I have.

Dad, you taught me to follow my heart, and it led me here. I love you. DFYP. Rachel Kellogg and Erin Philpot, you've been my cheerleaders for over a decade. Bonnie Smith Whitehouse and Amy Hodges-Hamilton, I found my voice and my passion for writing in your classes.

To my #NastyCousins for reminding me that the family you're born with can be the family you choose. To Galina, because these are my acknowledgments, and I can thank whoever I want. To Frankie, who sat on my lap when I wrote my first book, and still sits by my feet today. And finally, to Nick for your love, your jokes, and your help breaking this story. I wouldn't want to spend my life with anyone else.

Reading Group Guide for

In the Shadow Garden

Author's Note

They tell you to write what you know, and for me there are two things I've known most of my life: trauma and gardening. Over the years, I've found healing in both putting words on the page and burying my hands in the earth. I've seen the broken pieces of my heart transformed in time (and with a good amount of therapy) and my pain turned into something I can use to help myself and maybe even help others.

That is where the idea for this story came from. I wondered: What if there was a garden that lived on pain, a place where suffering could be physically transformed into something beautiful?

It wasn't easy to bring that idea to life on the page—no book is ever *easy*—but it was one of the most natural things in the world to me. I've been a lover of plants and teas for as long as I can remember, from pulling up carrots and picking raspberries as a kid to researching the medicinal properties of teas as a teenager, to falling in love with each plant's spiritual meaning in my adulthood as I sowed my gardens from seed and watched them grow. I may not read my tea leaves every morning like the Haywoods (personally, I tend to have better insights from tarot), but I do turn to a meditative cup of tea and the images left in the dregs at least a few times a year.

My learnings from books like *Reading Tea Leaves* by a Highland Seer, *The Herbal Drugstore* by Linda B. White and Steven Foster, *Mother Nature's Herbal* by Judith Griffin, Taylor's Pocket Guides to *Annuals* and *Herbs and Edible Flowers* by Norman Taylor and Ann Reilly, and *Plant Witchery* by Juliet Diaz are not only all over these pages, they're also a part of my own spiritual and life practice. You'll see the results of some of that research (along with my own interpretations) in the glossary I've included in this reading group guide for both the Haywoods' tea-leaf symbology and the plant auras.

While the shadow garden came first, this book wouldn't have been complete without the memory magic. My own journey through healing has included confronting the idea of forgiving and forgetting—that, somehow, a survivor is expected to be the bigger person without apology or remorse on the other end (my therapist politely informed me that was bullshit). And thus, the Bonners' magic was born. If you're looking to learn more about bourbon, I've included a few bourbon-related terms in the glossary. I also can't recommend the documentary *Neat: The Story of Bourbon* enough.

That being said, the memory magic also speaks to the hold alcoholism can have on a person. If you or someone you love is struggling with mental health or substance abuse, the Substance Abuse and Mental Health Services Administration's national helpline is free, confidential, and available all day, every day at 1-800-662-HELP (4357).

Lastly, this is a story of family—the family we're born into, the family we choose, and the family we leave behind. Even a family as loving as the Haywoods has room for growth.

Discussion Questions

1. Addison's tea-leaf reading appears several times throughout the book—an ear of corn, a sprig of rosemary, a ladybug, and a fern. The characters offer a number of interpretations as the story unfolds. What do you think the reading represents?

2. Each of the Haywoods' happiness draws a different creature from Yarrow—Addison and the ladybugs, Irene and the butterflies, Quinn and the dragonflies, even Maura and the honeybees. When they're angry, cicadas come calling. Similarly, the fireflies aren't only drawn to the gloom, but to the garden. What do you think this says about the shadow garden and how it relates to the Haywoods?

3. As a parent of an adult child, Irene wants to protect Addison but also has to come to terms with the fact that she must let Addison make her own choices, all while falling in love herself. How does she balance Addison's needs with her own?

4. When Addison goes in search of what she took from River, the shadow garden gives it up even though it is starving. How does this speak to the garden's role as a character in the novel? What do you think this could be a metaphor for?

5. Quinn views her immunity as an absence of magic, something that sets her apart from the rest of the Haywoods, but in the end it is that immunity that allows her to find her family's memories in the bourbon. What role do you think this plays in her own healing from the loss of her father?

6. Kaden leaves Yarrow to escape his family, and even when he returns, he finds his place among the Haywoods, not the Bonners. When do you think it is okay to break up with family?

7. The Haywoods and the Bonners each have their own legacy. Addison finds that her magic is both and neither, something all her own. How does this speak to finding ourselves both within and outside of our families of origin?

8. Because of their history with memory magic, the entire town chooses to accept that they gave up a summer of their own free will. How might this be a metaphor for trust and the cycle of abuse?

9. Sylvia is a victim of abuse herself, but in the end, she doesn't break the cycle of abuse for her children. Could there have been redemption for her character after what she'd done in the summer of '97 and then to Addison? If so, what might that have looked like?

10. Kaden used to think the memory harvest wasn't all that different from the Haywoods' healing magic. If you could give up any memory, what would it be? Do you think that would help you heal?

Glossary

Tea-Leaf Symbols

Anchor: Success in business or love
Apple tree: Change for the better
Balloon: An impending celebration or party
Bull: Slander by an enemy
Butterfly: Irene Haywood
Cat: Difficulties caused by treachery
Clouds: Serious trouble
Comet: Misfortune and trouble; treachery
Corn: Success and prosperity; at the bottom of the cup, new beginnings. Depending on the subject of the reading, it may also be tied to bourbon, more specifically the Bonner distillery.
Dragon: Great and sudden changes
Dragonfly: Quinn Haywood
Fern: Magic
Flowers: Luck or love
Fruit: Abundance, prosperity
Hand: Assists in the reading based on other symbols. The meaning comes from whichever symbols the hand points to.
Hawk: An enemy
Hourglass: Imminent peril
Kettle: Death

Ladybug: Addison Haywood

Leaves: Usually a lucky symbol. If small, they denote a choice that may cause a drastic change.

Man: A visitor arriving, typically read in conjunction with other symbols in the cup to determine the visitor's intentions

Mirror: Revelation of the truth

Owl: A dark omen that points to disgrace or sickness. If the reader is in love, they will be deceived.

Pitchfork: Deliberately stirring up trouble

Rooster: A wake-up call

Rosemary: Memory

Snail: Infidelity

Snake: Treachery and disloyalty. Betrayal. Possibly hidden danger.

Swan: Loyalty

Bourbon Terms

Angel's share: Bourbon that evaporates through the wood in the barrel

Bonded bourbon: Straight bourbon that has been aged and bottled according to Bottled and Bond Act of 1897 requirements. Bonded whiskey is not blended and has been stored continuously for at least four years in wooden barrels; it must all be the product of a single distillery during a single season and year.

Honey barrel: A particularly good barrel of bourbon

Mash: Liquid fermenting grains

Mash bill: A specific bourbon's list of ingredients

Proof: Denotes alcohol content. Proof is two times the percentage of alcohol by volume.

Single barrel: A bottle of bourbon that comes from a single barrel

Small batch: A bottle of bourbon that comes from a mix of a limited number of barrels, typically ten to fifty

Sour mash: A portion of the previous day's mash that is added to new mash for consistent quality and character

Straight bourbon: At least two years old. If it's younger than four years, the bottle must carry an age statement. Cannot contain any added colors or flavors.

White dog: The colorless, unaged alcohol that comes from the still, before it goes into the barrel

Auras

Adder's-tongue: Jealousy

Amaryllis: Pride

Ambrosia: Reciprocated love

Basil: Common basil suggests hatred; sweet basil a possibility for love

Begonia: Anxiety or unwanted thoughts

Bindweed: Uncertainty

Butterfly weed: Hope from sorrow

Camellia: Longing

Carnations, yellow: Disappointment

Cedar trees: Integrity

Chrysanthemum, white: Honesty

Chrysanthemum, yellow: Neglected love

Columbine, orange: Nervousness

Daffodils: Fondness; depending on the situation, sisterly love

Dead leaves: Sadness and disappointment

Dog's-bane: Falsehood

Forsythia: Anticipation

Gladiolas: Memory; if wilted, loss of memory

Hollyhock: Ambition, creativity

Hyacinth: Sorrow, grief

Iris: Hopefulness

King's spear: Regret

Lavender: Love and devotion

Marigold: Despair or jealousy

Marjoram: Happiness

Monkshood: Hatred
Morning glory: Affection
Oleander: Distrust
Petunia: Resentment or anger
Rosemary: Remembrance
Roses, yellow: Joy
Snapdragons: Deception
Sorrel: Affection
Spurge: Persistence
Sycamore: Curiosity
Tansy: A declaration of war
Weeping willow: Sadness, hopelessness
Yarrow: Everlasting love; sometimes a cure for heartache and sorrow